AMERICA'S
TOKEN
of
FREEDOM

AMERICA'S
TOKEN
of
FREEDOM

NEIL LEVESQUE

LIBERTY HILL PUBLISHING

Liberty Hill Press
2301 Lucien Way #415
Maitland, FL 32751
407.339.4217
www.libertyhillpublishing.com

Printed in the United States of America.

Paperback ISBN-13: 978-1-6312-9380-1
Ebook ISBN-13: 978-1-6312-9381-8

PROLOGUE

IN EXETER, NEW HAMPSHIRE, ON MAY 3, 1994, AFTER watching his Saturday morning cartoons, eleven-year-old Nirad Euksevel was in the thick, hilly, two-acre oak forest that surrounded his family home. He was throwing an oak stick to his dog, Mason, an English springer spaniel, when the dog suddenly stopped playing. Mason dropped his stick about twenty yards from his buddy Nirad, then he started digging in the forest floor next to the stick. After a frenzied minute of digging, Mason stepped back from his project and started barking like crazy.

Nirad ran toward his dog. "Hey, bring that stick to me or shut up!" he said. He reached down and grabbed the oak stick. As he did, he looked at the spot where Mason had peeled the oak leaves off the forest floor and dug out some dirt. Something in the ground caught his attention. He flung the dog's oak stick way off into the forest down the west side of the hill, and Mason took off hunting for it.

Nirad knelt down to look at the flat, six-inch-square, half-inch-thick granite rock Mason had uncovered. He brushed the dark dirt off the rock and from around it, then he saw that this rock was sitting atop another larger granite stone, about a square foot in size. Nirad picked up the top stone piece and looked under it. There was an old-looking brown coin about the size of a quarter sitting in a small hole carved into the bigger stone's top. The granite rocks looked like a box intended to store this coin.

He said, "What's this?" He picked up the coin, put the top stone back in place, kicked some leaves and dirt over the stones,

v

and then headed toward the house to show Mom and Dad what he'd found.

When Nirad walked into the house, his dad, Lien, his mom, Coleen, and his sister, Haras, were in the kitchen preparing the family's lunch.

Nirad said, "Hey, Dad, we've talked about the research you do on the history of this property." He pointed to a spot up on the post and beam shelves. "And we have these horseshoes and jars and things from that old farm that was here. Now look. I just found this coin buried out there by our stone bench. Well, not really buried. It was in a kind of stone box." He held up the coin.

His dad reached out and took it. He turned it over a couple of times then angled it so that it caught the lamplight. "Wow. It's an elephant coin."

Mr. Euksevel walked over to his wife and showed her the piece. "Hey, dear. This is amazing. This coin has an elephant on one side, and on the other side it says, 'God Preserve New England,' and the date is 1694. Oh, my gosh! This coin is from three hundred years ago. Why would this ancient coin have been here on this eighteenth-century farmland?"

Nirad turned his palms up. "Yah, wow. Three hundred years ago. That's not what you told me about the age of the old farmhouse you found the remains off, is it? Dad, what's the name of this farm? Something Corner?"

His dad nodded. "You're right. Our two acres of land here was part of a huge farmland from this corner here in Exeter up a mile there into Newfields. This whole massive countryside farm was known as Zebulon Thing Corner back in the 1800s. It may be two hundred and fifty years old, this farmland. Of all the stuff we found when we dug up the stone foundation from the house that burned down in the 1894 Great Oaklands fire, we never found any coins. I've always hoped we'd find a whole treasure chest of gold coins buried in this old farmland, but not yet. So, hey, maybe this old coin is some incredibly valuable treasure. And think about it. This coin was made in 1694. This farm burned down two hundred years later, in 1894, and now you found this coin three hundred years later, in 1994. Really coincidental! I wonder what will be up with this coin in 2094. We'll keep it with our other Thing antiques as part of this property's history. More important, though, I'm going to look up this coin's background, and I'll let you know what I find out about the history and significance of this old piece, if there's anything."

His son led him to the spot where he and Mason had found the stone box. Mr. Euksevel thought, "Wow. Why would this old coin have been buried in a stone box at Zebulon Thing's farm in 1894 when the farmhouse burned down? It will be interesting to figure out the life of this elephant coin."

NEET BOOK 1:

1673–1850

CHAPTER 1

CAPE COAST, AFRICA, 1673–1692

IN THE SECOND HALF OF THE SEVENTEENTH CENTURY, the western African region (eventually known as Ghana, Niger, and Cameroon) was rife with sadness and evil, like so many other African regions. Local leaders supported the European human trafficking markets by aggressively capturing African tribespeople and selling them to European slaving companies. Most African kingdom leaders advanced their personal wealth by trading individuals and entire families for European goods such as textiles, sugar, alcohol, and firearms.

Mehna Abhoola was born in 1673 in the town called Techiman, days north of the Ashanti tribal region of West Africa. She grew up with her older brother Jasok in her family's small village, Agosa, ten kilometers west of Techiman. Agosa and Techiman were located about nine day's travel north of the Cape Coast, where African kings and local workers were trafficking and selling native Africans to the British, after years of selling them to the Portuguese and Danish. Three days south of the area where Mehna's family lived, the drive for more slavery was beginning to take off by 1687, because the Ashanti Kingdom was getting better at using slavery to improve the economy in their capital, Kumasi. As teenagers, Mehna and her friends were hearing rumors of increasing challenges to families around their region. No kidnapping of people for enslavement had happened yet in their small village, but everyone was starting to get nervous.

Twenty-eight thatched huts made up the entire hamlet in which Mehna grew up. Hers was a close-knit community of families who worked together, ate meals together, and helped each other survive. Like fourteen-year-old Mehna and her mother usually did, most of the teens and women in Agosa spent their days in and around community fields, carrying vegetables back to their homes in the village. Most of the men of the community worked for local leaders, mining for gold and silver.

One morning, like they did just about every day before starting work, Mehna and seven of her neighborhood friends ambled toward the garden areas. When they got beyond the view of their parents and other villagers, they slipped into the woods and gathered together in their usual spot. As always, Mehna flitted about, working her way into random conversations about life in general.

"Hey, friends," she said with a smile. "Wasn't that a great dance party last night? Can some of you help me sing those songs next time?"

Jummy, one of the teen boys, smiled at Mehna. "Of course," he said. "I'll teach some more of them to you. And I'm speaking for all of us, Mehna, when I say you're so amazing. As you always do, you did such a great job setting up the party last night and organizing the food, the singing, and the great hugging, dancing, and celebrating that makes our lives so gratifying. Thank you, Mehna!"

Jummy turned to address the whole group. "Hey, friends. For most of my years, my dad and mom have been talking about all the people to the east of us that have been kidnapped. Then they are sold to white people, who bring alcohol and other stuff here on ships. How much longer will we hear these stories about people being stolen by our neighbors, sold, and shipped away? It's starting to get scary, how much we hear about it. Last week, I ran around with some boys miles east of here. One guy my age is now living out in the jungle full time because all the teenage boys in his town have been captured by the soldiers of one of the neighboring kingdoms and hauled away. He told me about the terrible months he's been through. His whole family has been separated from each other, most of them stolen away."

Mehna jumped in. "You're right, Jummy. It's getting scary, and we don't know what to do if those mean kingdom dictators eventually come here to kidnap us, our parents, and our brothers and sisters. I think someone here in our homeland should start figuring ways to protect our freedom from those dreadful leaders who are ruining families. If no one else starts working to protect us, it will have to be us, right here. I say let's start meeting here in our secret jungle spot every day and sharing what we see happening. Then we'll be able to discover ways to protect our parents and little brothers and sisters. You're all so sweet, kind, and fun. Let's use our awesome team here to defend our families. So look, starting tomorrow morning, before our parents come out to the fields, let's all meet right here, early on. See you tomorrow, friends." Mehna twirled, and waved. "We will make freedom ring," she whispered to each friend as she hugged them.

Throughout their tough years growing up, the children in the village thought of Mehna as their queen, because she had organized kids' events and taught teens how to work, play, and treat each other kindly and fairly. She had also coached them on being truthful—not telling lies to parents or to each other. For years, she had been providing positive feedback to the village's younger children, showing them all kindness and love. For the past nine years, the children of the village had heard more and more about the danger of human trafficking by African kingdoms.

Because of Mehna's compassionate character, her concerns about the lives of enslaved people had grown to amazing heights. At age fourteen, she was researching, analyzing, and targeting every rumor about enslavement in the areas near them, and she was constantly trying to figure out how to help the enslaved. She felt that, someday, she would find good people who wanted to stop the kidnapping businesses in Africa. Mehna had not yet seen or spoken with any already enslaved people, but in her head, she constantly thought of the deep sadness separated families must have felt.

Days after the teen team spoke about the growing business of slavery, things began to change drastically for Mehna's family and for the other families in the village.

CHAPTER 2

FAMILY WELFARE, WARFARE

AT THEIR TEEN HIDING PLACE IN THE JUNGLE, ONE OF the boys spoke up as soon as Mehna arrived. "Hey, good morning, Queen Moses. I'm calling you that because you remind us of that nice man that the churchers tell us about. So, hey, I talked with my dad and mom last night about the kidnapping stuff we discussed. They both told me about things that are worse than I've ever heard. The Ashanti king, just days south of here in Kumasi, is sending marketers out to all these villages like ours, and they try to convince people that they should sell their children to the Ashanti Kingdom for new products or to pay for things they already own. Oh, my goodness! How evil is that?"

"Right, Dirg," said Mehna. "That's inhuman evil that any town leader should never be allowed to do. And the rest of that story is that the parents must sell their kids, or the king will kidnap or kill the mom and dad."

Just as she stopped talking, their short and athletic sixteen-year-old friend, Jummy, came sprinting into the teen meeting area. His mission was obviously not just to visit with his friends at their daily morning event. Jummy was clearly upset, shaking and flailing about with his arms, his face streaming with tears. As he got to the middle of the group, he cupped both hands around his mouth and yelled, "Hey, quiet, quiet, quiet! There's a ferocious gang walking around our houses with weapons. I was out in the woods behind our home when I heard my little sister, Yumi, yelling

7

and screaming, 'Daddy, Daddy, what's the matter?' It must be like we discussed yesterday. Those armies from that Kumasi king are coming here to break up our families and steal us from each other!"

Mehna stepped toward Jummy and sat on the ground, speaking in her low, always-righteous voice. "Hey, come closer everyone. Sit on the ground right next to Jummy so we can talk in whispers. Quiet. Quiet now, friends."

After all seven of them had moved closer to Mehna, she said, "Let's come up with a plan. Jummy, do you think those hunters will not find us here? Or should we hide deeper in the woods?"

With a hand on his mouth and eyes aimed at the sky, Jummy thought for half a minute, then he said, "One of the things I've heard before is that these armies of Africans prefer to find kids and teenagers like us already separated from our parents, so they can just grab us with no fighting. Let's stay together, but in two groups to try to protect each other. Yes, Mehna, we must get out of this spot, because there are several trails from our homes out to here. So we need to move. Now!"

Mehna stood up. "Okay, two of you go with Jummy. And two go with Dirg. I'm going to sneak back around the woods next to the town center to see if they are still here or gone, so we can make the right choices tonight. I'll come back here and look for you. Talk with you soon."

While the other teens hustled off with Jummy and Dirg farther into the jungle, Mehna headed southeast toward the village, staying off the trail. She had her bright white robe on, because it wasn't really warm that time of year. She came across a giant tree that she had known her whole life. To make her less visible to the terrible people-haters, she put her bright robe up on the massive branch.

Then she patted and talked to her tree friend. "I'm here with you, Big. You're so awesome. I'll be back for my robe someday soon, I hope. Bye, Big." Mehna waved at her longtime friend and walked on to the village.

She had grown up in these jungles, so she made her way through fairly thick underbrush until she was able to see one village alley between a couple of houses on the north end. She didn't see any people, but she heard some angry yelling and screaming near the town center. As her fear and anger grew, she started toward the south end of town, running behind the homes on the east side. As she got a bit closer to the noise, Mehna turned left, heading back into the undergrowth to try to stay hidden. She stopped, sat, and listened further. She couldn't tell what was being said by the people who were yelling and screaming, but she still felt the emotions in the air.

Because of the elevated tension she was hearing, Mehna knew she must remain unnoticed. She stayed in the jungle undergrowth and kept moving south of the village. When she saw the main road to Kumasi, she found a hiding place in the bushes. There she sat and waited to see what was going on. She still heard the emotional voices of horror, fear, and violence to her north.

She didn't often get time by herself, so while Mehna was alone during this event, she sat with emotions blasting at her like a high wind, and she started thinking more about the terrible human tragedies that were happening in Africa. Those thoughts of the world's inhumane practices led Mehna to think about what it would take to stop the horrible practice of human ownership.

Sitting there brainstorming for an hour, she got to the point at which she wanted to learn more about the hateful dictators of the African kingdoms and the world of slavery. Mehna loved her parents and brother so much. She was upset that any human would be so supportive of family separation and human trafficking. She wanted to start figuring out how to learn more about it all. But as time moved on, she's was interrupted.

She couldn't see them yet, but the screaming and yelling led her to realize that the villagers were on the road only slightly north of where Mehna was hiding. They were moving toward Kumasi. As she looked toward the shrieking, she realized she was hearing kid's voices mostly. She thought, "Are they stealing my friends' little brothers and sisters?"

As she kept looking through the bushes toward the yelling, something changed. Out on the main street, she saw a parade of men coming from the north, heading south. She recognized most of the guys who were roped together, over a dozen of them. They were surrounded by other African men with clubs, swords, and maybe something else. The worst of the worst for Mehna happened as her eyes searched the crowd. She hoped not to see her dad or her brother Jasok. But there they both were, roped together in a human train with her friends' dads and brothers.

After she wiped the tears from her face, Mehna still heard the kids on the road, getting closer to her. They were following and screaming at the black pirates who were stealing their men and boys from them. She took off running north so she could reach the screaming kids and join them in shrieking about how terrible this was.

As she moved near the screaming parade, Mehna started hugging each of the children, the smaller ones first. Moms were also walking in this parade, so within minutes, Mehna's mom patted her back and then gave her the most important hug ever. As the screaming and crying continued and the parade kept heading south toward the dreadful enclave of soldiers and prisoners, Mehna felt that something must change. She hustled to the front of the sad villager parade, turned around to face them, raised her hands, and yelled, "Hey, hey, hey. Please hang on here. Stop, please. Look, we're all at a loss. Let's go back to the village. Those kingdom men down the road are forced by the king to do this. So we must be careful not to anger them too much, or they will kill us or steal us. Let's go back now and figure out what to do. I am so sorry for your families. There must be some way this can change. Okay? Head back please." She pointed north with both hands, and the moms started herding all the younger kids back to town out of their respect for Mehna Abhoola's opinion on safety. After they turned and marched away from their imprisoned guys, the emotions in the parade were clearly dreadful, a sense of sadness and loss filling the air.

While they walked the half-mile back, Mehna's mom held her daughter's hand, and said, "I'm so sorry, dear. Be careful. There are a few of those army men still back by our home. They might have more awful plans for us. Their boss man told me I must speak with him later today to address the new situation in our town. I guess he means we will be living without our guys for a while."

As they got closer to home, Mehna's mom told her to slide into the woods before any of the soldiers saw her. While watching her mom from the woods, Mehna saw one of those kingdom men grab her mother by the arm and invite her into the Abhoola family hut.

As her mom entered their home, Mehna started cruising around the village and telling the young villagers that it was time to do the garden work. They were all worried about their dads and older brothers. The young boys and girls around the village were still crying and screaming. When she met most of them in the gardens, Mehna held her arms up. "Come here, come here, you all," she said. "Let's share our love." As they gathered around her, Mehna hugged each child and teen. Ever the optimist, Mehna said, "Don't worry, friends. Our dads and brothers are good people, and they are strong, so let's be confident that we will see them again soon."

Before they started their daily work of gathering vegetables, Mehna encouraged the group of young villagers to dance and sing, holding hands and engaging in positive love-sharing moments.

The man who had taken Mehna's mom into the hut left the village after about an hour. As Mehna returned from the community garden, she removed the basket of squash from the top of her head and set it on the log table outside their home. Then she headed inside. "Mom, what is going on? Where are Dad and Jasok going? Who are those mean men? My friends say they are sent here by the Ashanti king, in Kumasi, to separate our families so he can build his own wealth."

Her mom said, "Come, dear, and sit."

Mehna walked slowly to her mom and sat, putting a hand on her mom's shoulder.

Mom said, "There's a weird situation. Your friends are kind of right. The new king in Kumasi, Osei Tutu, is building up his army to take people prisoner so he can sell them. He sent his armed men here to enslave our guys to work in his army to collect families and people to sell. The king is escalating his business plans to sell more people. Our guys will travel far and often to fight the tribes southeast of here. We have to pray and hope we will see them again some months or years from now. I have been asked by the kingdom to be the *ohemmaa* of our village people while our men are gone. This is kind of ironic. I named you Mehna so that your name would remind me of the word *ohemmaa*, which means 'female ruler.' That's who you appear to be."

Mehna looked down at the dirt floor and was quiet for a minute. Then she asked, "Why does Daddy have to go fight the other tribe people? Are they mean or dangerous to us or to King Tutu's family?"

"I can only hope our guys don't have to fight with the other people," said her mother. "Maybe I will get the answer to your question. I'm being forced to travel to Kumasi next week to get information on how to lead our village to support Tutu's kingdom. The king's guardsman told me that our villagers must now become brethren of Tutu's kingdom. I want you to travel with me, darling.

We'll travel down there to Kumasi, and then, when we come back, you can help me share the king's expectations with our people."

Mom asked Mehna to accompany her, because everyone— her parents, her brother, and the other community members—all knew that Mehna was and always had been a special person, with resilient and unifying characteristics. She had always gathered people together, encouraged comforting behaviors, and shown positive reinforcement to the other children. After the family men left the village, each day for a week, Mehna visited every hut and told each village child, in her sweet voice, that everything was going to be okay.

CHAPTER 3

MEHNA IN KUMASI, CAPITAL OF THE ASHANTI KINGDOM, RULED BY KING TUTU

MEHNA TRAVELED WITH HER MOTHER AND SEVERAL female leaders from other villages on the three-day journey south by camel cart to King Tutu's village, Kumasi. She had been really looking forward to this opportunity so she could figure out if anything could be done to help the kidnapped families and to someday figure out how to force an end to this horror.

Within hours of their arrival, as her mother was busy in private meetings with the king's assistants, Mehna began to sense that the Ashanti Kingdom was only here to support enslavement. In the afternoon, she sat on a log seat to watch people moving along the muddy roadway. Two twelve-year-old girls sat down with her and started talking. They were inhabitants of other villages similar to Mehna's, within days of Kumasi, and they were also here with their moms, who were also on a visit to meet the king.

As the afternoon passed, the world as they knew it changed. From several hundred meters to their left down the muddy road, they heard yelling and screaming. As they looked to see what was going on, the unbelievable happened.

Everyone was tense, so the kindhearted Mehna took over. She stood and moved to sit between the other two young ladies. Mehna put her arms around the shoulders of each of her new friends. Then she spoke softly. "Oh, my goodness, girls. What are we seeing?" For the next thirty-minutes, they became even more bewildered, as hundreds of Africans of all ages, male and female, paraded up the settlement's main road. The girls quickly realized that these people were not marching of their own will. African men with swords and clubs were surrounding the marching crowd. The yelling and screaming was mostly from the army of native men with weapons shouting orders at the marchers.

One of the girls with Mehna began yelling, "No, this can't be. They are all tied together with ropes. Ahhh, look, he's whipping them across their faces and backs. No! No! Why is this happening?"

Perceptive as she was, Mehna realized she and her new friends must not appear to be opposed to or upset by what was happening. "Ladies, take a deep breath and look away from this mess. We'll talk with our mom's and try to understand what we're seeing. But let's not get the attention of those soldiers, okay?"

When Mehna's mother walked out of the shack after the parade had gone by, her girl jumped up and ran to her. "Mom, I'm crying inside," said Mehna. "We saw the enslaved people—kids, parents, everyone—on their way to the coast. It looks like their entire tribes are being sold by this African king to the light-skinned English. Such a sad thing to see humans treating humans so badly. What can we do, Mom?"

Mom reached out and touched her daughter's shoulder with a gentle hand. "Dear, this human trafficking has been going on for many years, and it's probably all over the world, not just here. So thinking that only a few of us have enough desire to stop the trading of humans means it is probably not really going to happen. It's too grand in scale, I think, and it's all about using evil to create wealth for a few."

"Mama, we're seeing massive hatred from the enslavers. Their rotten beliefs and goals should not be allowed to continue against other people. I can't live with what we've been seeing getting worse and worse for years. Now my dad and Jasok are gone because of these African kingdoms. Even if it takes years to end slavery and to make our people equal in the world, stopping the horrendous leaders both here and around the world needs to start somehow—now. I feel like I need to spend more time here in Kumasi or down at the Cape Coast Castle, where they are shipping people away."

Mehna and her mother made several of these trips from Agosa to Kumasi over the next two years. Each time she took the journey, the loving girl with the wonderfully compassionate and generous nature was overwhelmed by the dark clouds of this inhuman slavery business. She spent hours by herself praying for the spirits to help the family members she'd seen separated, imprisoned, and beaten by the terrible king's army.

Because of her special intelligence, Mehna realized that in order to help the people of Africa, she had to learn more and become more involved in the marketing processes of kingdoms like Tutu's Ashanti. So, as she and her mother traveled for these two years to Kumasi, Mehna found ways to speak with King Tutu's mangers and leaders so she could understand the full processes and the core moralities for these kingdom leaders.

The kingdom leaders realized early on that this one young lady from Agosa, to the north, was special. She had always analyzed, designed, led, and corrected every process to improve the work of the workers and managers around her so that the enslaved were more protected and comfortable. She was so helpful and engaged by the time she was sixteen years old that King Tutu's management team forced Mehna to stay in Kumasi to work with other teens doing the kingdom's antifreedom work. Undoubtedly, the kingdom leaders who forced her to stay in Kumasi didn't realize that this was exactly what Mehna was hoping for.

Mehna's new job was to feed the captured tribal members during their stay, and to prepare them for their six-day journey to the coast, during which they were all chained or roped together in camel carts. She was happy to be working in the kingdom, so she could learn more about the people driving human sadness and come up with ways of helping the people who were processed through King Tutu's human trafficking business.

CHAPTER 4

GOLDEN STOOL OF ASHANTI, 1689–1691

THE ASHANTI KINGDOM IN AND AROUND KUMASI HAD been successfully selling tribal members down on the coast to foreigners, whom Mehna's coworkers call English or Brits. The king of Ashanti traded slaves for modern weapons, which were helping him win the local wars along Africa's west coast. As more people were sold for extra weapons, the kingdom became more effective in capturing African tribal members and selling them. Most of the millions of African tribal members had never even seen guns, and now their own countrymen were using such weapons to force individuals and entire families into lives of slavery.

For the two years that Mehna worked in Kumasi, she became even more disheartened. Nothing but tears, fear, and sadness filled the eyes and faces of the people she fed every day. She figured out in the first few months that the local regime kept weapons away from the people as one of the most effective strategies for making Ashanti Kingdom successful in human trafficking.

One of the prisoners she occasionally fed told her, "If we the people now had our own guns, this horrid local government process of human trafficking for slavery would be fought down and ended forever."

One day, the king's guards took her and some of her teen coworkers into the royal hall to clean the floors. There, Mehna saw several of the king's entourage and family members sitting in a tight circle, with an amazingly beautiful golden chair in the middle of their gathering. They appeared to be waiting for the king to arrive and sit with them.

After she and other laborers left the hall, Mehna turned to one of her male coworkers. "Zebu, have you seen that golden stool? That must be where the king sits and creates his cruel ideas to hurt people. I wish that stool could enslave him."

Zebu, a tall boy about Mehna's age, was worried about Mehna's comment. "Mehna, if the guards hear you say any bad words like that about the king, they will kill you or sell you to the English to be a slave. Please be careful."

"Okay, thanks, Zebu. I'll keep it between us. That golden stool is stunning, but what it represents is what bothers me. It is Tutu's safe place, and his safety is something he steals from other people."

Zebu said, "Interesting that you noticed that. You'll be amazed at the twenty-year legacy of this stool, and what it really represents. It's called the Golden Stool of Ashanti. It has a history that the good people of the Kumasi region recall and share with deep sadness. That's how I heard about this."

Mehna leaned closer, eager to hear the tale.

"Twenty years ago, right after he became king, Tutu held an event to get the rural queens to support his developing culture of the kingdom," said Zebu. "Apparently, the king heard from his event organizers that some of the queens were angered about his increasing support for human marketing. Ultimately, he set the event up in a roofless backroom where gold was being melted in fire pits. Within the first minutes of the event, life ending moments unfolded, according to town history. He showed the liquid-filled gold pots to the group. Tutu introduced his plan for making a gold chair. He talked about the future marketing plans he was creating for the Ashanti Kingdom, and then he told the dozens of female village leader that they must support him, or else. Tutu had his soldiers grab two women who had been organizing slavery protests earlier that day. They were moved over next to the hot gold pots.

19

Tutu put a hand on each of them, and the two ladies were killed and thrown into the boiling liquid gold pots. The liquid gold was later made solid and used to make this golden stool. So nasty, this king. Because of his evil, this famous altar that the king sits on has always been a highly revered piece of the compassionate people of Kumasi, a symbol of two respected ladies who were watching and getting ready to stop the king's plans for enslavement. Today, the elites of Tutu's Ashanti Kingdom consider the golden stool a unifying symbol, and they use it to send phony intentions out to the rest of the kingdom's people. The nice people of Kumasi consider the golden stool to be a symbol of the king's repression and hate. They continue to hope that someday those two nice, antislavery ladies that he murdered will raise up their arms and squeeze the king to death when he sits down on the golden stool."

Mehna's mouth was wide open with surprise. "Oh, wow, Zebu," she said. "I'm going to hug that stool every chance I get. Those awesome ladies' blood is in the gold. So they are here, and to some extent, their actions and their burial site will support the end of human trafficking around the world. Let's keep paying attention and see how that goes."

Mehna walked back up the hallway and into the meeting room, which had become empty of staffers. She got on her knees behind the Golden Stool of Ashanti with teary eyes, and she hugged it and kissed it. "Thank you, ladies," she said. "I will find ways to continue and expand your loving desires for freeing and protecting our people."

CHAPTER 5

INHUMANE LEADERS

AFTER WORKING THERE FOR A WHILE, MEHNA REALIZED she was sometimes within earshot of Tutu's leadership meetings. One day, while she was sweeping a hallway, she heard a good bit of conversation. The room was filled with a combination of local village leaders and Tutu's management team.

When several men within this group of fourteen kingdom leaders brought up concerns about the tough lives of slaves sent off to foreign lands, King Tutu jumped up and raised his voice. "Stop it!" he yelled. He ordered his leaders who trafficked families not to worry about the prisoners. "The enslaved people will only be helping the English for one or two years, and then they will be set free. This is what the English call an indentured servitude agreement, which makes sure they will not be imprisoned for life."

When she heard this, Mehna felt in her mind (and later confirmed) that this was a total lie created by Tutu to downplay the evil of slavery.

On another day, as Mehna worked in the meeting hall, the king had a white Englishman come in to speak to a dozen community leaders who helped him enslave others. The English leader told folks that the time aboard ship was good for the young at heart. He told them that the enslaved in Queen Mary Land had a chance for freedom and prosperity after completing a few years of work commitments. Just as Tutu had, this leader used the terms "indentured servitude" and "indentured servants" to advance the human trafficking business model in a way that people would not be afraid to support. Of all the people in the meeting, only the English leader and King Tutu knew the real truth—that indentured servitude law was only for English criminals, not for anyone from Africa.

After the light-skinned man left the room, Mehna heard the king coaching community leaders. Tutu said, "Hey, fellows, that was good to see the English captain so he could show us that slavery is not as totally horrible as some people believe. I also spoke with him privately earlier. After all we're learning, I'm asking you now to consider how to convince some of our regional people to think they should volunteer to go into enslavement. Start sharing with your communities that they could come back here to Africa in a few years, once their work is completed. The more we can do that, the more sugar, food, clothing, weaponry, and other produce we can have delivered here for improving our lives."

Mehna locked these leadership scam events into her brain. "Slavery opponents like me need to come up with some way of getting the enslaved families to realize that King Tutu has created false information about the enslaved being contracted as indentured servants," she thought. "In the future, in places around the world that practice slavery, we'll need to tell the people about Tutu's scamming. Someone needs to figure out how to show the local Ashanti people the facts about their king's lies. They need to refuse to volunteer for the king's fake offers of indentured servitude."

CHAPTER 6

ANTISLAVERY WHITE MAN, 1691

AFTER A COUPLE MORE YEARS OF WORKING AT THE Ashanti palace, eighteen-year-old Mehna and other young adults were assigned by the king's guards to escort prisoners on the six-day journey south from Kumasi to the Cape Coast Castle, where they would be sold. Each wooden cart held up to fifteen prisoners, along with a few young workers like Mehna, and a guard and driver, who carried whips and guns. Each cart was powered by two camels. Four or five carts made up the typical camel train from Kumasi to the coast.

At the end of her first camel-train journey to Cape Coast, Mehna was in awe of the castle itself, where the English and the African kings exchanged their human resources and other products. She had never seen such a large and solid building. The castle was several stories tall, rising above the rocky ocean edges. Walls of stone, taller than most trees, surrounded the entire castle.

On the inside, Mehna and her coworkers were taken through the terrible world where the African prisoners were living in worse conditions than one would ever imagine. Her first three days in the Cape Coast Castle seemed to be an inspirational visit. Several aspects of workday episodes with the prisoners ramped up Mehna's motivation to keep building a plan. At one point, she walked into the cavern where several prisoners were sitting, mostly roped together. Just as she entered, two prisoners started yelling at each other, and they started a fist fight. She charged toward these two guys and forced her way between them. "Hey, you guys. Let's not fight each other. Things are bad enough around here."

About an hour later, Mehna was approached by one of the English castle supervisors, Josh Green, while she was setting up some dinners. "Miss Mehna, I heard that you stopped two fellows from a fight earlier today. Great job. So now, the castle general's son, Martin Walpole, who helps with much of our business, wants to meet with you to talk about what you saw and how you fixed it. When you're done serving dinner downstairs later today, I'll be here to take you to see the general's son."

"Okay, thank you," she said, even though she was concerned about why the castle general's son wanted to see her.

Mr. Green found Mehna early in the evening, then he had her follow him outside the castle. They went to a building that had a storefront about a quarter mile from the castle entryway. The store had tables and chairs inside, so they sat down there, and the manager explained the current plan. "Okay, miss. Mr. Walpole will be here in a little while, but please don't be frightened about this meeting. We've heard good things about you from people who saw your work up in Kumasi. So Marty wants to meet you and work with you."

As they were waiting for the general's son, Mr. Green walked over to a counter and returned with two cups of dark water. "Here's a cup of coffee, miss," he said.

She took the cup and asked, "What is coffee, exactly? I think maybe I saw King Tutu's upper class drinking stuff like this, but I never tried it."

Josh said, "Well, around the world, there's this new product that is taking off. When you take a few sips, you'll see why. Not only does it taste good, but it gives you a little bit of energy. This stuff is getting so popular up in London that it has become a place where businesspeople hang out often with government workers. They use the new coffeehouses to get together, energize their brains, and then discuss business for hours."

"Yum, this does taste good, and I like the warmth. Let's keep an eye on my level of energy. I hope I don't get weird."

As she finished the comment, a short white man, a few years older than Mehna walked into the coffeehouse. "Hey there, Josh, and miss," he said. "Thank you so much for coming to meet me here. Hang on a minute, please, while I get a cup of coffee."

Martin Walpole came back with coffee and sat beside Josh, facing Mehna. "Maybe Josh told you who I am. Our castle leader, General Walpole, is my father. I'm here in Cape Coast maybe for a year or so, then I'm back to London to take care of some of my dad's needs up there, like checking on his sister, my Aunt Barbie. So, hey, Josh told me this is your first time here. How was your trip down from Tutu's kingdom? Please let us know if there's anything about the cart train processes that we could improve to lessen the disaster of imprisoning people."

Before she was able to respond, Mehna had to let the direction of his comment settle into her skull. She had assumed that because he was the son of the castle's leader, he too would be part of the human catastrophe. But when he said he wanted to lessen the disaster of imprisoning people, she had a moment of fusion with this man's goodness.

"Thank you, Mr. Martin. Good to meet you. My trip was okay, except for the normal difficulties of the cart train. But the sad life of the imprisoned families is the biggest problem." She paused for a minute to see if either Josh or Martin would scream back, angry about her caring for the enslaved. She wanted to holler that truly improving the cart train process can only come from ending slavery. But she needed to find out where these fellas stood before she could say any more about her position.

Mr. Walpole said, "You're right, Miss Mehna. Josh and I are both with you about the terrible plight we're generating for all of these nice people. I've heard enough feedback about you over the past few days to know that you're really close to the enslaved and that you want to improve their lives. I'm like you, Mehna. I talk to every prisoner whenever possible and try to get them to stay positive in life, even though I know it's not easy. I want this disgusting business to end during my life."

Josh nodded and smiled in agreement.

When Walpole called slavery a "disgusting business," Mehna became even more excited. She stood up, walked around the small coffee table, and gave Martin a hug. "I'm so happy to hear a white English guy be against the slavery thing." Then she stepped to their right and also patted the shoulder of Josh Green. "Thank you both so much for sharing with me your deep caring for my imprisoned people."

Martin nodded. "Okay, now we need to do a favor for each other. There are lots of people, some with light skin and some with dark skin, who are using slavery as a business for their own wealth and happiness. We have to be very careful not to let the slavery businesses and governments know where we stand. So, Mehna, please do not mention anything, anywhere, or ever about how Josh and I are truly slavery abolitionists within our hearts. We are here to help you. You want to help the good people, and we do too. So please let us know if there's ever anything we can do to support your great work, or to help you with your own life."

"Oh, Mr. Martin, you're awesome. I will never tell any of these awful kingdom leaders about your wonderful character and desire to put an end someday to human trafficking. Both of you are safe within my head. Do you know when I will be sent back to Tutu's kingdom? And if I'll ever get to see you again? We should have some more discussions."

Manager Green knew of the cart train scheduling plans, so he said, "There's a lot going on. Your king up there, Tutu, is becoming very interested in increasing the flow of European and world products into his kingdom. He wants to increase the flow of sugar, alcohol, and glass. And he wants to determine what other products are available in Europe so that he can take in even more. The sad fact is that enslaving a higher percentage of local people is the primary way the king increases his income. Marty and I have been talking about how we might be able to find an undercover agent who can tell us about the new strategies of enslavement being created by Tutu."

Martin chimed in. "I can try to help control the number of cart train tours you'll take in the future. King Tutu can override me, but I really think I can convince him that you're a major contributor to his business success. I know it must hurt such a nice person as you to know that the harder you work, the more enslavement could happen over time. But let's look at it the other way. We need to have you getting inside information on the king's goals, and we need to meet together to start seeing what else we can do to help these people."

The next day, Mehna began traveling north, back to Kumasi, the Ashanti Kingdom epicenter.

CHAPTER 7

SEEING THE ELEPHANT

ONCE SHE WAS BACK IN KING TUTU'S ASHANTI KINGDOM, Mehna began finding ways to talk with every local town leader, like her mom, when they came into Kumasi to visit the king. She spoke with each of these ohemmaa ladies secretly, to let them know about Tutu's lying and cheating ways to send people into enslavement. Mehna never actually saw changes to Tutu's objectives after she told the local ladies about his cheating in business. But at least she felt she was heading good people in the right direction, which was going to be her life forever.

About two months after she returned to Kumasi after her first journey to the coast, Mehna took off in the cart train for her second trip south, heading back to the disappointing market in human slaves, conducted in the Cape Coast Castle. The carts were rolling along at a safe pace to keep everyone in good shape.

After hours on the route, as they came out of thick wilderness onto an open field, a six-year-old girl whom Mehna had been feeding and supporting for days yelled, "Look, Miss Mehna. That tree over there looks like a giant monkey pointing at the clouds!" The little girl had a smile on her face, even though she was roped together with five other kids. Several of the children beside her pointed at the tree and laughed.

Every time Mehna saw a smile on a child-prisoner's face, deep sadness weighed heavily on her, and tears welled up in her eyes. On her first journey south since she met Martin Walpole, Mehna kept motivating herself in her head. "There's got to be a way we can help these unfortunate people," she kept telling herself.

On every trip south and north, the Kumasi camel cart trains always stopped at the Pra River to feed and water the camels. On day five of the tour, after all the captured tribespeople did their personal business in the woods and drank river water, they were loaded back into the carts beside the baskets of gold and pots of honey that were being sold to the English, along with the African families.

Seconds after the cart train began to roll, a young boy in Mehna's cart yelled, "Miss Mehna, look over there, over there!" He pointed east to the other side of the river.

One of the most stunning elephants Mehna had ever seen was standing alone on the riverbank, looking north, upriver. She nodded to this nice little boy to let him know she saw it, but she said nothing instantly because seeing this giant, stunning elephant, within view of all these families who were being enslaved, was deeply emotional.

While they could still see the beautiful African giant, Mehna stood up, pointed east, and yelled out to all of the carts, "Everyone, look at that beautiful creature. Remember this moment. It will have importance in your future lives." As she said this, the elephant slowly turned its head and looked right at the families whose lives were being stolen from them.

Because of her deep feelings for these people, Mehna felt that they would all need something tied to home in Africa to look forward to as they were shipped away. So, for the next few weeks, while she was feeding and escorting them around the castle, she often mentioned the elephant they saw on the trail ride.

Each day at the castle, Mehna asked some castle workers to let Mr. Green or the younger Mr. Walpole know she was there. On day two of Mehna's work visit, Josh came into the castle's prison area and found her. He escorted her to Martin's office.

Having not seen each other for months, Martin and Mehna were quite excited to join up. They gave each other a loving hug. "Hi, Mr. Martin," she said. "I'm glad to see you. How's it going?"

He touched one of her hands and said, "Me too. Glad to see you. I'm okay, but I'm still so sad about the traffic through here. Hey, Mehna, I have a personal request. Please, please call me Martin or Marty, not Mister. Because I just want to be one of your best friends. Not a person who wants to show supremacy over others. Okay?"

"Marty, you're a great man! So nice. Hey, on this trip down from Kumasi, something big came up. Before all the details, I just want to let you know I've really resolved for myself that the most important thing we can do these days, other than end slavery altogether, is find ways to give the people reasons to think positive and build optimism in themselves and their families. I'm sure you feel the same. So now, here's the detail of what has come up and where it might go. On this journey south, when we pulled over on the banks of the Pra River, the kids in the carts all saw quite a massive animal on the opposite bank. They were so excited, because everyone on the train felt this was the largest and most beautiful elephant we'd ever seen. And while they were all so happy to be seeing this great elephant, she acted upon their happiness by turning her head toward the train and waving her trunk at the families. So, just in this case, I'm reminding all of this train's travelers of the huge love we got from this elephant. If we see this giant in the future sending happiness toward the slaves, then you and I should start to figure how the memory of that elephant can somehow help these nice people."

Martin said, "I agree with your approach to coaching them in the direction of positive mental attitude to keep them from getting too deep into the low, negative emotions that are obviously an aspect of their situations. Wow, what a cool thing for those kids to see that large friend of theirs. We'll figure if any other positive-mental-attitude prompts can be applied as we work together."

CHAPTER 8

ELEPHANT IN THE ROOM

OVER THE NEXT TWO YEARS OF MEHNA'S CAMEL TRAIN voyages from Kumasi to Cape Coast, each time the train stopped at the Pra River to feed and water the camels and sad families, the elephant of remembrance was facing north, looking over at them and waving her trunk as they moved south past her. There was never one camel train ride heading south where their freedom friend was not there to remind them of a better future.

When the empty camel train brought Mehna and other workers back north to Kumasi to load up more imprisoned people, the elephant was never on the river. Mehna eventually knew for certain that a higher entity was making sure that the freedom elephant was on the river sending love whenever the enslaved families were passing by.

For the rest of her trips with the slaves on camel carts, and while working with them in the castle areas, she reminded these loving people that the elephant they saw would someday have a special meaning in their lives. Whenever she spoke with a prisoner out of earshot of the human traffickers, she always encouraged each teen or older individual she accompanied. "Please try to be happy," she would say. "Your new life of personal independence will begin when you or your future family members are joined by this elephant in your new land. The elephant will be your savior." And whenever she could do it without being seen by the thugs, she hugged the kids or adults with whom she was sharing ideas about their future life of freedom.

Mehna created this elephant savior remembrance plan for the future because she spent her entire days thinking about the heartbreaks of these enslaved people and families. She developed a clear path in her head, which was with her constantly during her workday. She said, "The only thing we can do for them before they board the vessels is to give them something positive to look forward to." She wanted them to know that something would eventually happen in their new land to help improve their lives.

Throughout the rest of her life, Mehna rejoiced every day when she remembered that seeing their influential elephant friend started the groundwork of her plan to free the enslaved from the world's awful rulers.

On every journey to the castle for these two years, she saw hundreds of people shackled in dark, unventilated dungeons. The floors of the dungeons were scattered with human waste. Mehna tried several times to get the local slave workforce to help clean up the dungeon floors, but the workers were mostly tasked with bringing food and water to the human harvest. They all knew that doing anything extra to help the prisoners could result in a beating or enslavement aboard one of the vessels in the bay. She still tried covertly to help ease the awful lives of many of them, but since she was starting to develop a long-range plan to help, she knew that anything compassionate she did had to remain unnoticed by the African army guards or the English.

On one trip to the coast in early 1692, while the prisoners, her new friends, were shackled together in those wet and moldy rooms of Cape Coast Castle, Mehna and other Ashanti teen workers were ordered to carry wooden boxes from a ship at the waterfront. The boxes were to be loaded into the Kumasi camel carts to prepare for the trip back to King Tutu's palace of human disgrace. These boxes were so heavy that it took at least four of the Ashanti workers to carry each box. Mehna stood near a camel cart as the last box was carried toward her. The boys carrying the box stumbled on loose ground and dropped the box. The wooden top popped opened. Inside were devices made of dark metal and wood. One of the older Ashanti boys said, "Look, these are those killer weapons that King Tutu is gathering to fight more tribal wars. The king's men call them guns."

During the next two days of labor in Cape Coast, Mehna over-heard discussions between the black Ashanti kidnappers and the white English buyers. The slave ship that her unfortunate friends would be placed on tomorrow was heading to a place the English call Mary Land, in honor of their queen.

She met up again with her friend Marty on this visit. In con-versation, when she mentioned the message she was giving to the enslaved about the elephant going around the world to free them, Marty responded with some information about Mary Land. "Hey, my lady friend. I love your idea to give them something good to look for. Let me add just a little detail about the land. Queen Mary, the ohemmaa of England, has named one colony after herself in a large place across the ocean called America. That's Mary Land, where a lot of your people are going. But other folks and kids are going to different colonies in America. I just want to let you know that when your message of love shows up in America, it will cover the people in Mary Land, but also your people in each other colony of enslavement."

Mehna's daily work at the castle, bringing food to the prisoners and escorting them out of the cave-like rooms to relieve them-selves, gave her frequent opportunities to talk with them. She spoke compassionately with the younger boys and girls, trying to ease the pain she saw on their faces. For several months, Mehna told all of the teens and younger kids that they would be free when the elephant they saw on the Pra River showed up in America. For days, she stated over and over, "After you get on the ship for your trip, I will make sure that our elephant friend begins its journey to help you be free and safe and happy. I promise—someday our people in Mary Land and other American colonies will somehow be united with an elephant of freedom."

Over all those journeys, Mehna determined that this elephant friend was a lady. On one of Mehna's journeys, a little girl in the first cart started screaming, "Ella Phant, Ella Phant," when they saw the elephant. From that time on, Mehna always called the loving elephant "Ella."

CHAPTER 9

THE FREEDOM JOURNAL, 1692

LATE IN THE SEVENTEENTH CENTURY, PRODUCTS FROM Europe included lamb and goat parchment pages and writing devices. Back in Kumasi, on a day when workers were cleaning in the king's turret, Mehna found her worker friend Zebu Thig and said, "Zebu, you told me you've read books before, and that you know about writing. I feel we should start writing down all of the hard feelings we see and feel every day. We should concentrate all the terrible stuff going on into one place and carry our thoughts forward to a better place and time. Do you know how we could get any writing gear?"

Zebu tilted his head back and forth, silently asking her to follow him out of the main room of the palace. Outside, Zebu said, "Hey, my friend, you're the nicest person I've ever known. I hear no one else talking like you about how to stop this horrible human trafficking. I have great respect for you, Mehna, and so I want to help. I think some writing materials have traveled in our camel carts back from Cape Coast. Of course, that means that King Tutu sold some people to buy writing supplies. I will try to find pages and writing tools for you."

"Thank you, Zebu. You're a great man." She gave him a big hug.

The next morning when she woke up on the dirt floor of the room she shared with the other workers, Mehna found something laying under her leather blanket. It was a leather-bound journal and two wooden writing tools. She picked up the journal and pencils and hid them under her housecoat as she left the room. As she did, she saw that Zebu was not in his thatch bed.

That same day was the start of another journey from Kumasi to the coast, with the usual cart train of eighty more prisoners. As they were in the process of getting prisoners into the carts, Mehna asked a coworker, "Koogie, have you seen Zebu yet today?"

The young lady looked down, covered her face, and walked away from Mehna. An hour later, as the last cart was being loaded with sad humans, Mehna saw something terrible and had to struggle to hold back a scream. Her friend Zebu was chained in a line with three other young men being loaded onto the cart. He had no shirt on, and his back was oozing blood from several swelling cuts. Apparently, he had been whipped with leather straps that the king's soldiers often used to beat the prisoners. Zebu avoided eye contact with Mehna.

As tears welled up in her eyes, Mehna casually walked over to Koogie and asked if she knew what had happened to Zebu. Koogie said, "He was seen going in and out of the storage hut last night, and then one of the guards said some of the writing products had been stolen."

Mehna didn't speak, but she felt like Zebu's loss of freedom was her fault. She realized she had to be more cautious if she ever again asked for help with her plan to fight the evil ones. Over the next month, she wrote a page of details into her new journal about Zebu's kindness and the deplorable turn of events in his life.

During this trip to the coast, Mehna's brain was swirling with what life her friend Zebu would now have and with what she might do to battle this world of human tragedy. She feared she could do nothing to stop the dreadful African leaders from selling their own people. They had dropped so far into outrageous, unloving, inhuman behavior toward native Africans that she knew she'd never see them change.

Mehna started to realize that the only path to higher life for her people was through the English masters. She decided she must go to their world to see if she could show them how they would feel if their families and friends were to become these chained prisoners being shipped away.

Because she could not think of anything else but going to London, Mehna came up with an idea. Over six months, she spoke to the king's guards and others in the castle about how many other products might be available in the English country—products that would support a better lifestyle for the Ashanti Kingdom. She was smart enough to know that more products coming from the English to Kumasi would mean more Africans traded into slavery. But she at least needed a plan that would get her to the central city of these slavers if she'd ever have a chance to somehow disrupt their evil marketing schemes.

CHAPTER 10

MOVE A MARKETER TO LONDON FOR MORE PRODUCTS

SHE MET WITH HER MOTHER WHEN THE OHEMMAA came down to Kumasi to meet with King Tutu and other female village leaders. With her mother's help, Mehna convinced King Tutu that she should travel to London to observe what other products could be brought back to Kumasi. The fact that she learned to speak the English language was one of the reasons the king agreed to send her to London to potentially improve future product trafficking back to Kumasi.

The king always traveled to Cape Coast Castle several times a year on his train of camel carts so that he could negotiate human sales with the British marketers. On the second hateful journey to Cape Coast in 1692, Mehna's mother joined her for the ride because she knew this could be the last time they would see each other for a long time. Mehna and her mom were in the last of six carts, and the king was in the first. Mehna sat facing the rear, so the guard driving the camels couldn't see when she pulled out the journal she kept strapped to her tummy under her clothes. When, on day five, the camel cart train stopped at the watering spot on the Pra River, Mehna saw the loving, beautiful elephant that had been at the riverbank during all of the passages of sadness. She quickly started a simple drawing in her journal and then hid the journal under her seat so she could start escorting prisoners out of the carts so they could relieve themselves and get water.

She hurried her cart members back into their seats so she could finish her drawing of the elephant of life on the first page of her journal of freedom.

The cart train arrived at Cape Coast Castle the next day. Mehna worked for the first day setting up the living areas for the new arrivals. While she did her work, her mom met with King Tutu to get ready for the business meeting between Ashanti Kingdom and the Cape Coast Castle tomorrow.

The standard meeting quorum when Tutu came down to market African lives included the king, two of his top female assistants, the Cape Coast Castle British general, the general's son, and one or more merchant ship captains. For this meeting, he also forced queen Abhoola and her daughter Mehna to be there. Because he'd decided he could benefit by sending a team of Kumasi African's to London, King Tutu started these conversations with the Brits.

"General Walpole," said the king. "I've invited some of my special people here to discuss a new recommendation we'd like to share with you. We'll cover that after I update you on the current production status. We've run lean on our mining for gold, but I'm working with other tribal leaders to the northeast to see if we can find more golden hills. We'll keep driving to meet your expectations for gold production."

The general said, "King, we appreciate your drive for more gold. We also want to discuss increasing your rate of delivery of teenage male and female farm hands. There's a large increase in European demand for sugar from Jamaica, Trinidad, and Tobago.

Also for tobacco and rice from America. So we need more workers on the ground to grow, mow, process, and ship the products. Can you increase your human supply chain?"

"Yes, sir. We will do our part to keep the production markets growing. I will increase our army's resources east of here to make that happen. To support your strategy, please ensure that the common people in the regions east of Kumasi are not given access to European firearms. Only governing leaders and their armies in kingdoms such as mine should have firearms, but not common folks. If the common people all have guns, we won't be able to overtake them and send them to you. The next time we meet, I'll have an additional five carts in the human train. General, we appreciate that you will allow our African resources to fulfill your people's needs. And this brings us to the recommendation I mentioned before."

As he gestured toward Mehna and the other two ladies from Kumasi, King Tutu said, "We want these special ladies from my kingdom to go with you to your villages in England. These young ladies will live in your society for perhaps six months. They will observe how your people live with the resources you have, and they will develop recommendations for you to ferry more of your wonderful products to us here in the Gold Coast. And as we've said, I'll make sure that you can get all of the natural resources you need from our land when the new products become available. You will see many more camel carts full of our people products."

As the king talked about selling more and more Africans, Mehna struggled to hold back from yelling, screaming, and crying. She hid her agony and emotion by immediately thinking of the Golden Stool of Ashanti and of the two angels in gold who would one day grab and squeeze the life out of this selfish man, King Tutu.

After the king's request to send Mehna and the other women to London, General Walpole rose from his chair, pointed to his son and said, "Marty, come with me. King Tutu, please wait here for a few minutes. We'll be right back."

The general led his nineteen-year-old son, Martin, across the castle epicenter to the flight of steps that went up to the top of the castle wall. As they headed up the stone stairway, Martin stared directly at the wooden door and stone archway to his right. This was the last place the African prisoners stepped on land on their home continent. Just beyond this doorway was the dock where the enslaved were boarded onto rowboats for the trip to the large slave ships. Martin didn't know what his dad wanted to talk about, but he knew it wouldn't be good. Martin had lived in this castle on and off for the past five years, watching the terrible treatment of these people by England's Whig Party.

As he climbed the stairs, his sad mind spoke to him. "This is the door of no return for these ill-fated people." This was Martin's constant grieving life, being so sad that his own father was such a large player in this human disaster. Beyond that sad aspect, he knew that his dad also expected him to be a big player in this cataclysm.

"Marty," said the general. "Those three ladies that the king is talking about should be sold as slaves. We already have enough Africans in London. In Maryland, where we're sending many of them, they can be part of the next generation. Let's not take them to London. Tomorrow, during our business improvement meeting with the ship captains, we'll ask who's got room aboard their boats for three more ladies."

Martin hid his anger over his dad's comment, then said, "Dad, let's be real. Some of them will always say they have room for three more ladies, but they'd never say they have more room for three more men. That's how the trafficking works. Overall, I see your point, but I don't think we should enslave any of the three of them. Two of those he's talking about should be just left here in Africa. But for his marketing desires, the girl called Mehna could meet his goals. This young lady is so much more engaging and smart than even white girls her age at home. Think of it. In her teen years, while helping our country's marketing needs, she has learned to speak and write our language. How about if she can help us to improve the passage of more products to these kings— the ones that sell their people for our goods and money?"

The next day, before he started his business improvement meeting with the captains of the seventeen ships anchored in the harbor, General Walpole took his son's recommendation into account. First thing in the morning, Mehna and her mom were told of the decision for Mehna to go to London and for the two other girls, Bixie and Modesty, to be enslaved and taken across the Atlantic to America.

They walked down a dark hallway to be by themselves for a minute, and then Mom said, "Oh, Mehna. This is incredible that you'll be going away to that place they call London. I'm worried about when I will see you again. The king says he thinks you'll spend about a year there, getting to know their marketing products and processes. He says he will request that General Walpole plans for your return after that one year. I'll miss you so much, as will all the village young people that you've fostered so well over the years. I heard that the boat ride is about ten weeks long to London, so that will be hard. Be safe up there, dear."

Mehna's mother and the king with his crew headed back to Kumasi on the camel train, each cart filled with products from London. The king's discussions with his staff during the trip north clearly showed how proud he was of these carts full of foreign products, which would benefit mostly the Ashanti elite—himself, his family, his management teams, and the Ashanti army leaders.

CHAPTER 11

ROYAL AFRICAN COMPANY FINANCIAL CRISIS

MARTIN WENT INTO THE RAC FINANCIAL CALAMITY meeting room before the captains arrived and he sat with the general, his dad. "I'm okay with your recommendation, son," said the general. "Lady Mehna will be going to London."

Martin immediately sensed some worry about Mehna traveling alone with these human traffickers, but then he became very pleased when his father asked him to travel with her to London and to set her up for the year-long plan to increase the volume of products sent to King Tutu. "Son, I really think we need you to help establish increased product flow from London, through here, and up to the king in Kumasi. So, with both you and the king's assistant, we should be able to create a plan over the next year to ramp up profits. You can help her become familiar with the Royal Exchange shops in London, the coffee shops, and more, so that she sees what might be good choices for the king's life north of us."

The seventeen slave-ship captains entered the meeting room. The assembly's agenda was specific to the improvement of the ocean crossing, not the castle business. Therefore, Martin was not expected at this meeting. He headed out to find Mehna, to give her the congratulations she deserved.

With all of the ship captains there, and after the arrival of one other person, General Walpole started the meeting. "Welcome, gentlemen. We know the difficulties of having to set sail on a very specific day and time. So, thank you for your efforts to be at this very important meeting. Most of us know that our Royal African Company is really in the middle of a financial catastrophe. More than anyone else, you know that the losses of lives of slaves during the ocean crossings are really contributing to our financial crisis. So today's meeting is a brainstorming session to see if we can figure ways to get more workers to their destinations. Now, I'm just here to listen in. Manager Gilbert is here to lead your conversations about changes that are needed." The general pointed to Mr. Gilbert, who stood up and waved.

"Thanks, General. Hi, guys. Mr. Stuart, your RAC president, is up in London very eagerly waiting to see the great improvements that will come from this meeting. Like General Walpole said, the primary goal of this meeting is to significantly lower the percentage of workers who die during transport. So there are eighteen of us here now. To get this improvement plan done in reasonably short order, let's break out into three teams of six. Each team will start by having deep discussions to highlight and understand the primary causes of death. In about three hours, we'll bring all three teams together to share the primary causes of death that each team has identified. After fusing the teams' ideas together, we'll separate again and come up with corrective actions to address those causes of death. Let's go. Break up into three teams and go find a place to talk. Let's get the RAC back to high profitability."

After a full day back and forth, the three teams and the full group got to a point where recommendations for improvement were agreed upon. They ended up with six potential changes that might increase the probability of a traveler staying alive. Four of the suggested upgrades were to improve the interior design of slave vessels to make it easier for the ship's sailors to see what was going on, to separate the enslaved more from each other, and to better process their mealtimes and bodily excretions. One recommendation for improvement was focused on managing the processes better by adding higher numbers of ship workers to handle the needs of the enslaved.

As the three troubleshooting teams got together for the last time, a major issue came up from the manager's opinion on these five recommendations. "Nice try, Caps," he said. "But there's a problem with these. I wouldn't dare bring these recommendations to President Stuart. I should have had us spend more time talking about finances and profitability. You're correct about these ship design changes and adding more resources to manage the vessel. But unfortunately, our Royal African Company doesn't have enough cash to rebuild all of our ships or to add more workers across the whole business. These things are needed, but we can't ask for them without a better plan. Comments, please."

The leader of team one spoke up. "We mentioned earlier one other recommendation, so I'd like to bring it up again. Us ship captains know full well that it's our responsibility to improve slaves' chances of living to keep our profits solid. However, we also know that we're so focused on sailing and our own lives that we often lose sight of what's going on down below decks. So we spent an hour just before this to reach a breakthrough on this problem and increase our focus on the issues below deck. Here's what we came up with. I think you'll agree. I can give this recommendation to you really quickly. Here goes. So, Captain Starr, if you board a hundred workers tomorrow morning, I'll hand you fifty pounds. When you get to America, if you have a hundred workers still alive, you'll get another fifty pounds. If you have fewer than seventy-five workers alive, then you have to give the first fifty pounds back to RAC. What do you think, Captains? Will that kind of a gratuity increase your focus on the living?" Mr. Gilbert ended the conference by telling the captains that he and Captain White would take the team's recommendation back to the RAC president to improve the company's profits.

CHAPTER 12

MEHNA'S RIDE TO LONDON

A CASTLE SLAVE PADDLED MARTIN AND MEHNA IN A canoe from the castle dock to the merchant sailboat which they climbed aboard for the nine- to eleven-week trip to London. The ship was anchored about a half-mile offshore with sixteen other British vessels. Martin knew this ship's crew members, and they knew he was General Walpole's son, so he shared with each of them that this African girl was a close friend of his and that the general was shipping her to London to help their marketing business. He shared this info to help protect Mehna from these human traffickers. He showed her around the vessel so she could see how they sustained life. Martin helped her get set up in one of the boat's empty cabins.

After the first full night on the vessel, when he was comfortable that Mehna was safe, Martin walked up on deck where the captain had an office. As they shook hands, Captain White said, "Hey, here you are, Marty. Your dad told me after our business improvement meeting that you'd be coming with us to London again. What's up? Are you heading home to stay, or just temporarily?"

"Well, Captain," said Martin. "I'm not really sure when or if I'll be coming back to the castle. I'm working for Dad and the kings to ramp up the product types, hoping to offset the Royal African Company's losses over the past year. You probably heard about increasing product types and quantities in that upgrade meeting.

What other ideas of improving the business were covered in the meeting yesterday?"

Captain White said, "You're right about the product upgrade discussions. The captains from all these ships out here in the bay were included in the discussions about the financial problems of our company. We heard the core of the company's plans to increase types of British products that the African kingdoms could use. As the African people become more familiar with and more in need of our stuff that will help those kingdoms increase their numbers of human assets they deliver to us. That was shared with the group, but here's the primary topic that was covered in the meeting. You probably know that most of our slave vessels lose over thirty-five percent of black lives when crossing the ocean. This is a big loss for our company. The meeting's week-long facilitator, a Whig commercial manager from England, challenged the team to figure out ways to reduce the high number of lives lost during the Atlantic crossing. Because this is another issue driven by the ongoing financial losses, the captains were motivated to come up with some universal improvements. That whole day was spent formulating how to save more of the lives so the Royal African Company can increase profits. Finally, an idea came to the forefront. All the shippers at the meeting, who make up only about five percent of the company's total ship captains, proposed that the slave-ship captains need some kind of special gratuity for each slave that makes it across the ocean alive."

Bewildered by the discussion of profit over life, Martin kicked in with a slightly emotional response. "To hear that so many lives continue to be lost means that something needs to change. Thanks for the update. Just so you know, my dad told me some of this already. He said you'd be taking the recommendation for a gratuity payment to the company's headquarters to try to get it moving. He wants me to roll with you into headquarters to see what might take off. Then I'll let him know the details of any changes he needs to incorporate into the slave boarding process at his castle."

Captain White said, "Okay, good. We'll go to headquarters to meet with Mr. Stuart and his managers. This shouldn't affect your dad's castle operations too much. He'll just have to set the ships up with whatever process Stuart approves to establish how many workers enter the ship in Africa and how many make it to the American colonies or the Caribbean Islands. We're already discussing the idea of asking the Royal Mint to create some kind of money for the gratuities to the ships' captains if they can improve their delivery status."

"All right," said Martin. "I have a few friends that work at the Tower Mint, so, as the process unfolds, from our discussions with Mr. Stuart's managers, maybe we'll be able to merge with the mint team to see if anything can tie this life-saving thing together."

"Okay, let's try that."

CHAPTER 13

THE JOURNEY NORTH, AFRICA TO ENGLAND

AS THEY SETTLED IN FOR THE LONG CRUISE, MARTIN surprised Mehna with a new topic. "Hey, dear. I'm a little concerned about some of these sailors. They don't usually see free black people, so I hope they won't be mean or weird to you. Here's what I'm going to suggest. I'm quite bored on these long trips, so I just wander around and help the crew with anything I'm comfortable with. Are you willing to do the same? Come around with me and help with meals or cleaning, just so they can see we're self-sufficient?"

"I'm okay with that. I think I might also be a bit bored on these days coming up. But don't forget that I'm going to be spending most of my unrestricted time writing the freedom journal to get Ella the elephant to Mary Land, which I now call America, thanks to you."

Fortunately, their trip came about during late summer, so the weather was okay. Throughout the final six weeks of travel, Marty and Mehna were spending a fair amount of time together sharing thoughts. Each morning, she continued the work on her journal, and then she let him know if any new ideas had popped up.

"So, my friend," Mehna said. "Let's keep talking about London. I'm both excited and nervous about getting there. You've told me about your past jobs with the Royal African Company and that you hate the human trafficking so much that you don't want to work for them anymore. But your dad expects you to keep it going. So how's that going to play out?"

He lowered his head and began to describe why he disagreed with his dad's business. "You're so sweet and kind, and so concerned for all humans being excluded from fair and honorable treatment. Let me share some of the reasons I'm with you on human kindness.

"A few years ago, I went with my dad's company to the new Carolina region in the American colonies. I was there for several weeks, so I found time to ride horses inland and meet some settlers. During that time, I was approached in the woods by some young native folks of a tribe called Neuse. They were heavily engaged in moving their families away from their land, which had been taken over by our settlers. It was so hard for them. They had to move because our mean people absorbed the land, the wildlife, and the vegetable fields away from the natives. Their day-to-day safe lives were taken away by our Whig settlers—the same ones that want your people to go there as slaves."

With a sad face and slow shake of his head, Martin continued. "Mehna, there's so much wrong with our Whig political ideologies and business practices supported by our racist government. It's incredible that they're the same immoral people as the African kings who sell people to get cash and goods. They are both so against the people's needs and desires. That's why they make up false stories to hide their evil plans from the people. Now that newspapers can be printed very routinely and shared with the public, King William cancelled our 1643 Licensing Act early this year, so companies and the government now have the right to pay news firms to report false information to the public. Most people don't know that reporters are printing false information to improve the profitability of slavery."

Martin put both elbows on the table and slowly laid his forehead into his hands. Mehna just stared at him, worried that he wasn't feeling okay.

Then Marty slowly lifted his head again and looked right into Mehna's eyes. "Mehna, dear, I just realized something else. The reason they're called the Whigs is because it's known that they hide the truth from all the public and convince folks with fabricated stories. They're hiding their real head of racism and slavery by using false stories and by not telling the public the truth of what's going on behind the scenes."

Mehna squeezed his hands and smiled at him. "Marty, if these racist asses are also in charge of government in America, then when she gets there, Ella will put an end to the Whigs hiding of the truth from all people there. I hope we can keep visiting together in London as you begin working, because I really love your true kindness, civility, and your thoughts about changing the world to a better place for all people. I'm with you all the way, Marty! You're the kindest person from England that I've met."

Marty said, "Good call, about Ella Phant restoring the truth for the people, so that government leaders like the Whigs can't just take care of their elites. So, your journal is going to get there, and somehow it will become exposed beyond reason, and then all the people will think they're seeing Ella the elephant. Let's talk about what might actually show up over there for them to see. Any ideas of that yet?"

Shaking her head, Mehna said, "I've got some potential ideas, but they're not ready yet. So far, this is what we have." She picked up the leather-bound journal that Zebu gave her before his life was stolen. After her sadness for Zebu, which she felt every time she touched the journal, she opened the cover to the first page and turned it toward Martin.

"This drawing is a combination of my favorite draft of Ella with a circle around her, which I added after you told me that your dad's company will be paying slave-ship captains more than they already do. I just tried to draw an elephant coin so you and I could discuss if this is a way for my people to get to the point of hoping for a future of freedom. What do you think?"

"Hey, my lady! You really have it. You already came up with a way to send the elephant to America. Not sure if that's our final choice, but good start. I do know a few workers at the Royal Mint who are expert at coin manufacturing. We also have a good relationship between the Royal African Company and the Royal Mint, because we deliver gold and silver from your region in Africa to the Royal Mint for their coins. Captain White told me that King William or Queen Mary or the mint master will not agree to make a real coin just for my dumb company to use for their own business improvement. He also said that President Stuart, who runs Royal African Company, will not use normal coins to engage his captains in this new gratuity game for better profits. He can't afford that right now, while RAC is heading into financial crisis. I'll be working with the mint and Captain White and maybe others from RAC to see what options we can find to implement a new plan for the gratuity. We need something that Mr. Stuart will agree to implement for his vessels around the world. Of course, you and I know that something has to change to stop the many deaths while crossing the ocean, so we'll do what we can to help design the new ship captains' gratuity coin."

For the final weeks of the journey, Mehna and Martin continued discussing all the issues with which they'd been dealing for several past years. Then they talked about which aspects of their conversations to carry into the elephant journal. At one point, Mehna put a title on page one of the journal: The Elephant Freedom Journal. As they neared the end of this journey, these two felt fairly confident that their upcoming time in London would result in some special outcomes.

A day before they entered the River Thames, which leads to London, Mehna and Martin pulled everything together from the past two years they'd known each other. They returned to the topic of what it would really take to end slavery.

Martin reminded her that they already had one solid idea that could be the answer. "We've used the word *abolitionist* to describe people like us who want to stop human enslavement. Except for real abolitionists, the greater population is either morally against people with different skin colors than themselves, or they're just too afraid to anger the human traffickers who only care about profits. You and I agree that we, as true abolitionists, need the help of many others who are willing to risk their lives to stop the enslavement of any human beings. So, from everything you've taught me and shared with me, I've come to a recommendation for us, Mehna. I think the whole basis for Ella showing up in America is that some version of her, whatever we choose, has to become aligned with years and years of abolitionism. Ella will have to, in some yet-to-be-determined manner, pull all of America's reputable and dedicated nice people together into one sophisticated group. We know they're there and will always be there, because good people are everywhere. I feel this abolitionist strategy is essential to obtaining enough clout from the good people of earth to end the horror driven by the world's racists."

Mehna agreed. "That's so good, Marty. You're right on with that strategy. And you're so righteous with your love of people and all that you do, sharing your virtue, decency, justice, morality, and honesty. So, because of you, I'm adding a page about our elephant plan. Ella was facing to the left every time we saw her. So, I'll report in the freedom journal that she's always facing to the left because she wants to protect the good people on the right, behind her, from the human traffickers she's facing on the left."

CHAPTER 14

SHIP ARRIVED IN LONDON IN SEPTEMBER 1692

DURING THE TEN-WEEK JOURNEY FROM CAPE COAST, Mehna and Martin developed a special relationship, one filled with a major project, figuring out how to get the elephant to be seen by Mehna's people in America.

The ship entered the Thames River east of London just an hour after sunrise. Martin woke Mehna up and helped her get ready to leave the ship. Once up and packed, they headed to the top deck of the ship with their bags of supplies and headed down the ship's ladder and into a rowboat in the middle of the river.

When they reached shore, Martin stepped off the rowboat onto the Royal African Company's dock. "Maybe I'll hire a hackney carriage tomorrow or Wednesday to give us a tour of the city." Marty kindheartedly held Mehna's hand and pointed toward the city streets. "Let's head up this road. There's a place called the Royal Exchange that I need to show you. Maybe we can set you up with a job there, since it's a huge marketing area. Then you can start doing the product-trafficking evaluations that King Tutu has assigned to you. More importantly, you'll also have a chance to absorb detail of the slavery insights that the Whigs continue to push on the world. If you work there, or wherever, be careful with whom you discuss your Ella plan. Many of those whom you'll meet this year will be those who've been tricked by the Whigs into thinking slavery is a necessary and good thing for the world. I don't think most of the Whig supporters are really awful people, but they get so much false information about black folks, economic strategies of slavery, and more. My point is, let's be careful with whom we share your Ella plan. Make sure we know that they're abolitionists, like us, before we bring them into your plan."

Mehna definitely agreed. "Oh, good to hear. We want this to be pulled together by abolitionist people like you and me, Marty. If I were to talk to the wrong Whig, it would just allow them to find ways to stop my people from meeting the elephant in America. That won't happen. Thanks."

They walked a few kilometers around the center of London. Mehna had never seen anything like this modern city, and she'd never been in a place with so many white folks and so few Africans. At first, Mehna zeroed in on every detail of the city streets and people walking around. There were so many aspects of infrastructure and clothing worn by people that she had never seen before. As they continued up a road from the river, she saw other trails to the left and right with signs showing street names. At one intersection, she saw a sign that said, "Lombard Street." As they crossed the intersection, looking down Lombard, she saw a sign on a building on the left for Lloyd's Coffeehouse. Pointing to it, she said, "Hey, Marty. I think you mentioned Lloyd's Coffeehouse to me a couple of times on our boat ride. Is that it?"

Holding her hand, he turned them to the right, down Lombard Street. "Yes, that's the business I mentioned, but not in this location. Mr. Lloyd just moved his coffee shop here from Tower Street last year, while I was in Africa with you. I used to visit them on Tower Street, but I've never been in his new location. Let's head in there now. I want to show you what they have for food and drink, and then we'll sit down and talk about what's next for today and this year."

They entered Lloyd's. Since it was the middle of the afternoon, the restaurant was only about 25 percent full of customers, so it was easy for them to just choose an open table. Mehna sat, and Martin went up to the counter. He ordered coffees and muffins and brought them back to Mehna. "You've had coffee once or twice at the castle, so here—try another one. Enjoy. After this, we'll head to my aunt's home. She's only about six kilometers from here, and it's a fun hike through the city. There are a couple of sheds out back of her home that Dad and I use when we come back here from Africa. We'll meet with Aunt Barbie and ask her to let us both use her sheds, maybe for the rest of this year."

After Mehna and Martin made their way north to his Aunt Barbie's house, they relaxed the rest of the day, visiting with his aunt and getting settled into the two sheds out back. His aunt was also a great antislavery, humanity advocate, the one who raised Martin to be caring and sweet to all people. She had been fully blind since she was eight years old. To Marty's way of thinking, her blindness was representative of her beliefs that skin color should have nothing to do with how governments treated various cultures. He saw her point of view as one where all people deserve equal rights, regardless of how they look.

The next morning, Mehna and Marty met up and made their way back down to Lloyd's for breakfast. They were both very ready to sit and start working on Mehna's plans for collaboration with American abolitionists.

As they were sitting again in the coffeehouse, Mehna shared her first thought to get the discussion going on the Ella plan. "I'm suggesting we really focus on the plan for Ella to end racial turmoil in America against my people. I can't work anymore on that product list for King Tutu to enslave more people. You okay with this approach?"

Marty said, "Oh, yeah. That sounds good. I agree that if we're going to start the world's focus on stronger abolitionism, we must do it as soon as possible to begin freeing your people. Even this plan of yours may take hundreds of years or several generations to overcome the heavy racial disparity of these Whigs, their businesspeople, and those African kingdom leaders. So let's keep it going. Don't forget, tomorrow or sometime in the next week, I'm meeting with Captain White at the Royal African Company's office on Threadneedle Street, not far from here. I'll be working with him and Mr. Stuart's managers to see about building that gratuity process for the ship captains."

As they were sitting in Lloyd's, Martin introduced Mehna to some of the workers and their boss. He mentioned to the supervisor, Bonnie Harper, that they would appreciate it if Lloyd's could hire Mehna for a temporary job for the next year or so. Bonnie came back out to them an hour later and asked to give Mehna a tour of the facility. Out in the restaurant seating area, none of the waitresses or bar maids were black Africans. But when Mehna followed Bonnie out to the kitchen, she saw several of her fellow Africans working out there, where the public could not see them.

Bonnie asked, "Would you be okay working out here with your people?"

Mehna looked around the kitchen, thinking of her answer to the question. "Oh, of course. But I'd also like to work out on the floor with your light-skinned waitresses so I can meet more of your Londoners. Would that be okay with you?"

"Oh, Miss Mehna, you're too brave. Most of our customers are merchants and their staff who come here to read newspapers and talk business. Because of their business motivations and support from the Whigs, most of them are tormenters of your people. That's why I ask these nice ladies to work out back here, away from those money-hungry thugs."

Several of the worker ladies overheard the discussion. They looked toward Bonnie and Mehna and smiled and waved.

Mehna was so happy that she'd met another sweet person who cared for all human beings. "Miss Bonnie, I'm happy to meet you. Thank you for caring for these ladies. Let me ask, though. Are they enslaved by this Lloyd Coffeehouse owner, or are they free to live for themselves?"

Bonnie slowly bowed her head and closed her eyes for seconds. Then she looked back at Mehna. "You're new here, so let me describe what's going on with Africans in London, so that you won't get surprised somehow. It's quite disgraceful here. The political Whigs and the slavery businesses are constantly saying that black people are not as intelligent as whites. They do it to make the general public believe that slavery is good and necessary for both sides. So hateful, these businessmen and women. I know these ladies well and love them very much. They live with my husband and me on our farm. Working with them here and hanging out around town and the farm, I know for certain we're all of same mental capacity, and the Whigs are so wrong. Oops! I might be a little wrong too. I'm sure that some of these ladies are way smarter than me."

Mehna touched her shoulder. "You're so sweet, Miss Bonnie."

Bonnie said, "Oh, thanks. But let me finish this point, because it's really something you need to be aware of to protect yourself. My husband, Jack, and I and some other farmers up our way, are so much against what the Whigs and businesspeople are doing to your people. We try as hard as we can to support you Africans. But here's the thing. I've heard many conversations out on the coffeehouse floor over the past year where business leaders are trying to convince the Whigs to pass a law that will make it illegal for any English persons like me and my husband to support slaves who escape from their owners anywhere in this country. They are pushing really hard for an escapee slave law. So, to protect them from Whig tyranny, my friends here in the kitchen must be represented as slaves, not escapees or free citizens. Jack and I have given them freedom to work, shop, and travel. But even that puts them into a dangerous position because of the racist politicians and business leaders. Therefore, to abolish that new reckless law that they are trying to design, we've been talking about some way to have these nice ladies show anyone who challenges them that they have their owner's permission to be wandering around freely. Not sure what the design will be, but something like a tattoo, a badge, a token, or a bracelet that they can show to anyone who challenges their appearance of living free. We will share information with the public about the badge, or whatever it is, so we might trick the terrible people into believing that these nice folks are not free but are enslaved with our permission to be out around the city doing errands for the farm."

Bonnie and Mehna headed back out and sat with Martin at the table. Fortunately, they were seated in a corner with no one within hearing distance, so they could continue their discussions.

Mehna said, "Wow. This is such a crazy world we live in. So many nice people are being hoodwinked into supporting the bad ones. I saw the same thing going on in Kumasi, Africa. The king there lies to everyone, telling them that it's not slavery. He calls it indentured servitude, and he tells them they only need to work for one year. With that lie, he asks them to volunteer to be slaves. Then if they say no, he kidnaps and sells them and their families for products to support his wealth. He's a lying, selfish leader, just like your Whigs."

Bonnie said, "And it's not just the political Whigs. They have close ties to London-area newsletter journalists who get paid top pounds to put the Whig's deceitful information out to the public. The reporters are paid probably hundreds of pounds to report the falsehoods made up by these selfish politicians. In my opinion, all of those men wear wigs on their heads because they want to look like someone nicer than who they really are."

After a bit more discussion between the three of them about the political supporters of slavery, Martin changed the subject. "We're all on the same side. That's great. So, listen. Mehna and I have a plan to meet with a friend of mine who is also a nice anti-slavery guy, and he's a coin maker at the Royal Mint, so he might talk with us about your ideas for badges, tokens, or something for your friends to be reminded of freedom. We're heading off now, and I'll let you and Jack know when we're going to have that meeting and maybe others."

"Oh, that's great," said Bonnie. "I'll check with managers here at Lloyd's to see if we can hire you, Mehna."

CHAPTER 15

GRATUITY PROCESS DESIGNERS

THE NEXT DAY, MEHNA STAYED BACK AT AUNT BARBIE'S shed and continued writing chapters in the Ella journal. Martin headed downtown to the Royal African Company's office on Threadneedle Street, half a kilometer east of the Royal Exchange, the world's largest marketing facility. He found Captain White at the RAC office, and the captain said he had already set up a meeting early that afternoon to start brainstorming for the new gratuity process.

The meeting included Martin, representing Cape Coast Castle; Captain White, representing the seventeen ship captains who met in Africa months back; Henry Harris, Chief Engraver at Royal Mint; and John Carlton, a vice president of the Royal African Company. Captain White started the meeting by making sure they all knew each other. Then he described the agenda as a brainstorming event to ramp up the effort to return RAC to higher profitability by improving the number of lives that would make it across the Atlantic. He told the other three men what took place in the Cape Coast Castle meeting, and then described with a dramatic delivery that the RAC team members came up with a solid solution.

In his summary statement of the prior meeting, he shared several points. "It didn't take long in that get-together of captains to see that the only path to improving the quality of passage is to provide significant gratuity to the ship captains for each life that makes it across the ocean. The team which included Whig commercial manager Gilbert who was there to facilitate the meeting is recommending that we come up with some kind of process to drive cash bonuses their way. There were hours of discussion on how to record the lives entering the ships in Africa in some way that will result in cash payment from our company when they get to America or the Caribbean Islands. Several guys even say they should get cash in Africa when the slaves enter the ships, and then they'd be totally motivated to keep the slaves alive. They'd give back to RAC any cash assigned to lives that don't cross. I've already checked with Mr. Stuart, and there is no way we'll provide a gratuity in Africa at the beginning of the voyages. Those captains are already getting paid plenty to make them and their families some of the wealthiest in England, so Mr. Stuart doesn't want to set up the cash transfers at each coastal slave entry point. Since I knew that we weren't going to give real money as gratuities, I asked Mr. Harris to come in today so we can talk about the copper tokens that we see all over London. Thanks for joining us, Henry. Let's see if we can come up with any other gratuity ideas here today. We'll talk about copper tokens first, since they're traveling around London and the colonies more and more lately."

For hours, the team used the info that came from the foundational meeting at Cape Coast. Eventually, the group agreed that some piece should be transferred with each African across the ocean. They concluded that if the slave and the badge or token both made it to America or the Caribbean, then some number of pounds would be awarded to the ship's captain. This plan became the basis of the gratuity plan that they decided to share with Mr. Stuart. Only slaves shipping directly from Africa would result in the captain getting the bonus. Just putting people onto a ship in America or the Caribbean without a token would not result in the cash award.

Marty, the youngest of the four, stood. "So now we've opened up all of the potential options to do the gratuity plan. Let's bring these ideas together, narrow them down, and close with final decisions and an action plan we can share with Mr. Stuart."

Henry shared his point of view from the Royal Mint. "As you fellows come up with the specific processes to share gratuity with the captains, I recommend you just consider the use of copper tokens, which now are fundamental marketing tools, easy to create, and not too costly for your Royal African Company."

Mr. Carlton, the RAC manager, said, "I agree on the copper tokens. Here's another idea we should consider. There are two basic avenues across the ocean. Mr. Stuart and I have discussed how we maybe should have two separate gratuity setups, one to encourage the Caribbean ship captains to improve passage, and one for the American colonies' ship captains to do the same. We think this might give both passage groups a bit of competition with each other, which could help to increase the percentage of lives making the passages. To support the competition, our company will publish the results, showing which group is doing better to increase our company's profits.

"Mr. Stuart's other position he told me to share with you is that he wants the governors of the American colonies to see that RAC is doing this to help bring more workers to them. Mr. Stuart is recommending that these tokens will also provide some benefit to our marketing in the colonies. So he wants at least the words 'God Preserve the Lord's Proprietors' to be on the tokens to show the governors that our company cares about them."

Given Mehna's relationship with Maryland slaves, Martin realized he should help steer the process toward Mehna's goals. So he stepped in. "Hey, Henry. Would something like 'God Preserve Maryland and the Lord's Proprietors' fit on the normal size copper tokens you make?"

"Sure. That will be fine for one side of a token."

John Carlton said, "Good try, Martin, but Stu wants to focus mostly on the American colony called Carolina for the next few years, because the plantations there are just starting up, while others are further along in building businesses. So, gentlemen, to follow Martin's suggestion, we would say 'God Preserve Carolina and the Lord's Proprietors' on these tokens. Mr. Stuart also wants us to discuss having another set of tokens, with some different wording or theme, to do gratuity for the captains who pull our slaves to the Caribbean or anywhere else in the world. His suggestion is to call this one a London token, to cover captains' gratuity anywhere in the world outside of America's colonies. Stu doesn't think the island slavery markets are going to keep going as much as they will in America, because they don't have the Whig political drive down in the islands like we have in American colonies."

Henry chimed in. "So that would be the wording? 'God Preserve London and the Lord's Proprietors'? Those words will also fit on one side of the basic copper tokens that we use today."

John jumped on that suggestion. "Oh, wait. The Carolina wording is okay. For the London token, since there are really no governing proprietors here in London, and not many in the Caribbean, on this set of tokens, let's just keep the wording 'God Preserve London,' with no mention of the colonial proprietors."

The meeting came to an end with the tokens partially designed. Mr. Harris told the team that he had a few token manufacturing questions that need to be answered before he could start making these. He mentioned things like thin or think planchet and asked what they wanted on the reverse side of the token.

Mr. Carlton said, "Henry, we'll have to get back to this after I update Mr. Stuart on what we've come up with so far. Let's have another meeting right here in March, when I get back from my tour of the colonies. The rest of you guys, please bring back some ideas for the reverse side of the tokens. The back side can be the same presentation for both gratuity types—Carolina and London. Let's come up with something that will help these people get across the ocean to their new homes to raise the profits of the Royal African Company."

CHAPTER 16

MEHNA GETS A JOB

THERE WERE MANY COFFEEHOUSES IN LONDON. OVER time, Mehna realized that the one called Carolina Coffeehouse, on Birching Street, just two blocks away from Lloyd's, was the most proslavery shop, because of its proximity to the Royal Exchange, the new Bank of England, and constant gatherings of ship captains, investors, bankers, lawyers, and storeowners. Anyone there for coffee or breakfast was working on business. That was why, in her third month, she decided to try to get a job at the Carolina Coffeehouse, so she could keep her motivations on high to get Ella to America.

While waiting for her job interview at the coffeehouse, she heard several marketers at the next table talking about the marketing of firearms. She was very intrigued by the discussion, because she was always thinking of the day her father got stolen from her. Dad was a pretty strong and confident guy, so she knew that if he'd owned a gun, he would not have been stolen by the local kingdom and would never have been forced to enslave other kind people.

With tears in her eyes after thinking of dad, and with her head turned away from that table of gun sellers, she said to Marty, "Hey, maybe you should start a company to sell guns to all the African people before they get stolen and sold by their own societies. Hard to believe that these awful marketers think people shouldn't be able to protect themselves."

Marty nodded. "Right, and that makes me think that in the American future, the Whig proprietors will always try to prevent the people, Africans or antislavery whites, from having weapons to protect themselves from government control. Perhaps your journal should show that free people must have their own weapons to prevent the terrible people in government from taking over their liberties and killing the drive for happiness for all."

By the middle of March, 1694, Mehna was working at the Carolina Coffeehouse. After several days of work, Mehna and Martin were having their daily journal meeting back at Aunt Barbie's. Marty's friend, a Royal Mint coin maker named Norbert Roettier, joined them at the picnic table near the sheds behind Barbie's house. Norbert showed up here because Martin knew that he was a great abolitionist, and Marty invited him to meet Mehna. While Mehna was at work that day, Martin and Norbert hung out and discussed how to best help her build and launch her freedom journal plan.

That evening, Norbert told Martin and Mehna that he'd over-heard some political staffers say that King William just set up a meeting in London with all of the American colonial proprietors three months from now in June. Both were silent for a few seconds. They were each thinking about whether or not those meet-ings with the colonies' governors could be used by Ella to start the journal plan. No ideas came out on how to use or intrude into that sorrowful meeting of proslavery governors.

After some of the random discussions she'd overheard at work that day, Mehna asked Norbert, "How about your English king and queen? Are they as proslavery and selfish as the king I know in Africa?"

Norbert said, "King William is really not so good. He's antireli-gion, so we've been at war with France for over six years because they are strong Christians, and King Billy hates them. He is also not so good toward women. He took his first cousin, Mary, from her family when she was fifteen years old and forced her to marry him. His favorite caffeine joint, Jonathan's Coffeehouse, doesn't even allow women to enter the building. Of course, he is also proslavery, because he's all about himself and his family, and he's really close to the Stuarts, who own the Royal African Company. He would never do anything to stop their racial business. In fact, he wants to secure his family name into the American slavery colonies, so just last year, on February eighth, he established a college in the American colony called Virginia. He named it the College of William and Mary to make sure his name and his cousin-wife's name will be sitting in the slavery colonies forever."

CHAPTER 17

RACIAL AGGRESSION

ONE DAY AT CAROLINA COFFEE, MEHNA OVERHEARD A bunch of businessmen talking about a fleet of treasure ships that got wrecked weeks earlier by a storm on March first down near Spain. She lingered around their table as the waitress, but she didn't let them know she was saddened by their talk. One of them said that those thirteen sunken ships killed over eleven hundred sailors. These proslavery coffee drinkers were so sad and upset over those lost lives. All Mehna could think of was how disappointing it was that they didn't care about any of the many African lives lost on slaving voyages, but they were so upset only over their own lost peoples. She thought they were probably not given information about the hundreds of African lives lost on ships each month.

On another day, months later, there was this guy at the Carolina shop who Mehna had seen every day, sitting and celebrating with various businesspeople. She heard over time that his name was Thomas Amy. He spent all his time in the house talking with potential Carolina investors and settlers. One day in June of 1694, Mehna saw people congratulating him. He'd been granted twelve thousand acres and then was given dictatorship as the Lord's Proprietor over forty-eight thousand acres in Carolina. The day after his assignment as proprietor with millions of pounds in value, Mr. Amy started his plan to move to America.

Mehna was doing her afternoon waitress work. Marty usually came in about then so he could walk home with her after work, but he was not there yet. There were only about nine guys in the shop for coffee. As she was cleaning up a newly vacated table, the front door came crashing open just to her left. She turned suddenly to look, and just a second before she was crushed, she saw two men charging at her, one of whom she recognized as Thomas Amy, the new Carolina Colony proprietor. They grabbed Mehna's arms and started to pull her out of the coffeehouse. She didn't scream or fight them off yet, because she expected that some non-Whig in the shop might step up and help her. But that didn't happen, so out the door they went.

Standing just outside the shop on Birching Lane, Amy confronted Mehna. "So you saw yesterday that our king granted me ownership of the colony of Carolina, where I'll be establishing government and distributing land to our business owners. I'm going to bring you with me to Carolina so you can be working to support my proprietor staff for the rest of your life. Here we go." They pulled Mehna south on Birching Lane, heading toward the river.

Martin was always so eager to meet up with his friend Mehna so they could enjoy their walk home and keep working on Ella's journal. He always increased his walking speed when heading to meet her. Now he turned right off from Cornhill Street onto Birching Lane. After his first ten steps down the sidewalk, he suddenly began to sprint because he saw two men walking out of the coffeehouse with Mehna held between them. He was afraid if he tackled these bullies, he'd hurt Mehna too, so he ran past the three of them, and swung back around. With fists up, he shouted, "What are you doing? This is my friend Mehna, not a slave and not your mistress. Let her go now, or we're going to have a fist fight, right here, right now."

Thomas Amy's comrade let go of her arm and took off right at Martin. As they began wrestling, Mr. Amy started pulling Mehna back toward Cornhill Street. She was confident Marty would win his fight and catch up to her in minutes.

"Mr. Amy, stop this," she yelled. "I promise I'll someday go to America's colonies, but not with you. I will be there to stop you terrible human traffickers and people haters."

Just as they reached the intersection of Birching and Cornhill, slaver Thomas Amy was slammed from behind and taken down onto the street. Marty quickly reached for Mehna's left hand and hurried off with her. They reached Threadneedle Street about four minutes after the Carolina proprietor's attack.

"Mehna, dear, sorry about those awful guys. Look, there's the New England Coffeehouse over there. We haven't tried it yet, but it's really known as one that's less Whig and more friendly than most of the shops. Let's sit in there and talk please."

They sat down inside, and Martin ordered them some drinks and food. Mehna said, "Thanks for saving me, Marty, my friend. They provided me with even more motivation to stop the horror. Tonight, with Norbert, we should really try to pull our freedom plan together. You told us last night that you have the final gratuity meeting in a couple of days, so we have to determine several aspects of our plan. Two particular open items are the back side of the Carolina and London gratuity tokens, and we still have to create an elephant token to support our journal and we have to decide how and where it will get launched."

After Marty came back with their dinner, Mehna continued. "Once Norbert looks at my drawing of Ella and determines that she fits and can be put on a copper token, you'll be able to recommend her for the gratuity tokens, so that any Africans might be enthused that Ella travelling with them across the ocean is maybe starting the fight for freedom. Even if it takes generations to raise the abolition process, the enslaved in the coming years will at least be able to feel that a better future for our people is on its way to them."

Martin said, "I agree so much that those two awful guys, who represent the entire Whig and business cultures of racism and slavery, just now gave us much greater motivations for your Ella plan. Let's get really specific this evening with Norbert, finally narrowing all of our findings and feelings into a grand plan for the abolishment of slavery in America."

Before they headed home, Marty shared one more idea with Mehna. "I was here at the New England Coffeehouse earlier today. One thing for sure. More abolitionist types hang out at this shop than at those Carolina and Lloyd shops, where only pro-slavers hang out. Today, we had several discussions about the colonies and slavery. The manager here told me that, for many kind English people, the name New England means that the American northeastern colonies will eventually stop the inhuman businesses. These nice people who come here to hang with angels and hide from the devils in the other coffee joints all think that New England, and especially the colony just appointed by King William last year called New Hampshire, will someday force and forever hold all peoples' freedom and happiness into the top of America's laws and culture. For these kind, caring folks, the word *new* in those titles represents the geographic home and the beginning of the end to slavery. So, for us, the combination of New England, New Hampshire, and the new Ella political group will lead to good overtaking evil. One more thing. On the way home, let's stop by Miss Bonnie's coffee shop and see if she and her husband, Jack, can meet with us tonight at Aunt Barbie's."

CHAPTER 18

ELEPHANT, LEFT OR RIGHT

THAT EVENING, BACK AT BARBIE'S PICNIC TABLE, ALL five of the abolitionists were meeting up: Mehna, Martin, Norbert, Bonnie, and Jack. Aunt Barbie asked her nephew Martin to guide her out to their meeting site so she could be part of the freedom team.

In her time in London, Mehna had seen lots of women wearing black patches of little stars or half-moons on their faces. That evening, when they were all together, Bonnie pointed to Mehna and said, "Hey, nice star patches you've gotten on your forehead. I used to do that. Looks good, dear."

Mehna had a friend at the coffeehouse put three stars on her forehead. "Some of my African lady friends at work wear these black stars. I feel like I'm carrying their needs forward from their foreheads to Ella's. I'll probably keep wearing these for the rest of my life."

Martin began the meeting with a detailed revelation of everything he and Mehna had been through over the past year. He let them all know how compassionate Mehna had been throughout her life and how serious she was about stopping the business of slavery. After people exchanged hugs and expressions of love and thanks, the conversations took off toward coming up with ways to ensure the slaves in America would someday be aware of an American elephant, as Mehna had told thousands of the enslaved over the past four years. Marty asked Mehna to share the elephant of freedom story with Norbert, Bonnie, Jack, and Aunt Barbie.

She held up the journal, showing her drawing of Ella. Mehna shared her life of sadness all the way back to when her dad and brother were stolen from their family, and how she traveled with and assisted so many enslaved children and their parents. She described the deep emotions she and the enslaved lived through when so many sad and loving kids were with her in the camel cart trains. Next, she told of an incredible event on the banks of the Pra River, where they always stopped to feed and water the camels and let the prisoners relieve themselves.

"After everything we've been through while developing the journal, I'm able to look back and describe that some divine being must have been overseeing the love of humanity. So I asked this amazing animal, the elephant, to give its love to the enslaved families. Every time we rode from King Tutu's prison-town down to the slave center on the coast, this animal friend was on the riverbank, facing left, and then always looking over at the children locked in the camel carts. She would waggle her tusks and trunk toward them, sending a message of love and caring. After slaves were offloaded into the castle, and as the king's staff drove us back to Kumasi to the north in the empty carts, this beautiful elephant was never there to look back at the slavers. Marty and I now call her Ella, which came from a kid that called her Ella Phant." She laughed. "In this journal, I've shown that she is facing left every time the camel train comes by to show that she is confronting the terrible people in Kumasi who promote slavery, and that she's facing this direction because the slaves are heading south toward her rear on their right, so she wants to protect them from the criminals upriver on the left. Other than loving care from a high up godly being, why else would she have been there every time the slave trains came by, and why else would she always be facing left, toward Kumasi? So the message for humanity is that Ella, as

73

shown in this drawing, is facing the left and wagging her tusks to send a message to King Tutu and other African kings that she will someday free the enslaved."

The team of good people all jumped up, arms to the sky, and responded with hugs, congratulations, and thanks for her journal work. Then Mehna told of her and Martin's plan to move the journal and maybe some tokens of Ella to the American colonies, where all the enslaved families she supported were told that when they see the elephant in America, their free lives would start to be recovered.

Martin shared with the group the new gratuity process, whereby the Royal African Company will use copper tokens to monitor the numbers of slaves that make it across the ocean and to pay pounds to the ship captains as they get more and more slaves to America. He let them know that the following week there would be another meeting, and he would suggest to the RAC that the backside of their gratuity tokens should use the African elephant drawing that he would show them, so that they could engage their marketers with an African mascot. "We want to create a set of tokens to combat the slavers. Since they say God Preserve Carolina and the Lord's Proprietors, and God Preserve London, our side of the token should say God Preserve New England, because it's going to be New England and New Hampshire that start the war. We will not include the words "Lord's Proprietors" on our abolishment tokens, because we don't want to honor those who use slaves. Let's assure ourselves that the Carolina and London gratuity token users won't know that Ella is pointing to the left to shut down their evil."

He also explained that Mehna's main goal was to assign the journal and tokens to top abolitionists in America who would adopt the journal's objectives by colluding to end the human struggles. As he patted Mehna's shoulder, he said, "The messages in this amazing woman's journal are so clear and convincing for any human beings who feel offended that some people want to own and control the lives of others. All good humans who read the journal's evidence and emotion will begin to understand how the evil ones lie and cheat to meet their financial objectives and how they financially ruin, imprison, or murder any person who doesn't agree with their governmental use of racism."

Mehna said, "Here's the next thing that will be added to the journal once we figure out the answer. We haven't yet reckoned exactly how the tokens will support the journal's messages to drive full righteousness in America. Initially, we wanted tokens or some image of Ella to be sent, somehow, to Maryland, where the slaves are shipped, so they could eventually see an elephant. It's hundreds of those people in Maryland who heard me share that phrase, 'seeing the elephant,' to motivate their lives. But our need for an abolitionist stronghold has brought Marty's research to the colony called the Royal Province of New Hampshire, in the northeast of America, in the region called New England. They are believed to have more antislavery people and town leaders than any other place over there. Let's take a break, and then maybe we'll come back and brainstorm about how a dozen serious abolitionists could read the journal and use the tokens to save the world. See you in a few minutes. Come on, Auntie. Let me show you back to your house." Mehna and Aunt Barbie hugged, feeling in each other the strength, emotion, tenacity, and love they each had.

Bonnie and Jack said goodnight and went home during the break. Aunt Barbie stayed inside for the rest of the evening. The three elephant abolitionists had one more discussion.

Norbert was actually excited with all that he'd seen and heard lately with his two friends, so he engaged with ideas and questions about the token. "So, Mehna, let's imagine the time, maybe soon or years from now, when your journal and tokens are in the hands of a core group of abolitionists. They're reading your communications and thinking of what to do with a handful or boxful of elephant tokens. Will the journal have specific instructions showing them what to do with the tokens?"

Mehna knew how to respond. "Thanks, Norbert. It's these conversations that help us innovate and find the right course to freedom. So far, I think the journal will tell the team of freedom pursuers in New Hampshire to at least use the figure of Ella from the tokens as the powerful new icon for their abolition efforts. It's not just about the tokens. It's the love being sent from Ella and the clear evidence of hatred, falsehood, and stealing freedom off to her left, which will drive the fortitude of the new team of abolitionists. Once slavery has been removed, maybe the new elephant team will use the tokens to protect the future from the terrible people who may always try to get back to their racist government controls."

Marty said, "That sounds great. Oh, my! You just gave me another idea. Your life of consistently seeing Ella on the river facing left toward evil has created the path to where we are today. Maybe we should consider that the biggest initial success we need to drive people to freedom is to get the grand team in New Hampshire to meet with Ella for the first time. We also hope that I can convince the slave-ship captains to have Ella on the backside of their gratuity tokens, so maybe some good people will start seeing the elephant that you love. How about if the journal confirms for the team of abolitionists in New Hampshire that their synergy and pledges to launch the Ella party to end slavery will begin the day they all agree to follow the journal's intentions? The journal will mandate that the day they all commit to the freedom plan, Ella will change to the right to point her love at the enslaved, and to show that she is changing her direction toward them to begin their view of the elephant which they've been waiting for. Turning her to the right will acknowledge their appointment of Ella as the team's icon of righteousness. And her ass should be aimed at the left, where the evil ones hang out to trash human rights. Just an idea. Your thoughts?"

Mehna and Norbert both thought this was a great idea. Mehna drew the righteous Ella in the journal, who would kick off the war against slavery when the abolitionists joined together in America.

By the next evening when they met up, she'd put together a drawing along the top of page nineteen of the journal's plan to end slavery, showing Marty's new right concept for freedom. Her drawing showed Ella today, Ella after the abolitionists sign up to end slavery in America, and Ella heading right to drive humanity into righteousness for all forever.

Page 19

CHAPTER 19

MORE OF THE ELLA PLAN

AFTER A FEW MORE DAYS OF WORK AND MORE JOURN-aling, Mehna came up with a different approach. She facilitated an hour-long discussion of how Ella's journal and tokens would end slavery. "Let's imagine you're the good fellow in America who receives the journal from us later this summer. I'll ask a series of questions that might lead us down the path of pulling together a solid number of abolitionists. Please answer these questions, and I'll jot down some notes."

She opens her journal and begins. "Hello, good man. I have a question, sir. Here in your colony in 1694, do you feel that you have enough antislavery leaders right now who can work together to stop the thievery of human freedom?"

Marty said, "No, ma'am. Even though I feel there are good people everywhere who agree with your plan, we don't have any consistent communications between all the good folks and no ways to share our desires for abolishment. Only the slavers control the government."

Norbert said, "I agree with Marty. The proprietors in our colonies are dictators assigned by Whig King William. The good folks have to remain hidden from the governments that support slavery. So be careful when building abolishment plans."

Mehna said, "Thanks. Now question two. With those responses, we need some way to find a very strong abolitionist who's now hiding in America and willing to take on the plan. Answer this question as that strong man in America hiding from the Whigs. How will you forward all of the strong influences and whatever else in our journal to a future time when the good people in your colonies start to step up and fight the Whigs? If you can't find enough abolitionist power in your lifetime, will you ever give up and throw the freedom journal away?"

Martin said, "Good question. I'll keep the package in my home and share it with any abolitionists I meet. If their combined effect doesn't happen enough over my next twenty years, I will give your wonderful package to one of my teen or adult children, if I have any, and I'll coach them up on how to look for the abolishers over their next twenty or thirty years. The mission for freedom will never be thrown away. Each of my journal holders will be driven by Ella's doctrines of righteousness to end slavery."

Norbert said, "Good one, Marty. I agree with your Ella prophecy that good must take over from evil. But we don't know how long it will take. It might take generations. Let's predict that the journal holder—and there may be more than one over the years—will make sure that Ella's freedom mission stays on track until the good abolitionists create strong leadership and teamwork. Someday, the journal holder will see a significant inspiration from decent antislavery people, which will inspire him to share Ella and her freedom plan with them. When this all comes together, your plan will launch their final war on slavery. Mehna, how about this idea? Let's say your journal has a page not yet filled in. When the primary journal holder finally sees that there is a path to abolishment, and when he or she gets the team of abolitionists together in an onset conference, should there be a page in your journal with a message that they each sign to show their full commitment to the war against slavery and racism?"

With increased excitement, Mehna said, "Oh, my goodness, Norbert. Great idea. Yes, there are still several open pages in my book. The day that Ella is turning to the right to be the team's icon of righteousness, your idea will be the same chapter where the heroes, men and/or women, sign up to commit to Ella's war against racial division and slavery. Beyond ending slavery, their signatures will also show commitment to destroying the many awful objectives of the Whigs, like lying to the public and paying money to news reporters to share false information.

"Now here's question three. Imagine that it takes three generations of my people being enslaved before our journal can find enough tough abolitionists to make Ella's dream come true. It saddens me to think it will take that long. However, the powerful Whig proprietors and black African kings will take a long time to overcome. So, let's say that over a hundred years from now is when the whole war starts up. Question: The journal will give you, the leader of the right team, serious encouragement to move forward. But what about the tokens you have with the journal? How many tokens do you have? What do they say? How will you use them to fight the freedom battle? Will the tokens be part of the reason that enslaved people begin feeling that the war is on? See what I mean, guys? We should start getting to some more details for the future of the token of Ella."

Marty said, "Your plan for humanity needs to last forever, even after the battle to end slavery is completed and beyond. Evil people might always be in the world, so your Ella tokens will be flourishing forever to keep fighting against the people who think they are special above all other humans. These tokens will show the extreme love that you've been providing to your people for your whole life. The first solid team we build from your plan will involve good people with smart strategies to win the fight. Your book will engage them with the love of your tokens and they will determine how best to use the pieces to win the battle and to keep people free moving forward even when the evil humans try to rebuild their skin-colored power over others. Because of Ella's work in the future of America, community folks will eventually see that there's one evil wing of politics, and they will offset it. Let's just make the tokens with the love of God and send them to the future of freedom in America. Norbert, tell us what you think of how many tokens we can make and ship with the book."

"Okay," Norbert said. "These will not be cash coins, so having too many tokens will not increase the value. Here's my thought. There are about a dozen colonies practicing slavery in America right now. Let's say that the journal holder can find a dozen abolitionists, and after that there might be a dozen antislavery events in each colony. Something like a hundred copper tokens would be the minimum we'd create. But it kind of has to do with what you two think will be the concept for them to use the tokens."

They talked a bit more, then decided that a hundred New England Elephant Tokens were okay as an initial number with which to build support for Mehna's plan. They decided that the journal would recommend using some of the tokens to honor antislavery war heroes, and holding a few tokens within the perpetual antislavery, anti-racial-division, anti-human-trafficking team.

CHAPTER 20

GRATUITY PROGRAM ELEPHANT TOKENS

AFTER SEVERAL OF THE ROYAL AFRICAN COMPANY
meetings to build the gratuity process to improve English ship captains' motivations to transfer people without losing so many lives,
Martin showed them a drawing of an elephant. He and Norbert
had already figured that the Royal Mint's copper token design had
the ability to put this drawing onto a die for manufacturing the
tokens. The leaders of the RAC agreed that the elephant was the
perfect image to add to their tokens to keep African marketing
alive. The mint began creating die tools for tokens with Marty's
elephant design on one side and their wording for Carolina and
London on the front. In the next few months, the mint leaders
manufactured several thousands of the 1694 Carolina and London
tokens and began putting them on the ships from Africa to America
and the Caribbean islands. Before they created the gratuity tokens,
one of their managers decided not to put the date of manufacture
on the London tokens because Queen Mary passed away that year
at thirty-two years old, and he didn't want the London elephant
token to celebrate her year of passing.

After the final gratuity token meeting that Marty attended,
he told Norbert and Mehna of the results. "We're finally getting
things to be more aligned with Ella's plan for success. Your elephant aiming at the left will be on all the gratuity tokens. We will
ask Ella on the freedom tokens to start the war to end slavery and
stop the gratuity process. Now, we're getting closer to solidifying

the plan. Last week, I talked with a ship captain who transports lumber from the town called Exeter, in New Hampshire. I told him I'm looking to take a trip to that location. That place is an oak wood haven, according to business owners here. Captain Patrick told me of some of the town's nice folks that he works with, and he offered me passage to Exeter on his ship. The only problem is that his ship is not going across until November or December. We might be ready sooner. Captain Patrick works with a Gilman family in Exeter who are big in the lumber business. When your package is ready for all the enslaved and their supporters to start hooking up with an elephant in America, we could sail over to Exeter, in the New Hampshire colony, with your package. I've heard that upper portions of New England, especially New Hampshire, have more abolitionists than Maryland and the other colonies to the south. Hopefully, we'll find some abolitionists who can help."

Mehna said, "Well, good that you have a potential tour boat, but you're right. We might get the journal plan done and ready months before that. And we might be driven to send Ella sooner by the terrible politics and disgusting inhuman culture around here. Like you've told me before, Ella should travel in the better weather of July or August."

"I agree," said Marty. "I'll keep working to find another vessel for an earlier ride this summer."

Mehna stood quickly. "You really think I can go over there with you? Great idea, but let's finish up the journal and the package and then talk about our travel plans."

Days later, Martin walked into the coffeehouse and stepped right up to Mehna as she was working in the back of the shop by herself. He asked, "Hey, baby doll! How's your day?" She set the rags down that she was using to clean. "Okay, but I'm so ready to be done with this place because of the terrible business owners who keep pushing their human trafficking strategies. Anything new about our travel plan?"

Martin said, "There's something new. On Monday, I went over to Norbert's coin-making room in the new exchange, a few miles to the west of here. Guess what. The name of the new exchange building is Exeter Exchange. What a coincidence. Exeter! That makes me feel like this plan of yours is again being supported by God, the same Master who always put Ella on the riverbank to help you help the people. While I was with Norbert in his new area, he told me he might be leaving his Royal Mint job and starting his own token-making facility at the Exeter Exchange. Because he agrees with us about the terrible Whigs, who are really big on human marketing, he's pulling away from his father's Royal Mint and their hard ties to the slave businesses. Norbert says he can't take the evil anymore. He has already used the elephant press they made for the gratuity tokens to make a new coin die with the same elephant. This week, he'll update the die with our words 'God Preserve New England.'"

Martin shared with Mehna that John Gilman, in Exeter, New Hampshire, was a member of the House of Representatives, and the previous year, 1693, he'd been elected speaker of the colony's council. Martin said Gilman was referred to as Honorable John.

Mehna said, "So when you're with Mr. Gilman, if you and he find that there are not enough strong abolitionists today, he needs to have a plan for the future. We need him or some other freedom supporter to monitor America's political evolution and try to determine when there are enough strong abolitionists to battle and win against the Whig's proslavery leaders. If for some reason Mr. Gilman doesn't want to do this, then we'll need to find someone else who will."

Martin nodded. "Well, my dear, if we can't find a righteous person for control of your plan, then I, or you and I, will remain in New Hampshire with your Ella package until your plan for the eventual union of abolitionists has a path to fruition."

Since they made the decision to take Ella to Exeter, Marty looked into shipping companies to see who may have a vessel scheduled for voyage to New Hampshire. He focused first on the British shipbuilders who liked the quality of hardwood from Exeter's oak forests. "Most of these companies buy the wood there in Exeter, then ship it down south to the Carolina low country, up a river called Goose Creek, where they have shipbuilding plants."

At the Royal Coffeeshop in the Exchange, Marty found a guy he knew who worked for Nye Shipping Company, and he discovered that they had a vessel leaving for New Hampshire on August 10. Joseph Nye's new shipbuilding business on the Isle of Wight was regularly using Exeter, New Hampshire wood resources, so Martin was able to buy tickets for the ocean crossing on a regular basis, now that he knew of Nye's location and his preference for New Hampshire oak.

That night, back at Aunt Barbie's, Marty shared the target date of August 10 with Mehna. "We have a potential ride for Ella to America on August ten. That's the earliest ride I found. So that's three and a half months from now. Do we have enough time to finish Ella's journal? Or should I plan for a later date?"

"Marty, now that we've pulled together the Abolitionist Conference plan and the plan for opening up true facts to the public, I want to get Ella and her journal to America as soon as possible. Please schedule the August tenth trip."

"When I set that up with the Nye guy tomorrow, should I tell them we're both traveling, or just one of us?"

Mehna appeared very distraught by his question. "That's a tough one. Several items to think of. My going to the slavery colonies could become a problem. Also, both King Tutu and my mother expect me to return to Africa this summer. I probably won't go back to Africa, but I haven't decided yet."

CHAPTER 21

THE WEEK OF THE PLUNGE INTO AMERICA

DURING HER FIRST FOURTEEN MONTHS IN LONDON, Mehna had overheard constant conversations in several coffee-houses about the upcoming political season of 1694. She was crushed emotionally by the supporters of the Whig Party, because of the party's self-interest and their constant investment in slavery and human trafficking of her people in Africa. She was torn, but she also saw their terrible hatred as beneficial to keeping her motivations sky high to someday end their human wreckage.

These selfish politicians won big on August 9, 1694, when the whole Whig Party came into control. By the end of that dark political day, Mehna and Marty were with Norbert over at the Exeter Exchange, getting ready to mold the final few New England copper pieces before the journal and the Ella tokens get on the ship the next day. They were all disappointed in the outcomes of that day's parliamentary voting. They talked about how each of them was sure the majority who voted for the Whigs would never have done so if they had known the real truths of the world's loving humans and the hateful English politicians and business owners.

Norbert and Martin continued working in the mill room, heating the copper melting tanks so they could mold a few more tokens before Martin and Mehna leave on the ship. While the guys were out in the mill room, Mehna was writing on the last two pages of her journal. She really wanted the whole book to be filled with the human recovery strategy, so she planned to fill the last two pages that night, before the ship leaves for Exeter.

Later in the evening, when Martin and Norbert were in the kitchen taking a break from the mill room, Mehna gave Marty a hug and handed him a note on a piece of parchment. Before he read the note, she quickly sprinted out toward Norbert's mill room out back. After he watched her hurry out of the room, Marty read her note, then he suddenly jumped up and hustled after his friend. "Mehna, Mehna," he yelled. "No! No! That's too much."

After seeing her run away, Martin headed up to his Aunt Barbie's to pack for tomorrow's trip to America. Then he went back to Norbert's mill room, where they continued to process the final twenty-five New England Elephant Tokens. Before they put any of the liquid copper into the die, Marty held up one of the first seventy-five tokens and asked Norbert if he could make a slight change to the die. "The elephant on these is slightly left, with its tusks reaching beyond the edge of the token. And on the back side, the rim is not straight. Only half of the token is outlined by the rim frame, but with two perimeters on that half. Can we put Ella more in the middle of the piece for these last twenty-five tokens? And square up the obverse message side of the token?"

Norbert agreed. "You know, Marty, that I brought this elephant token die tool from my dad's company after they finished all of the London and Carolina tokens. I also brought a second die tool, because he had another one after they misspelled the word Proprietors on their first round. They spelled it ending in 'ers', not 'ors'. But you are right about my first attempt. One of the dies had some letters that were a little crooked, like the letter D in *God* leans slightly forward. So I used a second die to start your package of tokens. Sorry, though. When I moved Ella to the tool with straight lettering, I guess I didn't align her to the middle of the die tap. So let's move the elephant die mold back to the tool with the original lettering. Then we'll align Ella closer to the middle of the token. Hey, we can say that the D leaning to the right means God is aligned with Mehna's plan for flipping Ella to the right to fight for righteousness."

They created the last set of twenty-five tokens using Norbert's rebuilt die tool. By mid-night, Martin had all one hundred New England Elephant Tokens placed in a leather bag for travel. Seventy-five of the tokens have Ella touching the side of the token with her tusks. The final twenty-five tokens have Ella's tusks moved away from the token edge, and the letter D in *God* leaning slightly right.

Marty was pleased that all one hundred tokens had the same elephant created from the same die press as the gratuity London and Carolina tokens.

CHAPTER 22

THE ELEPHANT ABOLITIONIST PLAN SETS OFF

THE NEXT DAY, MARTY ENTERED THE SHIP WITH HIS suitcase and a wooden box containing Mehna's journal and the bag of tokens. Off he headed to the American colonies. Mehna had decided the previous night that she would not go with Marty to live in the new colony. He hadn't spoken with her since she'd run off. In the first month of his voyage, Marty persistently studied Mehna's journal and reexperienced their mutual, loving creation of it. In his first full read, he found something astonishing on the last page of the journal. Apparently, over the last few days before he sailed away, Mehna added a plan for her future and how she might someday be able to help Ella facilitate the plan for freedom of all of humanity, even if she didn't end up living in America. As he read those last few pages of her final writings, he picked up the leather carrier holding all of the New England Elephant Tokens, and hugged the entire sack of tokens, thinking deeply of Mehna, her righteous loving hugs, and her wonderful drive for human rights.

During the seven-week voyage to America, Marty was disappointed about missing his time with his close friend, Mehna. She was the most loving, caring, and influential person he'd ever known.

After the ocean crossing, he was in the beautiful town of Exeter, in the colony of New Hampshire. On his first day there, at twenty-two years old, he wandered around and found a log hotel and a tavern restaurant. The people he met knew legislator John Gilman, whose family ran a lumber shipping business in the area. They explained where John and his family lived, near the Exeter River, in a log cabin.

Marty's strategy in Exeter was to find the best advocate who would promise to keep the plan for freedom safe and ready to launch until a strong team of abolitionists was formed and aligned with Mehna's journal.

After several months of getting to know people in the New Hampshire colony, Martin felt that John Gilman was a good man, but his lumber and shipbuilding businesses had kept him closely tied to the English government so that he could keep profits coming in. So Marty made a key decision that he, not Mr. Gilman, would be the handler of the Ella package until he met other good people. Martin felt that he being the first manager of the Ella plan was the right way for him to show his gratitude for the generous work Mehna had done to get the journal and tokens here to begin the end to slavery. Whenever he looked at page nineteen, the picture story motivated him to keep doing whatever it took to get Ella to someday flip to the right. He owed this gratefulness to Mehna, the princess of liberty.

After he moved his and Mehna's lifetime yearnings to New Hampshire, Martin worked for decades with several oak lumber companies in Exeter and Newfields. During his first few years in America, he built close ties with a local farming and lumbering family who owned eighteen hundred acres of wilderness along the Exeter and Newfields town lines in an expanse known as Piscassic River and the Oaklands Forest.

Michael and Sharron Giddings, landowners in charge in the area, met often with Martin during and after their workdays, always together at the Giddings' farming and lumbering area. Because Marty learned early on that they were true and solid antislavery people, he made sure that they reviewed and discussed the Mehna journal many times between 1695 and 1703. Whenever they read the journal, the Giddings were saddened by the profoundly described stories of enslavement. To unite their emotions with Mehna's life, they used her story to advance their family.

One day in the forest, Mike Giddings told Marty about he and his wife's reviewing of Mehna's journal the night before. "Like you know, Martin, my wife is pregnant, and the baby is coming along soon. If we have a baby boy, to honor your close friend Mehna and her buddy Zebu from the journal, we are going to name our son Zebulon. If our new baby is a daughter, maybe she will be Mehna." Their new baby boy, Zebulon Giddings, was born May 10, 1703.

By the 1720s, Marty, Mike Giddings, and Mike's son Zebulon were working and meeting frequently with another strong Christian abolitionist. Their new coworker friend, Benjamin Thing, was ready to move permanently from Massachusetts to Exeter to upgrade his work and life with the Giddings farmland families. From their years of close ties, Mr. Giddings built a farm cabin on hundreds of acres on the south side of the Oaklands Forest in Exeter and he sold it to Mr. Thing's family when they moved north.

Throughout those years of freedom and godly motivations, Marty was very gratified to have had these descent people understand and merge with Mehna's plan for humanity.

Years after the Things moved north to Exeter, their son, Winthrop Thing, was born on January 10, 1728.

In his family's home just a half-mile north of the Things' cabin, Zebulon Giddings's son, Zebulon, Jr. was born in 1733, and he was allotted the same name to continue the worship of Mehna's friend Zebu.

Mr. Giddings's next child, a brother of Zeb Jr., was born in 1736. The new boy was named Eliphalet Giddings because the Giddings were strong Christians, and they wanted to align their next child's name with Ella the elephant. Eliphalet was a name often used in the eighteenth century, meaning the God of deliverance. In his adult life, Eliphalet Giddings lived in the Oaklands forest region on the south end of the farmland, near the cabin owned by the Thing family.

As Martin shared Mehna's freedom plan for years with families around the Oaklands forest expanse in Exeter and Newfields, several families promised their future support of Mehna Abhoola's freedom plan. Throughout the eighteenth century, several children were named both Eliphalet and Zebulon by the Giddings and Thing families in the Oakland Forest, Piscassic River area to keep the honoring of Zebu and Ella moving forward in America.

By 1743, Marty, now retired, was spending more time in the downtown taverns of Exeter with some of his prior coworkers. His closest friends involved in the Mehna plan were the parents of one of the Thing families. After years of meeting with Winthrop and Judith, Marty realized for certain that the young couple was really against the slavery mess, as was everyone in the Thing woodland area. They were always angry about ships bringing Africans to Portsmouth, New Hampshire, where companies sold people. Win and Judy were among the many New Hampshire people who were angry with the British government for all their racial and minority separation strategies. Over the years, Marty shared a few aspects of a scheme to end slavery that he'd worked on with his friends back in London when he was young. Over the next three years, he ramped up the Ella information sharing with the Things. They became very close friends once they knew the entire Mehna story. By March of 1750, at seventy-eight years old, Marty was getting more and more concerned about his time remaining and how to share the Ella plan with a strong abolitionist before his life ended. He was feeling high levels of fatigue and despair. To continue his accountability as the responsible Ella holder, he started spending several days at a time with the Things, four miles out of town at their farmhouse. He was really thrilled to be sharing the total Ella plan with them.

"So good to finally give you this, Winnie and Judy. I've shown you the journal and spoken with you about this thing for years, but now I need to ask for your help. First off, as I've always said, I can't say enough about the incredible kindness, toughness, and intelligence of my friend Mehna Abhoola, from Africa, the author of this journal and creator of a freedom plan. You've revealed to me that you are amazed at her life and her hard work to build this proposal. Even though she was always under the pressure of becoming enslaved at any point in time, she always remained on a course to set this plan in motion, ever since her dad and brother were stolen and she met so many enslaved children and their parents."

He asked the Things to hang onto the journal and bag of tokens for a week or two so they could fully engage with the details and feel the emotions of the plan for ending slavery in America. Only three days later, while walking with his cane across the Exeter River Bridge, Martin met Winnie just across from Gilman's house. Before Marty even said hello, Win called to him. "Wow, my friend, I wish I had asked to fully inspect your journal long before now. Incredible. I think you'll agree right now that we don't have the ability to publicly ask for abolitionists to unite, because the southern colony business owners and their government will attack anything that they see that's pushing against slavery."

Martin had a positive feeling from what Winnie said. "True. You've shown me for years that people here in New England are becoming very opposed to the British government's dictatorial controls over the colonies. We know they're getting so deep in debt in England, so their parliament is making more and more taxes for us here. I think Americans are starting to feel they are getting overtaxed without representation. You and me and the enslaved feel like it's slavery in our lands without representation.

If this keeps going, these colonies might fight for their own government. If that happens, let's hope that the new government will not keep slavery going forward."

CHAPTER 23

THE RIGHT THING TO END SLAVERY

BEFORE HIS PASSING, IN MAY OF 1750, MARTY HEARD from Winthrop Thing that he and his wife wanted very much to be the new Ella plan holders and abolitionist trackers. Five years after they became the owners and controllers of Ella's plan, Winthrop and Judith had their sixth and final child, a son, Winthrop Thing Jr., born in 1755.

When Win Jr. was eighteen years old, in 1773, a bunch of Americans jumped onto a British merchant ship in Boston and pushed 342 boxes of tea into the bay. Within the next three years, American anger and disappointment ramped up so much that the colonies went to war with Britain and created the United States of America. The new country was an innovative style of government that let individuals vote for people to represent their desires for life, liberty, and happiness.

In 1779, three years after the new democracy was created, Winthrop Thing Sr. transferred the Ella package to his son, Win Jr., when the boy was twenty-four years old. His parents felt sure that Win Jr. had grown up to be a fair and kind human being, fully on the side of ending slavery.

Winthrop Thing Jr. married Lydia Gilman in 1794. They carried forward the whole Mehna Abhoola freedom journal box and emotional desires, just like their friends and families had done for the past seventy-years. They had a son in 1796 whom they named Winthrop to honor their ancestors. Their next son was born on

April 22, 1800. To honor ancient society members by using specific key names like their family trees had done over the past century, the Things named their second son, Zebulon G. Thing. They added the letter *G* as his middle name, to honor the Giddings family's close eighteenth-century ties to the Things.

Staying in line with the Ella plan, Win passed the journal and tokens to his son, Zebulon, in 1825, when Zeb was twenty-five years old. Like his dad and granddad, after reading and feeling the universal freedom and fairness tactics and emotions that Mehna wrote about in her journal, Zeb was excited to become the Ella freedom plan proprietor. He had worked with African workers, some free and some enslaved. Zebulon always felt they were his close friends, and he was always in high disagreement with the proslavery politicians.

In 1830, Zeb married Sarah York, from Brentwood, a town just west of Exeter. They built their family while living at his parents' farm in the Oakland forest area, on the border of Exeter and Newfields, near the Piscassic River. From this Thing family's active life, the whole Oakland forest area became locally known as Zebulon Thing Corner. Zebulon and Sarah became increasingly involved in following and assessing America's politics. Exeter was then a center of political activity in the state of New Hampshire.

Zebulon and Sarah Thing were members of the Methodist Church on the east side of town, across the river. He felt deeply rooted to his family's responsibility for monitoring the state of politics toward ending slavery in America, so Zebulon was pleased to learn that the church's reverend, George Storrs, was a huge advocate for the abolishment of slavery.

Reverend Storrs delivered a sermon telling all the good people of this area to begin alliances with abolitionists. At his event, on August 10, 1836, Reverend Storrs joined forces with Zebulon and dozens of others who supported the reverend's godly position on ending slavery in America. Moments after he began his freedom lecture, talking about how God wanted all humans to be treated equally and lovingly, a gang of fifteen men from Salem, Massachusetts, showed up at the Methodist meetinghouse. Massachusetts was a much more proslavery state than New Hampshire, so this gang pushed their political ideas north, because they heard that abolitionists were starting to gather in Exeter. The yelling, screaming gang started throwing rocks and swinging clubs at the meetinghouse walls and windows. "We hear that you're going against our Democratic leaders and us Democratic voters! You want to let those slaves wander around. You suck."

No one was injured. The reverend's lecture ended when the first window was smashed. He asked the Exeter freedom team to stay safe and head out the back door.

The proslavery gang left the area after they'd prevented the reverend's speech against slavery. Zebulon and three other men waited until the Democratic gang was gone, then they headed downtown to Folsom Tavern, a local watering hole that President George Washington visited on November 4, 1789, to lay the foundation of the Society of the Cincinnati's New Hampshire chapter.

Zebulon and his buddies had deep discussions about how America was still a country of sadness and contempt for minorities, and about how the Democrats were so awful in their desires for continuing slavery.

One of the guys at the tavern was Amos Tuck, a recent Dartmouth College graduate. He'd grown up in Hampton, on the coast east of Exeter, and at that time, in 1836, he was headmaster of Hampton Academy. The attack by Democratic voters against freedom of opinion at the church in Exeter became a major moment on the way to Tuck's future as one of the world's strongest abolitionists. Five years later, because of Democratic legislators in 1841, Reverend Storrs was ordered by local sheriffs to stop antislavery lectures. In Pittsfield, NH, North West of Exeter, the reverend was arrested twice because of his events against slavery. He was imprisoned for three months with hard labor for being a publicly notable abolitionist. This illegitimate court order added even greater fuel to Amos and Zeb's drive to help free enslaved people.

Over the first several years of their commitment to fight back, Zebulon and Amos constantly talked about entering politics to battle the proslavery Democrats. Zebulon shared the entire Ella journal and its strategic abolitionist concepts with Amos. They became highly engaged with discussions about how to gather the good, strong antislavery people in America together into a political army to take down the leadership of the group that continued to push their hate for Africans and Native Americans, and any American who wanted to free and support all human beings in the country.

Because he knew enough of the proslavery politicians' anger and struggle against any antislavery peoples, Amos came up with an idea to use the Democratic Party's practice of fake votes to move himself into Congress by hiding his abolitionist beliefs. In 1842, he ran as a Democrat and was elected to the US House of Representatives, and then he tried to work against slavery from within the party. But his plan to disrupt their push for continued slavery and minority suppression didn't work from within the party. In 1844, Tuck was formally removed from the Democratic Party by its leaders because of his antislavery position. He continued to run for office and was elected as an Independent to the US Congress, in Washington, DC.

In 1845, Amos Tuck started a convention in Exeter to bring decent voters together to oppose the proslavery Democrats and to show support for a strong abolitionist US Senate candidate, John Hale. Senator Hale won and became one of the strongest antislavery senators in America.

Amos Tuck continued to stay in politics to drive and support Mehna's plan. He ran for US Congress as a Free Soil Party candidate,

Free Soil being totally a party of abolitionism. He held office in the US Congress for three consecutive terms.

During those ten years of seeing directly how the Democratic political arm was doing whatever they could to keep slavery alive in America, Amos Tuck shared his frustrations with Zebulon and other local Exeter anti-slavers. Over time, with the terrible politics, Amos and Zebulon vigorously committed to each other that their relationship with Mehna and Marty's plan for the Ella journal and tokens would eventually become the driving force for a new abolitionist group to battle the pro-slavers until freedom became available to all. What drove their commitment so high was the lying and cheating of the slavery party to get voters to support the Democrats. By 1850, because of a new federal law, both Zeb and Amos knew that their battle was entering a new phase.

NEET BOOK 2:

1850–1853

CHAPTER 24

HUNTING FOR AN ELEPHANT

IN THE YEAR 1850, A HUNDRED YEARS AFTER THE HERO of freedom, Martin Walpole, passed away, and seventy-four years after America broke away from the British government, the republic government of the United States of America was under the power of a group known as the Democratic Party. For all those years since the country of freedom had begun, this pro-slavery party had been driven only by a desire for business and wealth, not by individual freedom rights. They would not support the freedom, fairness, happiness, and individual rights of slaves, Native Americans, women, or anyone who did not support their desires to continue with slavery, even though most of the world had ended lawful slavery over the past thirty years.

Because escaping slaves and their supporters in the north were becoming more successful at building a path to freedom, businesses that owned human workers were seeing lower profits. Therefore, their political arm, the Democrats, passed the Fugitive Slave Act of 1850 to criminalize any supporters of escaped slaves within northern abolitionist communities. This passage of such a discriminatory law by the Democratic Party elevated the anti-slavery emotions of the good people in America who wanted to free the African Americans and get them to be treated equally as US citizens.

A year before the Fugitive Slave Act was created and passed by the Democrats to stop support for escapees, on Monday,

September 17, 1849, Harriet Tubman, a twenty-eight-year-old female slave from Dorchester County, Maryland, risked her life to escape from her owner's farm. Harriet began finding routes from Maryland to Pennsylvania through fields, woods, valleys, and small towns to help escaping people get safely out of their owner's control. She traveled routes, which became known as the Underground Railroad, and she used churches, homes, and farms offered by kind and loving non-Democrats to support fugitive travels. As her underground process grew, she met antislavery politicians, abolitionists, and other people of love and integrity.

Because the Democrats' Fugitive Slave Act was passed only one year after she escaped, things became much more difficult for Harriet's freedom-building processes. She had to start steering fugitives to Canada through northern New England and New York. Serious assistance from several New Hampshire political and non-political abolitionists helped her create a freedom trail through Exeter, Newfields, and Lee, New Hampshire, up to Canada.

During the four years between 1849 and 1853 that Harriet ran her Underground Railroad, Zebulon Thing and Amos Tuck were continuing to communicate with as many antislavery politicians and businesspeople as they could. Because the Democrat's Fugitive Slave Act was causing difficulties with helping people, more and more folks and politicians across America, and especially in New Hampshire, were exceedingly frustrated with the government. Since the new act to stop escapees and imprison their supporters was so unfair, and since Amos was so enthralled with the Ella plan, he started sending messages to known abolitionists to ask for their commitment to a coalescing conference later that year.

CHAPTER 25

September, 1853:
Lee, New Hampshire,
along the Freedom Trail

MOSES CARTLAND'S FAMILY IN LEE, NEW HAMPSHIRE, had for many years been supporting antislavery positions and programs, and sharing their farm with escaped slaves who were along the Freedom Trail.

That year, Mrs. Tubman's Underground Railroad brought several groups of freedom-seekers to the Cartland farm for multiple-night stays on their trip to Canada.

Harriet, the most freedom-engaged fugitive slave in US history, had been to Cartland Farm several times since her personal escape from the Maryland farm four years earlier. One day, Harriet was approaching Cartland farm in a horse cart, traveling with a family of five escaped slaves on their run to northern New England and Canada.

When they got to the farm, Harriet first went right over to her escapee friend, African American Oliver Gilbert. Oliver had escaped from his enslaved life in Maryland a year before Harriet and had been living at the Cartland farm for several years.

"Oli, good to see you again," she said. She stomped forward and gave him the well-known Tubman hug. Leaning back from that, she said, "Hey, I heard about a month ago from some of our travel assistants that you've been saying you need to speak with me about something huge. What's up?"

Oliver said, "Been a while, Harriet. I hope you had a good trip up here this time. Those kids you brought today look in pretty good shape. Nice job. I bet you showed them how to use the North Star to travel here from Maryland. That's what all the kids and young adults coming through Lee have told me you do."

Oliver pointed to the oak picnic table across the yard, began walking, and said, "Hey, let's sit so I can tell you about that huge thing you mentioned. You're going to be so amazed by what I recently discovered with one of your freedom-trail supporters right over there in Exeter."

They sat at the oak picnic table, and he continued. "As we both know, we from Maryland have the same tribal history coming from the Ashanti Kingdom in Ghana and the Igbo peoples in Nigeria. We and everyone born into slavery around us grew up with our parents and grandparents constantly sending positive messages that there would be freedom, happiness, self-worth, and family worth in our future. We both know that our people have always said our future of freedom and the good life begins when an elephant shows up in Maryland or America."

Harriet smiled and nodded as he shared what they both knew of their future set by their ancestors. Oliver said, "We've talked about this before, you and I and others, always trying to come up with ways of getting this elephant to show up in America to free our people from the terrible political group that fights to confine, oppress, rape, and murder our wonderful men, women, and children."

Harriet raised her arms, and with a happy face she said, "Oh, Oli. What? Do you have an elephant hiding out in your red barn over there? Like I've told you before, as I was preparing my parents and most others to escape over the past few years, just about everyone raised their arms and cheered, 'We're going to see the elephant.' Now you're bringing up something about the huge mascot for freedom that our ancestors promised us. This makes me crazy excited, my friend. Tell me." With tears in her eyes and an eager look on her face, she reached across the picnic table with both hands and took Oli's hands.

Oliver said, "You've met Zebulon Thing, over at his farm, Zebulon Thing Corner, between here and downtown Exeter. You rode right by his farmhouse this morning. He's got something to show you."

Harriet said, "Oh, I love Mr. Thing and his wife Sarah. I've even stayed there overnight and spent good times with Zeb's wife and their kids. They are very nice. He's so caring and works hard like you do at getting our people from Maryland to here and on their way to Canada. Of all the nice people who are trying to help us blacks, the Thing family is one of the most fantastic. You feel this like I do, Oli, I'm sure. Mr. and Mrs. Thing, Mr. and Mrs. Cartland, and their families have been so engaged in our freedom trail even after the Democrats voted to make it illegal for good people to provide any assistance to slaves like us looking to be free."

Oliver said, "Right. Zeb and I, and his two sons, Jim and Ben, spend a lot of time together helping folks get on to Canada. When you and your allies bring folks here from the South along your secret trails, it's so good that nice people such as the Things and Cartlands in this area work hard as they do to feed and provide overnight lodging to our travelers. Now let me tell you what's happened.

"Last week, right here in the back yard, Zeb heard some of our escapees from Maryland rejoicing about finally expecting an elephant in America. As you know, that's how our people feel on their way to Canada. So I often mention the animal just to honor their escape. As we were standing here celebrating their freedom, I was awestruck by Zeb's facial expression when he heard that the elephant is a longstanding freedom symbol for our people in America.

He smiled big, his eyes opened wide, then he came close and put an arm around my shoulder. He whispered in my ear to let me know he was extremely interested in hearing about the elephant they wanted in their life. We moseyed away from the other folks a little, toward the creek behind the barn."

Oliver pointed out toward the woods. "See that log bench over there? Zeb and I sat down to talk. I explained to him that generations of our parents have taught all slaves who grew up in Maryland and some in other colonies that our freedom and happiness will begin to grow when the elephant shows up here in America. Then, an amazing moment happened. Zebulon's eyes opened wide, as did his mouth, and he gave me a solid handshake. As we shook, which had an energetic feeling like a huge achievement, he said he had to show me something. Then he said he had an old historical journal with an elephant story that he thought would amaze me. So, you know how I feel about this stuff, Harriet. I was super anxious, so I went over to Zebulon Thing Corner the next day, and he showed me an old wooden box with a journal and some old coins inside. I haven't read the whole journal yet, but I'm sure he wants us to."

Before Oliver told Harriet any of the details inside Zebulon's package, one of the travelers over by the barn yelled, "Hey, Oliver, can you help us here please?"

Oli stood, waved his hand, and nodded yes. To Harriet he said, "I'm busy the rest of the day, and your family of travelers is here in Lee for several days. We should go over to Zebulon Thing's tomorrow and meet up with the elephant. I already told him you were probably coming up this week. He's really excited to show you what he has. And you'll be amazed."

Oliver walked over to Ralph, the traveler who'd just asked for help. Ralph said, "Hey, I think I heard you say this farm owner's name is Moses. Moses Cartland. That's good. We're all so grateful for what Harriet does for all our people. She works so hard to help us stay clear of meanness. She is so awesome that we just had a discussion where we all said we should start calling her our Moses. She really is that, right?"

Oli smiled and said, "You're so right about her, Ralph. She's the most influential person I've ever known. I agree that she is the Moses of our people. Let's keep sharing that. And Moses Cartland here is also so much a devoted abolitionist. You'll even see him ask to take your children into the barn out back for some fun teaching. Both these Moses are great people."

CHAPTER 26

OCTOBER 6, 1853: HUGE ANIMAL AT ZEBULON THING CORNER

THE NEXT MORNING, IN A CARTLAND FARM ONE-HORSE cart, Harriet and Oli moved down the well-used road from Lee to Exeter. As they reached the wooden bridge at Wadleigh Falls, Harriet pointed down at the bridge and river. "Oli, this river has been a key part of our travels here. I was so impressed last summer when you showed me that you bring the younger travelers to this river to let them swim and play in these pools at the falls. Those kids who come through here in the summer always remember Wadleigh Falls. And we'll always remember that great guy named Oliver, who has worked so hard to help our people be free and happy."

Oli turned the cart onto Oaklands Road and headed south from Newfields to Exeter. Right at the town line, Oliver stopped the cart and pointed into a field of the Zebulon Thing Corner farmland. "Look there! Those two gravestones right there are Zebulon's parents, Winthrop Thing Jr. and Lydia Gilman Thing."

They pulled into Zebulon Thing's farmhouse yard along Oaklands Road, in the heavily forested region on the northwest side of Exeter.

Zebulon's wife, Sarah, and their two adult sons were just pulling out of the barn, which was just about thirty yards west of their farmhouse. When Mrs. Thing saw Harriet in Oli's horse cart, she handed the reins to her son and climbed quickly out. She walked right at Harriet with arms extended for hug. Sarah knew that she was getting the biggest, best, most loving hug from the famous hugger Harriet Tubman. "Hi, dear! Zeb is inside the house. He told me you might be coming over. We're heading downtown to get some groceries. Take care. See you later."

Harriet waved and said, "Hello, boys. How ya doin'? Bye."

While looking around the beautiful Zebulon Thing Corner farmland, Oliver and Harriet made their way from the barn toward the house at the corner of Oaklands Road. Harriet stopped and looked off to her left, toward the northwest. "Look at that nice hill right there, Oli. I would have built a house right on the hill, with all those oaks and the nice view it must have."

Oli said, "I've been up there. You're right. It's pretty nice. Maybe we can take a hike just so you can tell the Things how great their farmland really is."

Harriet changed the subject, pointing at the house. "Let's get in here with Mr. Thing."

They knocked on the farmhouse door. The door opened and Zebulon and Harriet got the usual hug and hello, then the three settled down at the Thing kitchen table. Zebulon said, "Hey, you two. Good to see you. Thanks for coming."

Before he said anything else, Harriet jumped in and said, "Hi, Mr. Zeb. First time I've seen you this year. Oli tells me you heard some of our travelers talking about wanting an elephant to show up in America. He says that you have some assortment that might do an elephant thing for our enslaved families and friends. Are you the elephant Thing?"

Zebulon smiled and nodded. "Ya. Funny. Elephant Thing. I guess that's me. Here's why I was so excited to hear your folks talking about needing to see the elephant. In that box over there, there's a leather-bound, handwritten historic journal of over thirty pages. And with that book, there's a leather pouch of one hundred antique coins, which we call tokens because they are not money coins. Both the journal and the tokens have an incredible elephant story. So, listen, this book was written by a young lady, an ancestor of your people a hundred and fifty-nine years ago. When you read this, you'll be amazed at the high twist of fate between this book, the elephant, and your people."

"Oh, my goodness!" said Harriet. "Generations of us in Maryland have been taught that somehow, someday, an elephant from Africa would arrive here and start the end of our enslavement. Wow! Is this it?"

"Yes it is! You'll be astounded," said Zebulon. "First, let me tell you how I got this box of stuff, then we'll go through it in detail. My dad always grew me up with knowledge and heartbreak of the terrible lives your people are living in slavery. By the time I was about eighteen, my dad said with high energy that he must show me this journal that a man originally from London, named Martin Walpole, gave to my granddad back in the 1740s. Let me show you."

He got up and opened his storage chest and brought a wooden box over to the kitchen table. As he did that, Harriet and Oli were staring right at each other with wide open eyes and faces of surprise. Zeb lifted the lid off the wooden box, then pulled out an antique, leather-bound journal and set it in the middle of the kitchen table. He also pulled out a leather sack that sounded like a bag of coins as he set it down.

He said, "That day way back, Dad opened this box, showed us and talked about what's in it. The discussions around the family members got really assertive in the abolitionist way of thinking. At that time, all of us had some African friends here in town, some of them free and some enslaved working in area farmhouses. Because we've always felt sad and angry about how these friends are treated, this whole topic that dad shared was very energizing for my parents and my siblings. He shared the incredible intentions of this journal and tokens with me for several years, and he coached me up on how to harmonize with slavery abolitionist leaders in the area. That is what the holder of this journal is expected to do. My dad transferred the obligation of fulfilling this box's plan to me when I was twenty-five, giving me the responsibility of coordinating more abolitionists wherever and however possible. Since we moved right here into Thing Corner twenty-three years ago, your elephant story has been here with me and Sarah. Since then, a lot has happened."

Oliver said, "Zebulon will tell you next, I bet, about his really strong antislavery friend, Amos Tuck. We all feel that Mr. Tuck, now holding office and a member of the Free Soil party, is highly committed to us being freed from the Democrats' desire for slavery."

Zebulon continued. "Oli's right. Since my dad shared this historical information with me, it's amazing that this town of Exeter has become the center of decent political principles for New Hampshire and beyond. Because of Exeter's character toward helping your people, I've been able to start a dialogue with several good folks about the abolishment of slavery. Of course, the most aligned person with abolishment is our friend, Amos Tuck. I think you might have met him downtown before."

Zebulon shared with Harriet an attack he saw against freedom. "Seventeen years ago, in 1836, when I was trying to start sharing the elephant plan from this journal with good people who want equal rights for everyone, a dozen of us were invited to a church lecture downtown with a great pastor who was against the whole inhumane behavior of this government. As he started one of his slavery abolishment speeches, a gang of Democrats from Massachusetts attacked his church's front wall with rocks and clubs to fight against any abolitionist gatherings. After that attack, I started sharing with Mr. Tuck the journal details that you will soon see. Being at that church of freedom when that evil clan attacked us became a major beginning of Mr. Tuck's political career so he could fight the evil. This great man will never stop working to end slavery."

Harriet added, "I can't wait to meet him again. We need more and more people like you and Mr. Tuck to rise up on the fight."

"Right," said Zeb. "So this is why we believe in God. Having you here this week is amazing. Mr. Tuck has been working this year to coordinate the political antislavery factions. In five days, next Wednesday, October twelve, Amos is facilitating a grand event right here in Exeter with major antislavery politicians and other good people from across America. Most of them know of you, Harriet, and all you've done to help people. They know that you're the queen of abolishment. After you've studied up on this journal from your ancestors, can you meet with Mr. Tuck and me at his antislavery party next week?"

Oliver said, "You can stay at my barn on Cartland Farm for as long as you need, dear."

Zeb added, "And Sarah would love to have you stay here at Thing Corner, too."

She agreed. "I'll stay for the week or more. Whatever it takes. First, of course, I need to see the elephant, which I've been waiting to do for decades. Then, we'll meet with Mr. Tuck."

Zeb was so pleased. "Wow. So amazing that you're here within days of Amos's big event, which I've been helping him set up for years. God Preserves New England is what you being here means. You'll see what I'm saying in the journal. For us, this is New England, not old slavery England. After we end slavery, God will preserve the future of New England and America to honor your people forever."

Harriet was getting excited. "So great, all of this, Zeb. Please tell me more about what you heard of my people talking about an elephant."

Zebulon said, "A few months ago, I overheard this conversation by your folks up at Oli's farm about the history of the antislavery elephant that your people are excited to see at some point in their lives. When I heard that caring discussion, I felt deeply in my heart that God is taking action to tie your people's need for a future of freedom to this package that I've been safeguarding. I thought about what I heard, then wandered to his barn house and asked Oli what we could do to merge these two together—the elephant expected by your people and the elephant from your ancestor's journal. Oli said we'd need Harriet to help us answer that. So that's why we're here today. You're seeing the elephant today, Harriet."

Harriet stood up and pulled off her coat because the woodstove was keeping the Thing house really warm. "Oh, wow! I can't imagine what type of elephant we're gonna see, but I respect you guys so much, and I'm so excited. Zeb, before we get into the box, let me cool down please. It's really hot in here. I'll head outside in a minute. You Things have a lot of oak firewood stacked outside, more than most farms I've seen. Why so much oak?"

Zeb smiled. "This whole area is like ninety percent oak trees for several square miles. We call it the Oaklands Forest, and this road is Oaklands Road. The oak is a great source of heat for these cold New Hampshire winters."

Oli said, "Oh, yah, Thing Corner is a great source for lumber and firewood. Last year, the Cartlands and I built that barn that I live in. Zeb helped me move several giant oak trees up from the Oaklands to Lee to make the barn really solid. This area is a resource haven."

Harriet said, "That's familiar to me because my father was a lumberman. He worked hard cutting timber in the Maryland shipbuilding business. So I'm familiar with your forest work here. Maybe my dad's timber products were from New Hampshire, maybe from right here in Exeter. Wouldn't that be a coincidence?"

Harriet walked out the kitchen door at the back of the Thing farmhouse and felt the cool October air for about five minutes. She used the outhouse out back, then she stepped back into the kitchen. "I'm ready to see the elephant, you guys! This is amazing," she said with elevated excitement. "Just so incredible to find out after all these years that the elephant of freedom sent by our ancestors has been here in Exeter for over one hundred years. Zeb, may I have this journal for a day or two? I need to read and understand everything that the queen who did this was thinking."

Zebulon agreed. "Of course. It's pretty detailed, so you'll need several days. Let's have you study this up to make sure we're seeing the right elephant that your ancestry set up to free your people. After you investigate the details in the journal, let's meet back up, maybe later tomorrow or this weekend. We'll see if we can develop a plan to steer the elephant to freedom. We'll discuss how to share the journal plan, which your ancestor Mehna Abhoola called the Ella plan. Ella as in Ella Phant."

As Zebulon loaded the journal and tokens into the old box for Harriet to carry with her, she said, "This is the right elephant, Zeb. I'm sure. I'll do my review of the box tonight up at Mr. Cartland's farm, then we'll talk maybe before meeting with Mr. Tuck to see if we can share it in a way that will start the once and for all freedom movement for America."

Harriet and Oliver got back in the horse cart with the elephant token box and made their way back to Cartland farm before the sun went down. Oliver set Harriet up in the second floor of the barn where several bedrooms were available for travelers. He ignited the whale-oil lights that were kept in each bedroom.

"Good night, my friend," Oliver said, giving her a hug and kiss on her cheek. "This is exciting. We have a new day coming for our people now that the elephant in the room of slavery has decided to step forward and stop the evil inhumane politicians."

For hours that evening, Harriet went through the ancient pages of the book, carefully turning from one to the next, because the old historical parchment pages were quite inflexible compared to books with paper pages. The first hour of her studies brought Harriet to a place where she felt that she knows the author, Mehna. In Mehna's early days, she was pulling people together with dancing, merrymaking, and friendly gatherings. When enslavement started to happen in the villages around them and then in their own, Mehna Abhoola became the utmost supporter of her subverted people, always trying to help them improve their situations. The more she read of Mehna's life and ethics, the more Harriet became overwhelmed with joy for this wonderful woman who authored the Elephant Freedom Journal.

Harriet was so intrigued with the journal's story that she told herself, "Mehna Abhoola lived the same type of life I've lived, working throughout her life and beyond to help the people and end slavery. Wow. Now we will take the idea of seeing the elephant in America to a new level. Incredible. Finally, we will begin the end of my people's enslavement by changing the politics in this country."

CHAPTER 27

OCTOBER 7, 1853, WORLD'S STRONGEST ABOLITIONIST

EARLY THE NEXT MORNING, ZEBULON WENT WITH HIS wife to downtown Exeter. Sarah dropped Zeb off at retired congressman Amos Tuck's office in his brick building on Front Street next to the Phillips Exeter Academy. He walked right into Amos's office. "Hey, buddy. Guess what?" he said. "Now that you've set up the meeting next week with our abolitionists, a new thing has turned up. You have some time?"

Amos said, "So when you tell me you have a new thing, I have to ask. Did Sarah just have another baby? Is that your new Thing? Ha, ha. Just kidding. I'm still getting ready for next week's meeting, but I've got some time. What's up?"

Zeb said, "You know of the great lady, Harriet Tubman. Harriet's up here in New Hampshire again this week. I just spoke with her about this same thing that I'm sharing with you which happened back on August ninth. Here's why talking with her is a big deal. When my wife and I were doing our normal support for the fugitives heading from Exeter to the Cartland's in Lee and onto Canada, our abolitionist plan took on a new level of urgency. As Sarah was feeding folks and hanging out with them, I was over at Cartland's grill cooking. Some of the freedom trail travelers were right next to me on a picnic table. Take a deep breath, Tuck, because you know how incredible it is that the whole Ella journal plan has driven us to next week's meeting. As I listened, this family of adults, teens, and children were celebrating their new freedom. They kept saying how they now believe they would be seeing an elephant soon. Each of them from Maryland used that expression 'seeing the elephant' several times, making me feel that they've all grown up waiting for the elephant of freedom to show up. One of the little boys hollered 'Daddy, daddy, when will we see the elephant? I think the elephant should be joining us now.'"

Tuck couldn't hold off. "Wow, brother. You and I and our wives have been living with love and mentoring from Mehna, Martin, and Ella for the past seventeen years. Now we're building their abolitionist party to fulfill that incredible woman's strategy for freeing her people. Way back like ten or more years ago, I think one of us mentioned perhaps going down to Maryland to see if the enslaved knew anything about Mehna's plan for the elephant of freedom. But we never did go down to those plantations, because we know of the brutality of the proslavery business owners and politicians down there."

Zebulon nodded. "I asked Oliver about the happy discussion that family was having. He told me every slave in Maryland has for generations been given a promise throughout their lives from their parents that when an elephant shows up in America, they will begin to become free and equal citizens. Then, when Harriett showed up this week, I asked her about the elephant prospect. She said that she escaped from her farmland down there because she was not seeing the freedom elephant and she needed to go find it. Remarkable, huh? You and I have read this entire journal several times. We've known since reading it that Miss Mehna was sharing a plan for future freedom with slaves being shipped away from their own land in Africa. So here now is our first confirmation that the journal is real and that its plan has been ready to take off, waiting for someone to team up a strong group of abolitionists. That's us, teaming up the party for the Ella plan next week. This is an incredible hundred-and-fifty-nine-year plot for African freedom in America that will be launched soon to stop the terrible ones."

Amos Tuck was one of the most encouraging antislavery politicians in America. He had already developed the agenda for next week's meeting with several American abolitionists. But this new aspect of the elephant significantly expanded the agenda of his meeting. Amos said, "I'd like us to meet with her tomorrow, or sometime before our freedom kickoff meeting on Wednesday. We should ask her to join us in the meeting to show our team the emotional ties of the enslaved black Americans with our new group's agenda and to share her viewpoint of the Mehna story. Has she seen the journal yet?"

Zebulon said, "Yes. I gave her the journal last night, so she's going through it now. Imagine how it feels to her, having lived her whole life waiting for an elephant to show up, and now it's here in her hands. So energizing for such a kind, brave, and motivated person like her. I'll ask her to meet with you before Wednesday, and to join our new party team on Wednesday. You know, my friend that I feel like Harriet is the Mehna of our time. It'll be amazing to see what she thinks of the journal and the Ella plan."

Oliver brought Harriet down to Zebulon Thing Corner on Monday, then he headed back to continue his work at Cartland Farm. Zeb and Harriet went down to Exeter town center. They entered Amos Tuck's office with Mehna's box.

"Hello, Mrs. Tubman," said Amos. "We've met once or twice before down here in town. How are you doing? So happy that you're here for this incredible story of the elephant. It's amazing what Zeb told me last week about your life of waiting to see an elephant in America. Now Zeb tells me that you've been reviewing the Ella journal. What do you think?"

Harriet began sharing her findings from her review of the journal. She referred to notes she'd taken. "Oh, my heavens, you guys. There are so many awe-inspiring details in this journal. The first one that I'm so amazed with is the beginning of this wonderful lady author's life in Africa, and her ties to the same place as my ancestors! Listen to this. My great grandmother, named Modesty, was enslaved and shipped from the Ashanti Kingdom in Ghana, the same region where this amazing lady, Mehna Abhoola, was raised and where she started this amazing plan. When Mehna produced this idea of the freedom elephant coming to America, giving generations of us hope that the evil of slavery will someday end, my great gramma was right there, the years around 1678 to 1692. Wow. In terms of timing, this means my ancestors probably knew this righteous young lady, Mehna Abhoola. Her message about an elephant someday coming to America was likely shared with my grandma, by her mom when gramma Modesty was being enslaved. Amazing coincidence that my ancestors and queen Abhoola were together those years ago."

Amos said, "Oh, my! What's happening here? I'm feeling like God is right now pulling together the world's two greatest slavery abolitionists, Mehna and Harriet."

Harriet reached right into the box, pulled out the leather sack of tokens, and hugged the whole bag with tearful eyes and a facial expression of love.

Zebulon asked, "So now that you've seen the journal plan, what do you think about the abolitionist party creation that Mehna made as her key strategy?"

"We can tell by her writings in this book that this woman was so intelligent, and so dedicated to the freeing of our people. Through her years, she met many really nice people who agreed with her that slavery is a human tragedy. She is so right that there needs to be an extreme consolidation of kind and strong people to rise up against the evil of slavery. So, Mr. Tuck, Zeb has told me that you have already set up a meeting with a bunch of our abolitionist friends. That sounds to me like the goal of Miss Mehna's plan for the alliance of strong people with antislavery passions. Can you tell me who has confirmed that they will meet with you on Wednesday?"

"Oh, yes," said Tuck. "We'll go through Wednesday's meeting participant list, then let's talk about how we can let you share some of the journal aspects to help merge these people together into one strong, consistent entity to fight the slavers. You, Harriet, probably already know some of these people." Amos handed her a piece of paper showing the expected attendees and a brief summary of the meeting agenda. "Here's the list of gentlemen who've confirmed that they will be here for Queen Mehna's first abolishment meeting. Of course, none of them know about Miss Mehna yet. As you know for sure, your very strong black abolitionist leader, Frederick Douglass, is often here in Exeter and at Cartland's farm supporting your freedom trail families. Zeb and I invited that great guy to this event. But Fred told me that he might not be able to get here this week. So I told him that we'll share with him the outcomes of our party fusion attempt."

Harriet reviewed his list.

American Slavery Abolishment Team Conference

Date: October 12, 1853

Location: Squamscott Hotel, Front Street, Exeter, New Hampshire

Agenda: Our Thirty-Second Congress (1851–1853) has included too many independent abolishment parties, so we don't convince the voters enough of our combined yearnings to stop the Democrats from advocating slavery. The parties in this conference are the antislavery faction of Whigs, Free Soilers, States Rights, and Independent Whigs. The objective of this conference is to consolidate our deep cravings into one strong party to end slavery once and for all in our country of freedom.

Member List

- Amos Tuck: Former US House of Representatives congressman, Free Soil Party advocate
- John Hale: US Senator from New Hampshire. Free Soil Party advocate
- William Seward: Prior New York Governor, now US Senator
- Moses Cartland: NH farm owner, fugitive slave devotee, and local teacher
- John Greenleaf Whittier: Author and poet from Amesbury, Massachusetts
- Abraham Lincoln: US congressman from Illinois, Free Soil Party advocate
- Zebulon Thing: Exeter, NH lumberjack and fugitive slave disciple
- Alvan Bovay: Lawyer from Adams, New York, now in Ripon, Wisconsin, Free Soil Party advocate
- Joe Josephs: Commercial marketer in Buffalo, New York Originator and facilitator of Free Soil National Convention in Buffalo
- Horace Greeley: Founder and editor of New York Tribune newspaper
- Harriet Tubman: Founder and facilitator of America's Underground Railroad, major advocate for freeing slaves

Harriet reviewed the list of abolitionists who had confirmed they'd be at Tuck's conference. "Oh, Mr. Tuck. You already added me to your list. That's great. Thanks. Hey, shouldn't we add Ella Abhoola and Mehna Abhoola to your meeting? They will be there, now that I'm on your list."

Tuck said, "Oh, great idea. That will open the curiosity of our team as they'll be wondering who these other two abolitionists on the list are and when these ladies will show up for introduction. Of course, we'll ask you to introduce them."

Harriet handed the list back to Amos, and he wrote two more names onto the committee list.

- Mehna Abhoola: World's first and foremost abolitionist and equal rights warrior
- Ella Abhoola: World's future and forever abolitionist and human rights defender

As he wrote these names on the list, she said, "I didn't see a name for the new party on this page. Is there one?"

Zebulon said, "For about a year, as we've worked to pull together a resilient team here in Exeter, Amos and I have been trying to come up with a strong, meaningful name for a new party of antislavery politicians. We're also talking about how to show voters that our party is the true party of our republic democracy. The liars in the other party call themselves Democrats, but they are against allowing the people to have power over government. They want power over the people. So, we might ask the team to name our new party Republican, to try and offset their use of the term *democracy*, which they don't represent well. We'll talk about it Wednesday, the Right Party or the Republic Party, or something else. Either way, we will be the party of righteousness to fight evil."

Amos held up the agenda paper. "Now that you added Mehna and Ella to our conference, here's another new idea. Let me know if this sounds all right to you two. When we send this agenda document around the room, or maybe I'll give them each a copy, they will not see Ella and Mehna in the room. It will raise their curiosity about the meeting essentials we'll be presenting. That's great. What would they think if they also see your name Harriet, but they don't see you in the room at the start of the meeting? Just an empty chair. Then when we start introductions, I will invite all three of you into the meeting. You'll walk into the room with a book and a bag of tokens, then you'll introduce these two other ladies, our new party girls. Could this help drive our new team's focus toward the Ella plan?"

Harriet had to speak up. "Oh, my goodness, you guys. Let's do it that way. You have organized the finest efforts ever to drive us to the end of enslavement in this country. This conference on Wednesday will be the most influential event I've ever heard to get us African Americans to start seeing Mehna's elephant. I'm so astounded. The aftermaths of this conference will mean that it is the world's most important good-fortune event for all of humanity."

She said that she doesn't think it will be beneficial to the freedom project to show the incredible final action Mehna Abhoola took to ensure the journal would be successful for American abolitionism. She said she thinks the last two pages of the journal will be too distracting from the overall message of Miss Mehna. Zeb agreed.

CHAPTER 28

ELEPHANT IN THE ROOM AT SQUAMSCOTT HOTEL

Exeter, New Hampshire, Wednesday, October 12, 1853

AS AMOS CARRIED A STACK OF PAPER AND WALKED toward Phillips Exeter Academy along Front Street to get ready for this meeting at the hotel, his mind was completely engrossed in the centuries-old connections that Harriet and Zeb shared earlier that week. He walked briskly as he felt the total weight of his meeting's objective to abolish slavery. Just as he reached the academy's front lawn, Amos stubbed a toe and stumbled a few feet forward. He tried to continue walking hastily, but his right knee got so sore that he hobbled in pain over the next two blocks to the hotel.

As he reached the hotel's front steps, he saw Zebulon and Harriet sitting next to the wooden box, waiting for him.

Zeb said, "Good morning. Wow, you're really limping. You okay?"

"Morning. Yes, I just stepped in a hole and twisted my knee. Damn it hurts. But I'll be okay. Harriet, you look awesome this morning with that new hair style. Are you all set to present the story of Mehna and Ella?"

"Zeb's wife, Sarah, set me up with this hair this morning," said Harriet. "She's so awesome. She and Zeb both helped me practice the presentation several times yesterday, so I'm definitely all set to get my people to start seeing the elephant. Let's do it."

Amos said, "Good. Zeb, please wait here, and tell everyone when they arrive that we're up in room two nineteen. Here's a dozen copies of the agenda document, so please hand one of these to each teammate, then send them in. Harriet and I will go up and set her up in a room near ours, so that she can get ready for her giant delivery which we're all so eager to see."

"Okay, will do. Cartland and I met some of our teammates last night at Hutchins Tavern. We spoke with Joe, Abe, and Alvan. Each of them feels the same as we do about the need to consolidate our efforts. I told them something big is entering into the conference, but I didn't give them any details. Seems to me like they are pretty excited to be here. A couple of the guys are staying right here in the hotel, so I'll hang out in the lobby to see them when they are ready."

Harriet and Amos headed into the hotel with Ella's box and went up to the meeting room, which was already set up with over a dozen chairs and a chalk board. After checking out the room where she would be introducing Mehna and Ella, Harriet took the box into a room across the hall that Amos had rented from the owner, Major Abraham Blake. Before anyone showed up, Amos went into the room where Harriet was. They spent about fifteen minutes talking about the best way for Harriet to start her presentation of the elephant in the room.

Amos went back into the conference room. Alvan Bovay, a lawyer and Free Soil politician from Wisconsin, was already there, so they were the first two to hook up. Bovay said, "Hey, Mr. Tuck. I read your agenda paper just now. Wow, good group of us abolitionists coming in here. It's about time. But who are these ladies? I've heard of Mrs. Tubman, but not the Abhoola sisters."

"Hi, Alvan. Good to meet you. My friend Zebulon, who just let you into the hotel, told me that he met you last night at the tavern.

So you're from Wisconsin. Out there, you're doing a great job looking to stop the western states from becoming slavery states to back up the Democrats. Thanks for all you do. It's because of your great work that we decided to add you to our meeting list. And thanks for adding your buddy Joe Josephs to our committee. He's going to help a bunch from what you told me. And thanks for also making sure that we included Mr. Lincoln, who was already on my list. You're right. We need to pull together a larger and stronger abolitionist team. That's what these ladies are going to help us with. They are experts at abolishment planning, so you'll be amazed to see what they have to offer."

As everyone else entered the conference room, there were examples both of strangers meeting each other for the first time and people meeting with guys they'd known for a while. When he saw that everyone, including Zeb, had arrived, Amos moved to the front of the room near the chalkboard and started speaking. "Hello everyone. Thanks so much for coming here to build this team. I know that many of you traveled far and long to get here, so thank you for coming to Exeter. This is the right place for us to combine our thoughts toward ending slavery in America. As you'll sense when you speak with locals, New Hampshire residents are increasingly moving toward abolishment since the stupid 1850 Fugitive Slave Act and since more horrors of the physical abuse of enslavement are being shown to the NH public these days rather than hidden from voters as in the past. Let me start with the big picture. Many of us have been discussing for several years, in both private and congressional settings, how to offset the terrible inhumane ideologies of the Democratic Party.

"We fought and departed from the dictatorial British Empire eighty years ago to build a government that can protect individual freedoms. Ten years ago this August, the British House of Commons ended legalized slavery in all world areas of British rule. Now, in the nineteenth century, we in the USA have gangs of pro-human traffickers in a major political party. As you all know, we currently are the most proslavery democracy in the world, because of the Democrats. As I implied in my invitations for you to come here to Exeter for this meeting, there is new information about our country's white-supremacist history and how one political party is working openly and also secretly to keep that human-trafficking culture alive. To rollout this new fact-based information which you will find godly, I'll outline the meeting agenda first. Then let's go around the room with personal introductions, followed by opening ideas and recommendations from each and all of us."

Mr. Tuck continued. "Of course our ultimate conference objective is to end slavery and racial separation in our wonderful country, but we also must build a plan that will forever prevent the Democrats from taking back the government and restarting their desires for continued slavery of our African friends in America. In general, we will today brainstorm and outline our plan for unification of our abolitionist strategies to drive for the future betterment of all lives in the USA. To get the movement started, we have some new and incredible information to share with you that will help send this meeting's agenda to quick closure. After this new huge discovery is shared with you, the antislavery elephant in the room will be so massive that the slavery party will not be able to remove the elephant from the room—not ever. Now let's get started with introductions, because we don't all know each other yet. So, tell us who you are and give a brief intro of your background and future plans, if any. We'll go around the room. I'll start.

"Amos Tuck. I've been a local lawyer here in Exeter since 1838. As some of you know, I began politics in the NH House of Representatives in 1842. But soon after I got to work, I found the inhumane characteristics of the slavery party's leaders. They always work so hard to fake out the voting public with lies and hidden agendas. For the past eight years, Senator Hale and I have been talking about how to unify our positions on ending slavery to drive for all families' prosperity and happiness. I've held offices in Congress for Democrats, Whigs, and the Free Soil Party. My initial efforts to change the Democrats in the House to antislavery didn't sit well with them, so they kicked me out of their party. Now, it's time to pull us all together with one unified party across the whole country. That's the objective of our agenda." Amos sat down and pointed to the man on his left, New Hampshire Senator John Hale.

Senator Hale stood. "John Hale. From Rochester, New Hampshire. I'm embarrassed to admit that I began politically in the Democratic Party. Some of you know that I was thrown out of the US District Attorney position by President Tyler twenty-one years ago, because I could not stand behind their slavery position. Turns out I'm really pleased with his decision to kick me out of their party. As you all know, I was the Free Soil candidate for president last year. But we haven't organized enough of the abolishment aspects of several anti-Democrats to end slavery of all humans in the world. The racial division and dreadful antifreedom ideology of that party made me get away from them. With their slavery fight still holding strong, and now that my Bowden College colleague, Franklin Pierce, is our President, I have to reenter the fight. I'm so disappointed that a New Hampshire native, our new president, is leaning toward the protection of slavery laws. So we here in this meeting have to unify our plans to get him and other Democratic Party people-haters voted out of their seats. I'm here to work with you to finally stop the Democratic Party's ongoing fight for slavery." Senator Hale pointed at Mr. Bovay, next to him.

"I'm Alvan Bovay. Originally from Adams, New York. I attended Norwich University, in Vermont, not far from here. Now I'm a lawyer living with my family in Ripon, Wisconsin. I've been aligned for years with most of you trying to uplift the Free Soil Party to prevent more new western states from engaging in slavery. I came through New York a few weeks ago to visit family on my way to meet with you here. When passing through Buffalo, I asked my friend Joe if he could come to Amos's conference to help unify our parties." He touched Joe's shoulder. "This guy is so committed to freeing the Africans. He and I have been trying for years to find ways to unify soles and goals like yours and ours to support freedom and prosperity for all humanity. As for me, after we create our new party platform, name, and character, I will bring our fight for human rights to Wisconsin and other western states. I'm also a colleague of Mr. Lincoln over here. He's a strong and dedicated antislavery attorney and is talking about jumping back into politics to fight the foolhardy party's push to grow slavery out west. He and I talked of party unification needs several times this year, then we both got this conference request from Mr. Tuck. So astonishing, the timing of your request for us to come here. When I return home, I will share the outcome of this event with any other western abolitionists." Alvan handed the speaking over to Joe next to him.

"Joe Josephs. I'm from Buffalo, New York. I run a commercial advertising business. I use paintings, framework, flags, and other items to promote businesses' products. I also do the same to support antislavery politicians running for election. Since 1848, I've been helping facilitate the Free Soil National Convention in Buffalo. Something else, too. Where is Harriet? She and I have met several times, as Senator Seward and I have helped move her people north through western New York to Canada. Is she here?"

Zebulon Thing said, "Wonderful woman. She's here in Exeter. She'll join us in a little while."

Mr. Lincoln stood up next. "Abraham Lincoln. Hello, freedom leaders. I'm from the farmlands of Illinois. At twenty-five years old, I was happy to become a member of a group of abolitionists within the Whig party. But for years, half of our Whig party was lying like the old British Whigs; they were hidden Democrats pushing for slavery. That's why some of us started the Free Soil Party to firm up the fight against human enslavement. But it's been too un-unified this way. Last year, fifty-one percent of presidential voters voted for Democrats and forty-nine percent voted against the Dems and their push for continuing to treat the enslaved like they are animals. But it was both our Whig and our Free Soil parties in the voting outcomes, so we need to pull all of us and our voters together into one party to win the world of freedom for the people. We're very close to having the votes to reset the United States of America as a country of freedom and democracy, but our efforts are being hampered by the Democrats. But it will only happen if we combine our political parties into one strong legislative body against slavery. It's time to save the future of happiness in this country. Once we pull together and show the public what's really right and what's really wrong, and show the details which the Democrats hide from voters, then there will be no more of their evil policies." Mr. Lincoln turned toward the guy next to him.

"William Seward, US Senator. Most of us know each other. I'm so grateful for us all to be here for this battle. I was a lawyer in my hometown of Auburn, New York. I started in the state senate twenty-three years ago. Then I was elected governor in 1838. Then I met most of you after making the US Senate election four years ago. Let's make this happen once and for all."

The next man spoke up. "Horace Greeley. I'm the founder and editor of New York Tribune newspaper. Mr. Josephs told me about this meeting, and then we contacted Amos and got assigned to your conference. Thanks so much. I really want to make sure that your political direction is set forth to the public, so I'll make sure to help." Greeley nodded to the guy on his left.

"Moses Cartland, here," said the man. "Hello, Mr. Tuck and gentlemen. Thanks for having us all here. We really need this for the nice Africans in our country. I've got a farm over here in Lee. Because of the stupid slave law, please don't tell anyone, but my family and I open and share our farm as a haven for Harriet Tubman's Underground Railroad. All the people who visit our place on their way north or who stay with us are so nice and honorable. Knowing these good people has made it so difficult to live within our Democrat's slavery environment. Let's do this. We've got to take their sad policies down. Now, here's my cousin." He pointed to his left.

"John Greenleaf Whittier," said the next man. "Hello, team. I'm an author and poet from Haverhill, Massachusetts, originally, now living down in Amesbury. I come up here to Exeter often, because you have a higher concentration of people in favor of ending slavery than any other place in America that we know of. Mr. Cartland and I are cousins and best friends. We both are very much ready to help you with abolishment of the damn slavery of these people. I will write and publish messages with your righteousness, you guys. Thanks for doing this." He looked to his left, prompting the next man.

"Zebulon Thing. I'm a lumberman right here in Exeter, grown up here my whole life. I've been working with Mr. Tuck for years trying to coordinate this type of alignment for us. Like Joe and Moses both mentioned, my family also has been working with Mrs. Tubman for a couple of years as she's guided her people north through this region. When Harriet gets here today, we have something to show you which you'll be amazed to see." Zeb nodded toward Amos, indicating that he should start setting up an elephant in the room.

Amos Tuck felt very excited about the next phase of the conference's agenda. He started his leadership facilitation. "Okay, team. Thanks for your intros. You saw on the agenda sheet that there are three more people coming to meet with us. When they come in this morning, you will see a highly special event. These ladies will share with you a historical piece that aligns with each of your righteous personalities. Great to know that some of you have met Harriet Tubman. She's here in New Hampshire this week, so we invited her to your conference. She'll be here shortly with the other ladies.

Let's begin with a bit more discussion on the objectives of this meeting. John, Horace, and I walked down to Water Street last night to Widow Folsom's Tavern. President Washington ate at Folsom's Tavern just sixty-four years ago. So let's use this place and this meeting to reestablish our country's unity, respect for human rights, and freedom from government over-control, all of which the Democrats are trying to take away from America. We do not want dictatorial practices where the federal government allows states to supersede federal or state human rights laws so they can keep slavery alive forever. We prefer a republic form of government, on the concept that power resides with the people— *all* of the people, not just the white people, which is the strategy of the party currently in power. We're all here looking for the right Republican formula.

"The high levels of honesty, decency, justice, principles, and virtue that have brought you here tell of your high levels of righteousness. Our new party's full republic form of government will be firmly entrenched by your morality for all people. Now this, the name of the proslavery party is a lie. They call themselves a name taken from the word democracy, but they only want government control over individuals. True democracy is not supported by the Democrats' agendas. We need to get the voting public to have a chance to support real democracy. Our country is expected to be the world's most fair republic, where the supreme power is owned by all citizens, not monarchs. Our republic is one of true democracy, except for the aspects where voting citizens are tricked into voting against freedom. At the end of this meeting, we'll talk about the best name for our efforts, based on righteousness, republicanism, human rights, and the right things to do. But for now, get ready for a giant outburst. Zebulon, please bring Mrs. Tubman and her Abhoola friends in to meet the team and to share their commitment to freedom."

Zeb walked across the hall from the conference team room and saw Harriet sitting with the journal, still touring through Mehna's archives of love and heartache. "Hey, nice lady. The team's ready over there. Like we said yesterday, you'll be right in front of the chalkboard for your presentation. I'll be sitting right next to you with Ella's box on my lap, so you can jump into it at any moment in your discussion. You all set?"

Harriet put the journal into the box, handed it to Zeb, and then put an attractive hair cloth over her head and a scarf around her shoulders. "I'm more than all set. Like you and Amos also feel, I'm craving to share with our strong abolitionist squadron Mehna's life that she and Martin Walpole created. Let's go, Zebu."

CHAPTER 29

SPECIAL COLLUSION INCIDENT

ZEBULON THING ENTERED ROOM 219. "OKAY, GUYS. Listen up, please. We're heading to the really right place. Come on in, Queen." Amos had already prepped the entire room to honor Harriet Tubman as soon as she showed up, because they all knew of her incredible work for humanity. The beautiful champion of her people strolled through the doorway carrying an antique wooden box. Harriet was dressed in her business-looking jacket and skirt. All nine men stood up instantly with arms in the air, and started clapping, and cheering for her presence.

They cheered things like "You are great," "Such a princess," and other good words for a minute or two. Several of them had met Harriet before, so she and they shared hugs. Then there were more hugs and handshakes, and measures of high honor for this woman.

Zebulon asked them to sit. Then he said, "We're all so proud of you, Harriet. We've all been following stories of the hard work you're doing to help free your people. This must have been so crazy dangerous for you for the past few years, after they attacked your love with their Fugitive Slave Act. What a strong and brave person you are. Let's get started by telling the folks here what drove you to push the freedom train as hard as you have."

Harriet took over. "Thank you, thank you, gentlemen. I'll do the same kind of intro you just did, then I'll introduce two super women who will change our lives for the better. I was born down in Maryland thirty-two years ago. I don't have to tell you nice fellows of the terrible lives being lived by my people, because you've each proven that you're disgusted by the slavers. You understand the horrors of life that would drive someone to try to escape like I did. Several of you have helped us move people up to Canada through here and through western New York. Maybe you know that Joe Josephs and Senator Seward and his wife have been helping us over in western New York just like you Things and Cartlands do here. Thank you very, very much for helping free my people.

"Let's get right into it. I'm about to share with you some fascinating history. For a hundred and fifty-nine years, generations of the enslaved families in Maryland from the Ghana region of Africa have been living under a shroud of history that brought a giant message from our homeland. Let me start with this. Please raise your hand if you have ever seen an elephant here in America."

No one raised their hand. "Not yet, huh?" she said. "As I expected would be the case. I want you to know that there will be an elephant in our country sometime sooner than you think. I'll tell you in a minute how we know this. First though, let me share how I ended up with my lifelong desire to see an elephant. It's not just about the animal. It's about generations of my people being taught that there will someday be an elephant coming to America to set off the war against slavery.

From everything we were all taught growing up, I always told myself that I needed to meet the elephant before I was twenty years old. That didn't happen, so I decided to pull out of my farm in Maryland four years ago this month because I saw no signs that we would ever see the giant freedom icon that our ancestors told us would come along someday. I left the farm with my brothers, both of whom are chickens, so they went back within days. All of my people of African descent enslaved on Maryland's eastern shore plantations grew up with family folklore about a woman in Africa who will someday send a beautiful elephant to end their enslavement. Three or four generations have been waiting for the elephant to show up. But it never did in their lives, so my ancestors died after a full life of slavery and disappointment for not seeing the elephant. The enslaved today are still waiting for the giant to arrive so that they can begin their lives of freedom, equality, and happiness. If you see an elephant in Exeter today, please rise into high emotions for the beginning of the war against slavery."

Harriet turned toward Zebulon as he took the lid off the Ella box. "Here goes more. You're now meeting a great African woman named Mehna Abhoola. You don't see her, but trust me, Mehna Abhoola is here." Harriet holds the journal and the bag of tokens up high. "And now, I'll turn the discussion over to Zebulon to share with you what these things are and how he found them."

Zebulon set the box on the floor and stood up. "This box, with an old book and a bag of copper tokens in it, has been with my family since 1750. My granddad had a lumberjack friend here in Exeter named Martin Walpole. Mr. Walpole moved here from London in 1694. He lived here for fifty-six years. Before he passed in 1750, he shared this box with my grandpa and asked him to carry the package forward until the plans written in this journal can be applied to American life. When my dad made it to adulthood, Grandpa turned the package over to his son and asked him to protect and uphold the intentions of this box. Same thing happened to this Thing. My dad introduced me to this package about twenty-three years ago. I've been living with it and trying to figure what to do with it since then. Then something came to light. Seventeen years ago, Amos and I were hanging out at the tavern after an attack by Democrats at one of our church's abolitionist conferences. I shared the messages in this journal with Amos that night because of the impact we felt from the attack on slavery abolishment. Since then he and I have been trying to work this journal forward. Amos is up next. He's going to tell you what's in this journal that made us bring it here to show you." Zeb sat down next to Harriet.

Amos Tuck stood in the front of the room. "If any of you ever reads this old journal, written a hundred and fifty-nine years ago, you'll see that a group of young people in London in 1694, one of them from Africa, wanted somebody in America to eventually build a strong team to put an end to slavery. Harriet told you of this lady who was the initiator and leader of the plan in this book.

"At eighteen years old, when her father was captured by local black leaders, Mehna Abhoola, a young African woman in the 1690s, began a fight in her head for her people's freedom. To make themselves rich, those kings and their home-grown armies were selling any Africans they could kidnap. For a couple of years, Miss Mehna was enslaved by the local king to help feed the families of slaves on their way to the coast. What she did was show love for the enslaved families. She began showing them an elephant on their trip south to the coast, and she always reminded them to think positive of their future lives. She told hundreds, maybe thousands of families that this elephant on the river was going to someday become their path to freedom. Miss Abhoola's intelligence and her brashness toward helping her people allowed her to eventually learn the English language and make her way to London so that she could try to understand the motivations for slavery by the people there. For a couple of years in London, she developed a plan and wrote this journal to push her desires to end slavery into the colonies in a place called America.

"Some of you will want to read this whole book someday. Zeb and I have been focusing on this journal's intentions for decades. But we didn't ever confirm that the enslaved peoples in Maryland and beyond have been waiting to see the elephant for three generations. This summer, Zeb heard some nice fugitive families traveling through here talking about their new freedom. Some of the children were asking their parents where the elephant was, now that they were getting free. What an incredible discovery for us to hear. So we asked Harriet and her friend Oliver about their lives of waiting to see the elephant, and we showed her this manual and bag of tokens. So now, she is getting close to the elephant of free life. Do you feel that you have now seen the elephant along your freedom trail, Mrs. Tubman?" He asked her this to set up a special response.

Harriet responded eagerly, "There is an elephant in the room. We will all see it by the end of this meeting!"

Amos reached into the bag of tokens that Harriet held open for him. He pulled out a handful of New England Elephant Tokens and walked through the room handing one to each member. "Take a look at these antique tokens. Please discuss what we've shown you, then head to lunch. Come back around one o'clock so we can start narrowing our discussions."

As discussions picked up, Abraham Lincoln headed right over to Harriet as she was looking in Mehna's book. "Oh, dear. You have been the savior of your people, just like this lady in the book. It sounds like you and she are related, with emotional struggles to fight and end slavery." Horace Greeley stood with his camera and took a picture of Abraham standing with Harriet and the freedom journal.

"Thanks, Mr. Lincoln," said Harriet. "My great grandmother was there in the Ashanti Kingdom at the same time Miss Abhoola was there starting her plan for freedom. We could be related, but I feel like she is my sister anyway because of her life of helping people. I hope you get to read this journal, because it has so many concepts to get the freedom battle started."

Abe said, "Okay. I'll ask Zeb and Amos when I can read the book. Where's the other lady on the agenda? Ella?"

"She's here, too," said Harriet. She opened the leather cover of the journal and showed Abe the first drawing Miss Mehna did, a hundred and fifty-eight years ago.

"This is Mehna's drawing of the enslaved families' elephant savior, whom she named Ella, as in Ella Phant. See the elephant on your token? That's Ella too. She's here to start the war against slavery, Mr. Abe. But we need to do more teambuilding to head Miss Ella in the right direction to start the first battle for freedom. Here's the book. Please read page nineteen before you head out to lunch. See you soon."

Mr. Lincoln was feeling highly engaged with Harriet's feelings of eagerness to get a serious war going. He looked over the section she mentioned.

Amazed by the layout and message on this page, Abe went over to Amos, who was still in the meeting room talking with others. "Tuck, can I be one of the journal readers after the conference tonight? I just read page nineteen. May I have some time to speak this afternoon? I'm thrilled by what you three are doing. And even more amazed by what that young lady and her friends did over a century ago for their people."

Amos agreed that Abe could speak later that day and hang with the journal later in the evening. "When you do read the whole journal, Abe, you'll be even more amazed by what Mehna did and what she planned for the future of the world to stop racial division forever."

CHAPTER 30

NEW PARTY LAUNCHES

AFTER LUNCH, AMOS TUCK BEGAN THE SESSION WITH more information. "This young lady and the abolitionist friends she met in London went through a whole development process to figure out where in these American colonies they could pull people together who would fight the battle with enough power to win. They chose this New Hampshire colony which slavery leader King William certified in 1693. Mehna and her partner, Martin Walpole, received some evidence that the local people here were more against slavery than people in the southern colonies. So, Exeter, New Hampshire, became their point of focus for building their team to end slavery. Here we are. We're the team they worked to build. So now, Abe has asked to speak with us since he's looked at some of Mehna's journal details."

Lincoln spoke up. "Thanks, Tuck. Hey, team. Amos told me I could see the book later, but I couldn't wait. So I sat here and cruised through this book. Holy cow! Or should I say holy elephant? I saw a section that shows how the kingdom leaders in Africa were very experienced at lying to the people to keep them from knowing the true goals of the governing powers. Those were also the practices of the slavery proprietors and monarchs in England back then. And today, the falsehood narratives are a big part of US politics. Like Miss Mehna says here in her book, we need more righteousness in government.

"We lost the presidency last year because the voting public has not been shown the atrocities of the party who call themselves Democrats. Let's all of us in this room, including the Abhoola ladies, take this message of heavenly advice, and agree that a full political war against slavery will be underway no more than two elections from now. Let's promise as a team that if we don't win the 1856 election, we will win the presidency, the house, and the senate in 1860 because over the next seven years we will ensure that the true sadness of slavery and our antislavery messages are fully expressed to the voting public.

"I must tell you what I saw on page twenty-three. She wrote in the journal, 'Find several strong abolitionist leaders and get them to merge, merge, and merge until they have enough centralized power to win the war for freedom!' Then she added these empty lines on this page for a full team of humanists like us to each sign our signatures showing our commitment to start the battle. This incredibly intelligent lady who made this plan knew that good folks are everywhere, and she knew that good has to collaborate resolutely to beat immoral, because that seems to be everywhere too. Two strong abolitionists have already signed onto the battle plan. I won't tell you who, but you will see their names when you sign up. These two are our true leaders.

"I congratulate each of you for being here to join Mehna Abhoola and Harriet Tubman's team for driving freedom to all humans. Amos says we will sign the journal today to show our commitment. Let's start our new consolidated party of the elephant. From now until 1860 elections, we will accelerate communications to voters about the horror of slavery, so that voters vote for health and well-being rather than voting for slavery which the Democrats have them do today, because their party is good at falsehood management. Starting today, team, we're turning our country's government into the direction of righteousness forever."

Harriet was so thrilled by the whole event and Mr. Lincoln's speech. Sitting next to Zeb, she reached over and took the journal and a pencil from his hands. She opened the book to page nineteen and drew a quick version of Ella to the right, with Abe's wording, "Righteousness Forever." To document Mr. Lincoln's goal for the new party, she showed Zeb and Amos her version of Ella's right turn that she'd just added to Mehna's drawing.

Zebulon stood with the journal in hand. He opened it to page twenty-three and said, "Please, come right up and sign. After we all commit to the elephant party plan, let's talk about the goals and shape of our new party, which will win the day, like Abe says, no later than 1860."

Lots of open discussion took place on the shared historical information, while everyone in the room lined up to sign their commitment on page twenty-three of the journal. The whole team was astonished by the story from generations ago and its direct connection to the enslaved people in America at that time. The two team members whose signatures already existed on page twenty-three were Mehna Abhoola and Harriet Tubman. When the men saw these signatures, their hearts swelled with love and motivation to join these ladies' battle.

After most all of the team members had signed their commitment into the party of freedom, someone started knocking on the hotel room door from out in the hallway. Zebulon walked over and opened the door. A friend that he's known for a few years walked in, so Zebulon responded. "Oh hey, Fred, you made it here! Great to see you." Frederick Douglass was an American social reformer, abolitionist, orator, writer, and statesman. After escaping from slavery in Maryland in 1848, he became a national leader of the abolitionist movement in New Hampshire and New York, so he often spent time in Exeter and at the Cartland farm in Lee to keep freedom expanding. The team all cheered and spoke with Fred, then Zeb had Mr. Douglass sign into Mehna's journal for his commitment to the party of freedom.

Conference Findings and Corrective Actions

The last person to sign up for the new party plan was Joe Josephs. "Amos and Zeb, thanks so much for pulling together this strong list of comrades who've signed up to start the final war against slavery. Wow, Harriet! You and Mehna are the first members to sign up for commitment to the party of the elephant. Are we going to call our new group the Elephant Party, the Ella Party, or what?"

Amos said, "Good try, Joe. Yeah, we'll be the party of the elephant icon, now that we see the heavenly efforts from this African woman and Harriet. But the name of our new united party will be one that the voting public sees as important to freedom. Let's get going with the team's discussion toward the party's name, its foundations, and our plans for action."

Tuck stood at the front of the room to bring the discoveries, conversations, and opinions together, then to facilitate the team into establishing goals and pathways to achieve political triumph and slavery abolishment.

"Okay, team. Thanks for your commitment to support these ladies of human rights and to end slavery forever. Let's get it done. For the rest of this afternoon, there are three main topics that we should finalize to kick off our new battle for the people. We will discuss the best option for the name of our new assembly. Then, we'll talk about what each of us should do over the next decade to expose the hidden falsehood strategies of Democrats. Please be prepared, each of you, to share with us your primary strategies moving forward to support the main objectives of our new party and cover specifically how you will engage new politicians and voters to hook up with us. Lastly, we'll talk briefly about how to use our new icon, the elephant in the room."

Harriet had to respond to Amos's planned agenda for the afternoon. "Mr. Tuck, one more thing we should discuss today is the right direction of our new icon. This is important now that we've all signed on and agreed to the fight."

Amos agreed. "Okay. Let's start with that discussion. It's hugely important. So, team, now that you each have a New England Elephant Token in your hand, we want to share with you Mehna's plan for our use of her icon of liberty.

"The amazing story from her time in Africa while helping the enslaved during their awful journeys is one that sets our new icon's foundation. For years of travel with carts of families toward the coast where they were being sold, they all saw an elephant facing left along a riverbank. The elephant was there on the riverbank during each journey Mehna made with slaves to the coast, and the elephant always laid her eyes on the children chained in carts. She was never on the river when the empty carts went north as they were heading back to the kingdom in Kumasi to be filled with more families imprisoned by the local black king.

"Mehna felt that this was godly support, where the animal was always there for the enslaved to see and feel. In her journal, she wrote a concept that her elephant friend whom she called Ella was always facing to the left to show her anger toward the kingdoms to the north that were imprisoning and selling African people for years.

"Mehna wrote that when the true army of antislavery colludes together by signing page twenty-three like we have done today, Ella will at that moment flip to the right to show her people that she is now in America so the enslaved will start seeing the elephant of freedom coming toward them, no longer facing the immoral slavers on the left.

"Let's take a short bathroom break. When we get back, I'll show you how Mehna rolled Ella to the right on page nineteen of her book."

As all of the guys walked out, Harriet headed right up to the chalkboard on the wall behind Amos. She grabbed a piece of chalk, then held it out and smiled at Zeb, who was still sitting with the journal on his lap. He could tell exactly what she was asking for, so he opened the journal to page nineteen and took it over next to the chalkboard so she could see it. Harriet drew a copy of Mehna's picture of freedom.

As they all headed back in, the team members saw the fantastic message on the chalkboard that Mehna had presented to them in her book.

Harriet was still standing next to the chalkboard. She pointed to the far right. "Just so you know, I added this elephant hero on the right of Mehna's drawing while Mr. Lincoln was speaking. Like you said, Abe, Ella is here to turn our government into righteousness forever." She stepped back a bit, looking at the board, and was so overcome with emotion about finally meeting the elephant here with Mehna's abolitionist team. With tear-filled eyes, she turned to the team. "Oh, my God! The moment to flip the image right is here right now." She pointed to the flipping point between Ella left and Ella right.

As she wiped her face with her sleeve, she said, "You're all here as the team that this wonderful woman built to someday start the real war against slavery in America. Now that Ella has flipped to the right, the elephant in the room is your war against slavery politicians. Thank you, thank you, thank you, for all you're going to do to set off the war."

The whole team stood again, applauding and cheering for Harriet's passionate sharing of her close ties to the new party of freedom. She smiled, sat, and aimed her hand toward Amos so he could take over the discussion.

Amos began the discussion on the name of the right party. "Wow! What a sensation. This is the very moment that will eventually put an end to life's disaster for so many nice people in our country. Let's focus on the strongest name for our new party. Most of us here today know that we've had too many separate groups trying to start the fight to end slavery. Because we haven't been unified enough, the voters don't really know who's who out here in the world of politics. It's very important, as you know, that we consolidate all antiracial politics under one strong party. But the people need to feel the true foundations of our party by the heart of its name.

It's my opinion that the liars call themselves Democrats to trick voters into thinking they believe in the fundamentals of democracy and our constitution. But they are against allowing the people to have power over government. They want power over the people, so their use of the name Democrat is completely false, as we know from their desires to prevent all people from being free and voting. Because of the uninformed voters, we need a party name that shows how we really support our constitution. *Democrat* would be a name we believe in, but it's been stolen away from the people that believe in freedom. Our constitution is the world's best republic for setting people ahead of government. A few of us were down at the tavern last night brainstorming what our party name could be. We came up with a great name. To show the people who we are, we recommend the name Republican. Your thoughts?"

Horace Greeley stood right up. "Wow! That's it. From this moment on, in my editorials, you will be called the Republican Party. And you will be *right* because of Mehna's plan to launch your righteousness toward the people. In my writings, your opponents will be left, as in left behind because of their indecencies regarding human freedom and because that's the direction God set up Ella to point against the slavery leaders in Africa. The world's use of the terms *left* and *right* for politics started in 1789, in Paris, France, when the king held conferences and people who supported him were on one side and people who disagreed with him sat on the other side of the epicenter.

"Our whole Whig disaster has tried since then to use those terms, left wing and right wing to confuse the public. But from now on, because of this great event today and this new history you showed us of righteousness, the nice party of fairness and love in my newspapers with always be the right party, your newly organized Republican Party."

The whole committee discussed the name Republican Party for some time with super positive talk. No other name came forward, so Amos got back to the agenda. He started with both arms straight overhead. "Congratulations, all of you Republicans, for starting the war against slavery on this day, October twelfth, 1853. We're going to win the war."

The entire room of abolitionists stood up again, arms up, and cheered, "Yay," and "Hooray," and "Free the people," and "Awesome job, Mehna and Harriet", and "Down with the damn Democrats!"

After the cheers, hugs, and handshakes, Amos continued. "Thank you, Mehna Abhoola, for starting America's Republican Party to end slavery and stop racial division forever. Let's go around the room, individually sharing your thoughts on how we will each work to get Harriet's people to see the elephant of freedom as soon as possible, no later than the 1860 goal for starting the full war. Horace, you already told us where you are heading with our new party in your newspaper. Alvan, you go next, please."

CHAPTER 31

INDIVIDUAL STRATEGIES FOR THE FUTURE OF ELLA

ALVAN BOVAY SPOKE UP. "YOU ALL ARE SO AWESOME. Thanks, Amos, for this unifying event. I will launch our new party out in Wisconsin as soon as I get home. We need a high acceptance from the voters, so I'll convince them in my state to buy into the name Republican Party before the next election season. I will convince the people to fight the new western states away from accepting slavery. I'm with you all. I'm going to fight the battle every day until we fulfill Mehna's craving to free her people." Alvan looked left to his buddy, Joe Josephs.

"I promise I'll take our new party to new heights," said Joe. "Because of the deep sentiments you've provided to us today, the new party of the elephant will be the primary focus of my marketing business and products. From today on, Harriet, your people will start seeing the elephant, for real. Especially in Buffalo. And so will the American voters who've been tricked into detesting African Americans because of the Democrats' falsehoods. When I get home to Buffalo, our voting public will start to see thousands of elephants there to free the enslaved. I will encircle our entire Erie County with decades of Republican Party dealings, like conventions, parades, and merchandise. One more thing. I'm going to be the elephant guy in Buffalo, so I suggest that you, Amos, should consider changing your name to Amos Tusk because of all you've done to get America to start seeing the elephant of freedom." He laughed. "Just kidding! Good job, team!"

William Seward, said, "In New York, with you, Elephant Joe, I will continue to fight to end slavery, never giving up. Amazing what we've taken on today. I agree, Abe, that this is the day to begin the consolidated battle by merging us together for the next few elections until we win the president, house, and senate. I will always fight the battles with you in Washington, and my family will always help Harriet and her fugitive friends with their needs during escape. Next."

Moses Cartland spoke next. "You are right, Senator. What an incredible day we've had. Until we win the war that you are all starting today, I will continue to work with you Harriet to help all of your folks that you are able to send our way up your Underground Railroad. I'm a teacher too, so I will always teach the kids to treat all people the same, with love and caring. Go ahead, John."

John Greenleaf Whittier said, "Thanks, cousin. I will always be a writer, but today changes everything. Your stories shared here today will engage my writing efforts with ever more emotions toward the people who are treated so terribly. You will see significant messages toward ending slavery coming from my novels."

Next, John Hale spoke. "Now that we're starting our new gathering of strong abolition, I promise I will continue to run for office and do everything I can to stay in the US Senate for our next decade of ending slavery. I suggest that we have more of these Ella conferences some time before each presidential and congressional election until we win the offices and free the people from the Democrats. Amos and I might ask for your travel back here to Exeter several more times to continue the alliance that we've built today. Thank you so much Harriet for being here and for introducing your lady friends who brought the elephant into the room."

Amos Tuck was next. "I lost to congress last year, but never will I stop fighting this battle for Harriet and Mehna. Regardless which of you champions wins the seats we need to fill, I will still be there to support any aspect of our new Republican Party, the party of the elephant. In fact, Zeb and I will work with you to set up recurring Ella conferences, here in Exeter or elsewhere, to ensure we're fusing together to effectively combat all proslavery strategies of the Democrats. If there ever has to be real war, put me in the army or navy so I can battle face-to-face with those humanity haters. Okay, Mr. Thing, your turn."

"Fantastic day, my friends," said Zeb. "I will always be here in Exeter, so I'll keep working with Amos to support whatever you need to drive the party to full unity. As for this journal and these tokens, I will continue to hold them on the edge of your party, so they can be used to start and win the war against the Democrats.

"I will continue to have the Thing family control this bag for Ella's future. Just so you know, there are two slightly different types of Ella tokens in this box. You each have type one, where the D in the word *God* stands straight. The second set that Mehna and Martin Walpole made has the D in *God* leaning slightly forward because they want some of the tokens to drive freedom into the far, far future. As the political battles arise every few years over the next decade, we will keep sharing Mehna's plan for Harriet's people to start seeing the freedom elephant that they've been waiting for, for generations. I will keep the second set in hiding as we move forward beyond winning over the government and ending slavery. Trust me, please. The New England Elephant tokens will stay in battle as long as the evil Democrats continue to push for separation of people by skin color, which I believe they might do even after we put the end to slavery."

Joe Josephs joined with Zeb. "Mr. Thing. I'd like to work with you on establishing the future of the elephant for the Republican Party, so please let's meet tomorrow before I get on the train and later as often as needed to keep the elephant in the room against evil politics forever."

Zeb agreed with Joe. "Thanks, Joe. That's great. We'll meet tomorrow and later. I'll ask you, the marketing guy, how we might be able to create more New England Elephant Tokens someday." Zebulon pointed to Abraham Lincoln.

"Harriet, speak before me, please," said Abraham.

Harriet Tubman spoke. "Gentlemen, thanks so much for coming together for this grand union. I have always followed the North Star, Polaris, to guide me and my escapee friends to these great lands where you nice people live. Now we have a new trail where we will follow this great animal from God to the right for freedom and righteousness. Here's my primary plan. I want to continue to work with any of you as you win elections and take over control of our freedom. Please continue to ask for my assistance so we can fully meet Ella's and Mehna's goals for freeing everyone. When you ask, I will even consider attacking the slavers by hiding and faking them out and spying on their strategies, just like they do to your side. Hey, Zeb. Here's a concept that Mr. Lincoln and I talked about during the break. You might want to consider using some of Mehna's tokens as a way to honor political wins or real war battle victories. Ella on the tokens points toward the left today to stop their evil just like she did back on the river in Africa to fight the black slavers there. Thanks again so much. Please use this elephant in the room to free my people. Then keep them free forever by constantly fighting against the awful Democrats who are such true racists. Mr. Lincoln, your turn."

Abraham spoke, "You, dear, are the most influential abolitionist in American history. We will continue to work with you in several ways. Here are my visions of the next decade.

"We need a leader who will fully advocate for all citizens to be free and with open routes toward wealth and happiness for their families. With our new Republican Party, and with all of your strong commitments to the fight, the voting public will eventually realize that all of humanity needs our party.

"It's important that when Amos contacted each of us he asked us to make sure to keep this meeting secret from the open world of politics and falsehood reporters. Let's please keep some of our future meetings secreted while we collaborate and build the strongest possible strategies for full slavery abolishment.

"Lastly, let me say that from this day on, we're the party of the elephant. And the party of the right way to righteousness, established by Mehna Abhoola. Zeb and Amos, I'd like to speak with you about how to use Mehna's tokens. How about if you, Zeb, work with us in the Senate, House, or White House to award Ella tokens to strong abolitionists in our government or military? Like Harriet showed us, the tokens represent Ella standing up against proslavery people. So, it might be a godly message to let our abolitionist leaders start holding the elephant in their pocket so they can show it to the enslaved who will be freed.

"All right. Some of us are getting on the train to Boston tonight, so we've got to wrap up pretty soon. How incredible has today been? This wonderful woman wrote this book one hundred and fifty-nine years ago, and she focused it so much on the need for a super team of abolitionists to someday merge together to defeat the human slavers. That's us—the Republican Party, the party of Mehna's godly elephant. Yay!" He raised both hands.

The whole room stood up cheering and waving. The conference ended with individuals mentioning future get-togethers and the amazing story of their new icon for freedom.

NEET BOOK 3:

1854–1994

CHAPTER 32

ELLA COMMENCEMENT, 1854–1859

ON FEBRUARY 28, 1854, ONLY FOUR MONTHS AFTER the New Hampshire kickoff meeting, Alvan Bovay organized a new party assembly at a local church in Ripon, Wisconsin. By the end of his meeting, the politicians in Wisconsin were using the new Republican Party name to restart the fight against slavery in the western parts of America.

Eight months after the October 12, 1853, freedom meeting in Exeter, Horace Greeley published an editorial in the *New York Tribune* in which he said, "We should not care much whether those thus united (against slavery) were designated 'Whig, Free Democrat' or something else; though we think some simple name like 'Republican' would more fitly designate those who had united to restore the Union to its true mission of champion and promulgator of Liberty rather than propagandist of slavery." In 1854, Mr. Greeley wrote editorials exposing how the Democrat Party had always used propaganda as its main source of getting voters to unintentionally support slavery in America.

With help from most of the Exeter team, thousands of slavery protesters arrived in Jackson, Michigan, in July of 1854. Abe Lincoln and Alvan Bovay organized the convention under the name Republican Party.

By 1855, John Hale had become a Republican Party senator from New Hampshire. He was a senator within the abolitionist party for the next ten years.

William Seward was reelected to the US Senate in 1855. He and his family continued for years to assist the Underground Railroad fugitives in Western New York.

In 1856, Joe Josephs started Erie County, New York's first Republican Convention. For years after engaging in the foundation of the Republican Party, Joe was recognized as one of the world's most impassioned antislavery advocates by his extreme work to get the Democrats voted from office. For years, he handed out miniature elephants to support the goal of all humans seeing the elephant of freedom. He soon became known as Elephant Joe Josephs. Joe built parade floats, painted banners, organized rallies, gave speeches, and sang songs he had personally written to support the new party of freedom, truth, and equal opportunity.

In 1858, Harriet Tubman supported abolitionist John Brown as he made plans to build a militia to attack slaveholders at Harper's Ferry, West Virginia. After Brown was executed by the Democrat-controlled government in Virginia, Harriet always prayed for him as a hero for her people. That same year, Senator Seward and his wife, Frances, were so much in support of escaped slaves that they made a kind deal, giving their house in Auburn, New York, to Harriet Tubman.

In 1859, with assistance from Joe Josephs and Senator Seward, Harriet smuggled her parents out of Maryland and up to Auburn, New York.

Also in 1859, the Republican Party had two Exeter teammates running for party presidential nomination to the 1860 election. Abraham Lincoln and William Seward contended for several months, but Seward backed down and gave Mr. Lincoln the road to success with his support. Lincoln won the elephant party vote. He and Senator Seward were still much united to fight the war against slavery. After winning the nomination, President Lincoln's most faithful ally was Senator Seward. They became very close friends and strong American leaders.

In the spring of 1860, Mr. Lincoln, the Republican Party nominee for president, traveled back to Exeter, New Hampshire for his fourth time over the past seven years since the Ella launch. Two of his trips were for party upgrade meetings. He traveled up last September to bring his son, Robert, to Phillips Exeter Academy for a redo of his senior year in high school. Now, Mr. Lincoln was in Exeter to see his son and to give one of several New Hampshire pre-election speeches. On March 4, 1860, the evening before his speech at Exeter Town Hall, Abe met with Amos Tuck and Zebulon Thing at the tavern on Water Street.

"Hey, guys. Good that we're all here this week. Thanks for setting up this event tomorrow. Come November, we're going to win this election for Mehna and Harriet's good people."

President Lincoln won the election on November 6, 1860, seven years and one month after Mehna's team of abolitionists flipped Ella to the right and accepted her as their icon of righteousness.

CHAPTER 33

IN 1861, WE ARE SEEING THE ELEPHANT

SIX WEEKS AFTER PRESIDENT LINCOLN'S INAUGURATION, seven southern states tried to secede from the US, and they attacked the federal government's military at Fort Sumter, South Carolina.

After the Democrats' slavery states said they were leaving the United States following their attack on Fort Sumter, President Lincoln prepared the Union to stop the Democrats' drive for continuing slavery. With his close ties to the Exeter team, he asked for some of their services in the upcoming war to save our country.

In mid-1861, after the war had really ramped up, a new naval officer in Boston, Amos Tuck, contacted his good friend President Lincoln and set up a gathering for his Exeter teammates with the President. Zebulon Thing went down to DC and joined Joe Josephs and Harriet Tubman who just came down together from Auburn, New York. Now, Harriet, Elephant Joe, and Zebulon met at the White House with the President and one of his army leaders, General Winfield Scott.

The Ella team provided General Scott with a short description of the incredible history of the Republican Party and the party's icon of freedom. In the discussion, they showed a New England Elephant Token so that General Scott could see Ella standing up against the left.

As discussions moved on, Harriet kept asking to give more of her support for the whole freedom cause. She said, "Mr. President and Mr. General, I really want to get close. I'm willing to act as a spy to steal information that you need from the bad guys. If not that, or after that, I want to support the whole army of soldiers who are risking their lives to free my people. I can be a nurse or help feed our troops of freedom fighters."

General Scott said, "Mrs. Tubman, you are so incredible. And so is this story of the elephant from your people. We will definitely appreciate your help in this battle." General Scott told her how to connect with him and his officers later so they could celebrate their use of her skills.

Joe Josephs stepped into the conversation. "General, here's my thought. Our Republican Party is the only party of freedom for all humans in America. And we're the party of the elephant because of this wonderful woman's hundred-and-sixty-seven-year battle to end slavery for her people. Since this elephant icon for liberty and these tokens have such a rich history, we'd like to get the entire army of freedom soldiers to know of our icon's past and why Ella is standing up against the left, like she's doing on the token. How about if someone like Harriet and I go out to your army forces and teach them up on how their winning of the war for humanity will finally mean that the enslaved people will be 'seeing the elephant' for the rest of human existence?"

Looking into his general's eyes, President Lincoln agreed. "That's the right idea. Let's go with it."

Zebulon said, "That will be really neat. Here's another notion. The historical package still has sixty-eight more elephant pieces that Miss Mehna would love to share with heroes of righteousness. Do you think, General, that we could honor our soldiers' efforts by awarding a token to victorious leaders? These awesome antiques can be a trophy for your officers, soldiers, and staff members who lead their troops to the win."

General Scott and President Lincoln were extremely satisfied with these volunteers and their plans for supporting the Union military. "I am onboard with your suggestions," said General Scott. "Once we get you out to the fronts and share the Mehna story, our soldiers will feel that they are seeing the freedom elephant every time they can attack the crazy secessionist armies."

The president said, "You're all doing so much to drive our path to success. Think of this. Our soldiers will be screaming "seeing the elephant" each time they see a southern combatant, so they will be thinking deeply, emotionally of your people and the drive to free them. This godly phrase will be a total link of our soldiers' hearts to those of your enslaved people. Your idea will help our kind troops drive to extremes to win the war for freedom. Keep it going, friends."

After the meeting in DC, Harriet stayed in the capital for months to work with army leaders. They created plans to have officers let soldiers know that they are freeing slaves who are waiting to see the elephant of freedom. Zebulon Thing left sixty-five New England Elephant Tokens with Harriet so that she could work with Union officers to set up performance awards as the Civil War moved forward.

CHAPTER 34

HIDING THE ELEPHANT IN THE ROOM, 1861

ON THEIR WAY BACK NORTH, ELEPHANT JOE AND Zebulon got off the train in New York City, to move to two separate trains for their travels home, Joe to Buffalo and Zeb to Exeter.

Before their separate trains were ready to go, Elephant Joe came up with a new idea. "Hey, Zeb. I feel like there's a need to have more of your New England Elephant Tokens manufactured for Harriet and General Scott to use for the honoring of heroes in this war. Here's an idea I have for that. There's this huge Robinson Company, in Bristol, Connecticut. I know one of the owner's, Alfred Robinson, because he sells me paper supplies, printing machines, and flag poles. They also have bread and cheese businesses. Most importantly, he makes metal tokens and other devices for any business that wants them. Your train rail goes through Hartford. We could go see Alfred to see if he can create new Ella tokens so that we can give more awards to army heroes. Want to try?"

Zebulon liked this idea, so they both got on the train to Connecticut. They got to Robinson's shop and filled him in on the story behind the elephant of freedom. They showed him a 1694 copper token. Mr. Robinson was proud to support the military, so he agreed to produce more New England Elephant pieces. Joe and Zeb both payed him some cash to get him started. Alfred told them that he received dies made by a friend of his in Boston named Joseph Merriam.

They spent the night at a hotel in Hartford. Zebulon and Joe continued working on the creation of more concepts to keep fighting the Ella battle. They both were still distraught by the false news reports about the entire war on slavery. For years, they both received feedback from abolitionist congress members and from the president about how the Democrats continued to block the true facts of racism and the brutality of slavery from the voting public.

The evening after meeting with Alfred Robinson, Elephant Joe brought up a new point. "Zeb, I went to share some of my new rail-splitter drawings with President Lincoln a few minutes after we broke out from meeting with him. The president told me that he has received information about a secret mob hidden within the Democratic Party. He was contacted by the new president of Harvard University, Cornelius Felton, a good Republican. Mr. Felton told him some hard left Democrats from DC had been going to his school and meeting with the hugely liberal staff of the college and with editors from the left-aligned newspapers. Of course, we know that Harvard University has driven nothing but liberal, socialist concepts since super racist Sam Webber became Harvard president over fifty years ago. They've continued since he set up their rotten infrastructure to push his biased racial beliefs out to teachers and students. President Lincoln told me two days ago that Felton has been trying to undo the hard left behaviors within his staff, but he says that it's not going well so far. The last thing the president mentioned to me was a request for us Exeter team members like you and I to work to set up a secret society conference process for our new party. We know he's mentioned a deep state society since our fusion meeting in fifty-three, so now he wants us to set up a more frequent and more resolute brainstorming process."

Zeb said, "That's good to hear. President Lincoln is so dynamic and prevailing with his ideas for helping all people. Now we know that the Democrats have a secret bunch of politicians that get together with their reporters, but they remain secreted from their other party members and from anyone who might share the real meeting objectives with the public. That explains how their deep-state ideologies are created and locked in, but not fully shared with voters, or even with all their political less-informed party members. This also explains how they are implementing their strategies of sending money to the newspaper companies to purchase the lying and hiding of facts."

Joe said, "Right. They don't represent the American voting public because they obtain votes from totally deceived and uninformed voters. When the public becomes fully knowledgeable of the real ideologies and strategies of political parties, all voters will walk away from the Democratic Party's secret society. So, how can our party which cares for all the people compete with a hidden underground gang that creates minorities, convinces people that they are minorities, and uses them as a tool to win votes? We can't just sit back and let them keep winning elections with their lying and cheating schemes."

Their discussion launched a definite agenda. They spent hours this evening and the following day building a new plan for Ella to fight the Democrats' secret third party. Because the discussion took on such new concepts, they both decided to stay at the hotel in Hartford for another day or two while the new Ella plan took off.

Only weeks after their request, Alfred Robinson had a new coin die press in Hartford. To support the Union's first year of Civil War battles, Alfred manufactured forty-eight God Preserve New England 1694 elephant tokens using different metals; fifteen copper, fifteen brass, fifteen nickel, and three silver. He mailed these forty-eight tokens to an address in Washington, DC, which

Elephant Joe gave him to link the awards up with Harriet and the Union army leaders.

Secret Society Conversation

Zebulon had Mehna's journal traveling with him. He asked Joe to read the whole book before they go further with their brainstorming. Hours later when he was done his journal assessment, they were back at it, and Elephant Joe had a whole new attitude which Zeb could hear in his voice.

Joe said, "You know, I reviewed about half of Miss Mehna's book eight years ago in New Hampshire at your amazing conference. But there are so many more startling details she wrote that I just now read. Wow! She really, really knew deep down that this slavery thing and minority hating would probably continue for generations. So she wrote her long-range plan and brought her emotions forward to show that we need to continue to fight the terrible people, even after the Africans in America are freed. How amazing is that? We now see how right she was. These Democrats will continue to push their secret society goals even after we win this war and end slavery."

Zebulon said, "Yes. You're right on about her book. She definitely made this package to continue the fight indefinitely until the rotten parts of humanity are gone for good. So now, it's up to us, the abolitionist team from the Exeter event, and the Republican Party to continue with the Ella plan. But here's the thing, Joe. I'm sixty-one years old, now, and you're only mid-thirties. So, any long-term plans we devise will be with you for a long time after me. But let's get it going anyway. So our great president agrees with us that we need some type of underground secret society or team like the Democrats are using. We need regular, consistent meetings where we can drive our strategies for ending their racial division schemes. If we do any Ella ideological planning out in public, there will be physical attacks from the Democrats. So, let's talk about how to manage our secret society so it will engage this journal and these tokens through the full extent of the fake and aggressive Democratic Party. When they are finally turned down and away by the public, then Mehna's Ella plan can come to a successful end. Sound right?"

For the next few days, Zebulon Thing and Elephant Joe Josephs built a plan that they intend to share with the Republicans, by which Exeter, New Hampshire would be the primary location of Ella secret society conferences. Zebulon knew that he would continue to maintain Mehna's package for use by the conference members. They agreed that Zeb would begin to set up the conferences. Leading Republicans from the House, Senate, and President Lincoln's administration would be assigned to the secret meetings, only if it was agreed by Joe, Zeb, and Senators Hale and Seward that they are truly conservative Republican elephants, not rhinos (Republicans in name only). Joe recommended that he and his city of Buffalo should be the backup plan for alternate conferences by the new secret team.

1861: Secret Ella Society

Throughout the rest of this year, as the Civil War significantly intensified, Zebulon Thing and Elephant Joe communicated with the party in Washington to help set up a consistent quarterly schedule, so the secret team would meet at least every three months, usually in Exeter, and sometimes in Buffalo or Auburn, New York, and maybe even closer to the District of Columbia. Now that the secret society was meeting repeatedly, when local politicians like William Seward and John Hale were in their home state, they attended the secret conference so they could still support the long-range plan for standing Ella up against evil.

CHAPTER 35

ONE-HUNDRED-AND-THIRTY-THREE-YEAR HISTORICAL OVERVIEW (1861–1994)

1861: John Greenleaf Whittier

Mr. Whittier, a cousin of Underground Railroad humanist Moses Cartland, in Lee, New Hampshire, composed poetry and songs in support of freeing all African Americans as the Civil War accelerated. He was known as one of America's most righteous abolitionist authors.

1861–1865: Seeing the Elephant in the Civil War

Civil War Union soldiers constantly spoke about the importance of 'seeing the elephant'. Throughout the war, they habitually yelled 'seeing the elephant' when their proslavery enemies came within sight.

1862: As the Civil War ramped up to high levels of battle and death, the Democratic Party developed a new wing within their own party called Copperhead Democrats to try to get voters to end the war and allow Southern states to keep slavery legal by seceding from the United States of America.

In December of 1861, President Lincoln's Republican devotees introduced a bill in the US Senate to abolish slavery in Washington, DC. Even with the Civil War raging for nearly a year, the Democrats in Washington were still driving to keep slavery alive. The leading Democrat opposed to this bill, Democratic Senator Garrett Davis from Kentucky presented the following message in a Washington, DC, Congressional Speech on March 15, 1862 to push his party's protests against ending slavery anywhere.

The negroes that are liberated and that remain in this city, will become a sore and a burden and a charge upon the white population. They will be criminals; they will become paupers. They will be engaged in crimes and in petty misdemeanors. They will become a charge and a pest upon this society, and the power which undertakes to liberate them ought to relieve the white community in which they reside, and in which they will become a pest, from their presence.

The Democratic senator created and shared fake examples of how the freeing of slaves in the Caribbean islands had ruined the economies there. The honorable Republican senator and Ella-team abolitionist from New Hampshire, Senator John Hale, researched the actual facts of Caribbean emancipation and gave a speech to congress to show how those economies and people there were on their way to freedom and economic stability.

In his response to the Democrats who were pushing to keep slavery moving forward, Republican Senator John Hale from New Hampshire pushed back against the highly racist Democratic Party in his Congressional Speech on March 18, 1862.

Mr. President, there is nothing on earth that is more unjust, nothing more unkind than for this boasted white Caucasian race to enslave the colored race, to keep them in a state of ignorance, to keep them in a state where it is a penal offense to teach them to read; I say it is cruel and unjust to such a people, denied the right to bringing a suit in court, denied the right of testifying as to their own personal rights and wrongs; to pronounce them as degraded, ignorant, incapable of representation, because under the crushing weight of all these disabilities they have not made such progress as to enable them to step at once on an equality into a condition which their masters have enjoyed for many years.

It is cruel. Take off these burdens, give them a fair chance, let the light of science shine into their minds, make it no longer a crime punishable with imprisonment to open to them the pages of God's eternal truth, let them read something of the world that is about them, and something of the hope which leads to the world beyond them, give them the elevating influence of some of the motives that have elevated you.

On April 16, 1862 President Lincoln signed the bill passed by the Senate to free the enslaved in Washington, DC.

Harvard University Politics

The president of Harvard University, Cornelius Conway Felton's term of office was from 1860 to 1862. Because he was a supporter of President Lincoln, Mr. Felton hoped to stop the democratic staff in his college from holding those secret political meetings in the college basements. He was originally thought to be a Democrat, so no one opposed him being in a few of the secret meetings.

Nine months after the war began, after discovering with spies in classrooms that his staff was against President Lincoln and the Republican Party, Felton began to try to get his workforce to support President Lincoln's positions, but that did not go well. His staff members were all pissed off with their college president. Mr. Felton traveled from Cambridge to Hartford, Connecticut, to meet with abolitionists from the Republican Party. Within days of meeting in Hartford, Cornelius Conway Felton died for unknown reasons at his brother's house in Pennsylvania while on his way to Washington, DC.

1863: Harriet Tubman was working for the Union Army as a nurse and chef. After working so hard for the soldiers, she volunteered and was assigned as a spy and an armed scout leading army squads toward battles. Harriet was the first women to ever lead an American army raid. She freed more than seven hundred slaves in South Carolina when she led her troops to the Combahee River Raid. Later that year, General Grant awarded Harriet a New

England Elephant Token to honor her great work as a troop leader, a spy, and a nurse.

The Emancipation Proclamation

On January 1, 1863, due to his deep desire to end slavery, President Lincoln transformed the character of the Civil War by granting freedom to all slaves. His proclamation opened the Union Army and Navy to African Americans. Two hundred thousand black soldiers joined the war to support President Lincoln's and Mehna Abhoola's drive to end slavery. Over thirty-five thousand black Americans lost their lives battling the Democrats and the Confederate states to end their drive for a future of human slavery.

During the war, *Harper's Weekly* was the most read media in the county. The publication had declared itself in support of the freeing of slaves in America. In July of 1863, the newspaper published an article showing a photograph of an escaped slave Oliver Gordon with his severely scarred back from whippings he'd received. This article took the whole Union Army into higher respect and support. After that photograph of a mutilated man was published, over two hundred thousand freed slaves joined the Union Army to fight for their people.

1864: Ella Newsletters

A newspaper called *Father Abraham* was founded in 1864 in Reading, Pennsylvania, to help promote President Lincoln's reelection. The newspaper's publisher, Edward Rauch, knew Joe Josephs in Buffalo, NY. President Lincoln won his second term in office in the third year of the murderous Civil War. To celebrate the victory of the Exeter abolitionist team, Elephant Joe gave Mr. Rauch a New England Elephant Token. In his first newspaper publication after President Lincoln's victory, Mr. Rauch raised Ella's trunk above her head to honor the president's victory and gave Ella a flag which said, "The elephant is coming," to show readers that the fight for freedom just got a huge win. He displayed Ella running hard at the left. Edward wrote, "We'll rally round the flag, boys, rally once again, shouting the battle cry of freedom."

1865: Violent Left Secret Society

Five days after Robert E. Lee surrendered the Confederate Army to end the Civil War, a team of hard left slavery supporters engaged in a plan to tear down the Union government. They engaged a secret society plan to restore the Confederate states' war against freedom for African slaves. They planned to kidnap the president and to murder Vice President Andrew Johnson and Secretary of State William Seward all on the same day, to end the strong leadership which won the war, and which created the Emancipation Proclamation to free everyone equally. On April 14, 1865, John Wilkes Booth changed the secret left's plan from kidnapping to murder, and he killed President Lincoln. The other plans for murder were shut down by family members in the Seward and Johnson home sites. Several members of Secretary of State Seward's family were wounded, but they fought back with firearms, and Seward lived through the attack. The Copperhead Democrats carried their opposition to the abolition of slavery for decades after the Civil War ended.

1868: Violent Left Secret Society Political Attack

Following the Civil War, a military force called the Ku Klux Klan emerged among former slave owners to suppress and victimize newly freed slaves, and to serve the interests of the Democratic Party. The Klan quickly poured throughout the Southern States, terrorizing Republican leaders.

In 1868, just a few years after the Civil War ended, James Hinds, a thirty-five-year-old Republican Congressman from Arkansas was murdered by the KKK because he had persistently advocated for black Americans' rights to vote, to keep and bear arms, and to have access to equal public education. The Democrat's secret KKK army also murdered three South Carolina Republican Party legislative members and several other Republicans who served in constitutional conventions. After one of the attacks by the Democratic KKK army against Republicans, some wounded victims reported that they heard yelling from the murderers. Before guns were fired, they heard, "You're not going to be seeing the elephant anymore!" And, "We're going to kill your elephant!"

Also this year, devoted Africans in America became elected as legislators in constitutional conventions. The left's KKK army attacked over ten percent of the black legislators, injuring many and killing seven. The left's murderous gang also attacked African American schools and churches.

1874: Iconic America

During the Civil War and over the first post-war decade, Thomas Nast, a cartoonist and reporter for *Harpers Weekly*, shared with the public his understandings of both political parties in America. He met repeatedly over the years with Elephant Joe Josephs from Buffalo, and Amos Tuck from New Hampshire, two facilitators of the Secret Ella Society. Mr. Nast was prolific at calling out other reporters who wouldn't share the full facts and hidden ideologies of the Democrats with their public readers. In 1874, because the political party of racial turmoil and their deceitful news reporters were still so barbarous, Thomas Nast showed the public a new version of their party's icon, the donkey. By presenting their jackass icon hiding under a lion skin, he showed the tricked public that their party was one of pure scandal. His cartoon was in line with the left's hiding of their deep secret ideologies. Mr. Nast's reporting and drawings also helped align the Republican Party and the party's historical icon, the elephant, with the kind and humanistic American public. He created his version of the Republican elephant to appear similar to the New England Elephant Token he had received from his colleague, Elephant Joe Josephs. He even heard the story of the elephant waving its trunk at the enslaved children, so he included that in his published cartoon.

1879: After the war ended and he left the US Navy, Amos Tuck returned to New Hampshire and resumed his career as a lawyer. He also worked with railroad construction businesses. Over the past decade, Amos facilitated a few Secret Ella Society conferences each year and he traveled to Buffalo, New York, to attend some of the conferences there. That year, at sixty-nine years old, he only attended the Exeter conferences. He passed away on December 11, 1879.

1882: Things Take Off

For the previous twenty years, the Republican Party's secret conference team had been going through strategies to deliver total truths to the public in response to the inaccurate information and hidden facts used by the other party. Zebulon Thing had set up the first quarterly meeting of the Secret Ella Society this year in Exeter on April 14. He scheduled it later than the first quarter because of a terribly tough winter in New England. As seven secret Ella society members showed up for the April event in Exeter at the Squamscott Hotel, they were each given sad news that Mr. Thing passed away yesterday at eighty-two years old. On day one of their three-day conference, some team members sent gifts and flowers to Mrs. Thing at Zebulon Thing Corner.

Zebulon's wife, Sarah, and his son James showed up in room 219 of the hotel on day three of the conference. She entered the room carrying the old antique box which most of the team members had seen before at other team rallies. Secret Ella Society members shared their sorrow over Zeb's death, and they shared their appreciation for all of the fantastic work he and his ancestors did to unite the party of freedom and to steer the Ella plan forward to keep the war alive as long as the Democrats continue their drive for constant racial segregation.

Sarah Thing responded to their honorable comments. "Thanks for your adoration of my great guy, Zeb. We're really going to miss him. James and I want you to know that we will continue to hold the journal of freedom and the tokens of abolition out at our farm. I'm seventy years old, but my son here is only forty-five. He'll be available here in Exeter far more than I will, and he'll make sure your society gets to engage with the elephant in the room at all of your conferences. Most of you know that there are aspects of this book and these tokens that will only come to bear if the Democrats take their crap so far and so fake that Ella needs to step toward another war to defend freedom. Before I leave, one more thing. Two weeks ago, Zebulon told me that he added a paragraph to the last page of the Ella journal. I just read it. He says he buried one of the tokens into the ground in a granite box on the hill at our farm, Zebulon Thing Corner."

1891: The End of a Great Thing

Sarah Thing passed away on New Year's Day, 1891. Her son James moved the Ella box down to Exeter Town Hall. Exeter building inspector Douglas Westman had been helping organize the Secret Ella Society meetings in room 219 of Squamscott Hotel for nearly a decade. Mehna's historical box had been concealed at Zebulon Thing Corner for over one hundred and forty years. James Thing always helped his mom transfer the Ella package to Ella's conference meetings since his dad, Zebulon, passed away nine years ago. After his mom, Sarah, was gone, James decided to sell his parents' farm, so he asked his Republican friend, Mr. Westman, to find a place in town to hide and manage the box with the journal and the bag of tokens. He showed Mr. Westman that there were only twenty-four New England Elephant Tokens still left in the Ella box.

These were each of the second set of tokens Martin Walpole made in 1694 with the *D* in *God* leaning slight right. All of the other seventy-five tokens were awarded away to elephant party leaders and military heroes since the start of Ella's abolitionism team in 1853.

James Thing shared important aspects of the Ella plan with Westman. "Please, Doug, take a look at the last few pages of the great African lady's book on freedom. Because of the details at the end of her book, I found out that my dad planted one of these original tokens on the hill at our farm. It's hidden in the dirt, under a granite slab, right next to a solid granite bench. He added a paragraph to Mehna's journal to document that we have one protected token of freedom stashed on the hilltop at Zebulon Thing Corner. He hid this one in case the rest of them are ever lost or stolen before the next phase of Mehna's plan for freedom for all."

Mr. Westman showed the Ella box content to a solid friend who worked at The Society of the Cincinnati at Folsom Tavern on the corner of Front and Water Streets. His friend agreed to take over the honoring and holding of the Mehna plan to keep the package available for the Secret Ella Society conference meetings. He put Mehna's box into hiding in the tavern's attic.

James Thing sold his parents' farm to the Wentworth family in Exeter this year.

1894: Violent Left Secret Society

On March 6, 1894, in Troy, New York, poll supervisors discovered that a former town mayor who was now a US senator and a serious Democrat was setting up many of his left voters to allow and encourage them to vote unlimited times in each election. When the poll officers tried to end the Democrats' push for multiple votes from each left-wing citizen, the officers were attacked by a gang that worked directly for the senator. Poll Officer Robert Ross was shot and killed by the Democrats because he tried to stop their illegal multiple-vote strategies. His brother William was wounded by gunshots but survived. The Democratic gang leader who murdered Officer Ross was convicted of the crime and executed in 1896.

1894: A massive summer thunderstorm in Rockingham County, New Hampshire, started a forest fire, acres away from Zebulon Thing Corner. The fire became a giant blaze enlarged by the Oakland Forest's expanse of solid oak fuel. No one was harmed, but the Thing's historic farmhouse and barn were completely enflamed and lost. Only the granite foundations of the farmhouse and barn were still in place going forward.

1902: Progressive Secret Society

Thirty-seven years after they lost the Civil War, deep Democratic insiders labeled themselves as "progressives" to try to rebuild their white supremacy legacy. After announcing their desire for progressive supremacy over minorities, these hard-left Democrats skirmished for the next twenty-two years using falsehood to persuade voters to deny Native Americans and African Americans the right to vote.

1920: Harvard University president Lawrence Lowell continued to hold secret meetings within the college, both for political drive and to keep the college's segregation practices as strong as they had been since the early 1800s. He created a secret school court which made college rules against minorities and homosexual persons. Their strong Democratic positions and their excellence at hiding their policies made the college a school from which leftwing politicians often graduate.

1924: Fighting Segregation

On June 2, 1924, Republican President Calvin Coolidge signed an act granting full citizenship to all Americans born in the United States. He did this to offset the twenty-two years of continuing strategies of racial division of progressive Democrats.

1938: Progressive Secret Society

In 1938, a new Democratic Senator from Louisiana, Allen Ellender, introduced a bill to ban marriage between different races.

His bill failed to pass, but it again showed the core racial foundations of the Progressive wing of the Democratic Party.

1945: Because of the terribly racist policies being pushed by the Democrat's, the state legislature gave New Hampshire its official motto, 'Live Free or Die', which were written on the state's auto license plates to coach the people into remaining free.

1949: Progressive Secret Society

During a discussion of civil rights on NBC Radio on February 6, 1949, popular Democratic Senator Allen Ellender explained why he and his party's ideologies were against having federal laws that would eliminate states' rights to prevent or make it difficult for voting among different races. The civil rights improvements he tried to combat included Republican Party attempts to make human lynching illegal in all of America. Ellender and his congressional supporters tried to keep it legal for their secret KKK army to kidnap and hang African Americans. He shared on radio the racial flavor of the twentieth century progressive Democrats: "Now that you bring up the subject, I would say that the Negro himself cannot make progress unless he has white leadership. If you call that 'supremacy', why suit yourself. But I say that the Negro race as a whole, if permitted to go to itself, will in-variably go back to barbaric lunacy."

1954–1956: In 1954, the US Supreme Court determined that segregating public schools by race was unconstitutional and un-American. Most of the Democrats disagreed. In 1956, a declaration of constitutional principles known as the Southern Manifesto was written by Democratic leader Strom Thurman. The manifesto attempted to offset the Supreme Court's decision to end states' rights to keep public school segregation legal. Among members of the House and the Senate, ninety-nine Democrats and two rhino Republicans—from Alabama, Arkansas, Georgia, Louisiana, Mississippi, South Carolina, and Virginia—signed the manifesto to attempt its passage so that they could try to keep their racial division strategies moving forward. To defend against the progressive Democrats' ongoing racial attacks, Congress refused to pass the Southern Manifesto proposal.

1964: After the Republican Party battled for over sixty-years to get to equal rights for all citizens, the Civil Rights Act was passed in 1964. Before it was passed, Kentucky Senator Al Gore Sr. continued the Democrats' hundred-year battle to keep racial division active so they could always try to get more minority votes by falsely calling the Republicans racists. He and other Democrats launched a seventy-four-day filibuster against the bill. Fortunately, the Republican Party's push for full equal rights for minorities won the voting results. In the vote in the House, a higher percentage of Republicans (80 percent) than Democrats (63 percent) voted to approve. In the Senate, 82 percent of Republicans voted to approve, compared to 69 percent of Democrats. For the next fifty years, Democrat-controlled news outlets lied to the public, saying that the Democratic Party started and passed the Civil Rights Act.

In his first year as president, Democrat Lyndon Johnson gave a speech to show the public how important the Civil Rights Act is. In the speech, LBJ shared the fact that more Republicans were for equal rights than Democrats: "Whatever your views are, we have a Constitution and we have a Bill of Rights, and we have the law of the land, and two-thirds of the Democrats in the Senate voted for it and three-fourths of the Republicans."

1965: The Republican Party fought for many decades to offset the progressive secret society's drive for voting segregation. The Voting Rights Act to prevent states and cities from having laws that encumber minority voting was passed by Congress in 1965. Similar to the Civil Rights Act passed a year before, the Voting Rights Act was passed by a higher percentage of Republicans than Democrats in Congress. The vote in the House of Representatives was approved by 82 percent of House Republicans and 78 percent of House Democrats. The Senate approved the Act by votes from 94 percent of Republicans and 73 percent of Democrats.

1985: This year, the Euksevel family of New Hampshire purchased a two-acre piece of forest land in Exeter to build a post-and-beam home on a hill in the middle of the property. They moved into the house on September 28, just hours before Hurricane Gloria hit New England. The roof of their previous house, in East Kingston, New Hampshire, was smashed by three huge willow trees that Gloria took down. Mr. and Mrs. Euksevel went back to their previous home and took the trees off the roof to support the new homeowners.

After moving into the two-acre property in Exeter, the Euksevels discovered two granite foundations buried in the ground along the corner next to the road. For years, they found horseshoes and other antique pieces around the two acres of woods. Mr. Euksevel researched the history of the Oakland forest area and learned that there was a farmhouse here in the 1800s called Zebulon Thing Corner which burned down in 1894.

NEET BOOK 4:

1994–2094

CHAPTER 36

1994 ANCIENT DISCOVERY

IN APRIL OF 1994, AN ELEVEN-YEAR-OLD BOY IN EXETER, New Hampshire found an ancient coin-like piece in the woods outside his home on Oaklands Road. The token he revealed had an elephant on one side, and said GOD PRESERVE NEW ENGLAND on the other side with the date 1694. His dad, Lien Euksevel, did months of research on the piece and learned there was an interesting history behind these copper tokens made in London three hundred years ago. He decided to try to participate in a coin auction because some of these New England Elephant Tokens had been sold at auction for over fifty-thousand dollars.

Mr. Euksevel met with David Bessey, a coin expert in Wolfeboro, New Hampshire, in July. He showed Mr. Bessey the New England Elephant Token that his son found in Exeter and asked if there are any upcoming coin auctions in New England where this piece could be retailed.

Bessey said, "Well, thanks for coming up here. First off, you might know that any coin or token up for auction has to be determined as original or counterfeit by the Professional Coin Grading Service (PCGS). I'll help you get the PCGS review if you want. As for right now, I'm not adept enough on these historical elephant tokens to give you an opinion as to this one's originality. But if you leave it here with me for a couple hours, I'll speak with my staff and try to give you a recommendation on this."

Mr. Euksevel returned later in the afternoon after hanging out around the beautiful edge of Lake Winnipesaukee watching the local boaters and fishing families.

Mr. Bessey shared the results of his assessment of the token. "While you were out, I contacted one of my staff members who knows the details of several 1694 copper elephant tokens. I sent a couple of photos of your piece to my staffer Jean White. She took a look and said that there are two original styles of these tokens. There's another New England Elephant Token where the elephant is not centered on the coin like this one is. It has the elephant to the left where its tusks are shorter and touching the token's edge. The letters on these two types are a little different in their alignment. Jean says that the PCGS reviews have set up the piece with the elephant not in the center as the only genuine token. However, her review and others have judged that the elephant itself on both types of tokens is exactly the same, which implies that both token types were made by the same elephant die, with lettering that was altered from one to the next. She tells me that this style, with the elephant in the center, has never been auctioned as an original. This is where my conversation with Jean took on a special direction. Are you an Exeter native? If you are, you'll be stunned by this."

Lien said, "Well, I'm a Maine, New Hampshire native living in Exeter for about nine years. What's going to stun me?"

With eyebrows sticking up, Bessey shared the stunning story. "Jean said that last year there were two men from Exeter at a New York auction who were there specifically for the elephant token trades. She says they were the ones there who told her about the second style of token which she had never seen before. Jean told me that you being from Exeter and finding this token buried there is so remarkable. Here's why. A guy named Tom Ginnam whom she met in New York at the auction is a manager down at the American Independence Museum in your downtown. He told her about this same style of token that you found. She said he has an extensive history for this particular one. So her recommendation is that you should try to meet with Mr. Ginnam and see what he thinks about what you found and where."

Mr. Bessey said that his staffer told him that most numismatists think that there are only three original New England Elephant tokens. He said that those have been bought at auction for between fifty and one hundred and twenty thousand dollars.

Mr. Euksevel drove back home to Exeter and headed right into the American Independence Museum downtown on Water Street, which is the antique building known as the Gilman-Ladd House built in the eighteenth century. He had been to the museum with his family a few times, so he was aware that this property, which also included the house called Folsom Tavern, was operated by a historical group called The Society of the Cincinnati. The Exeter section of The Society of the Cincinnati was formed in 1783 to honor the negotiators and authors of the Declaration of Independence and Revolutionary War leaders and heroes. The Society opened the American Independence Museum in 1991, six years after an electrician found an original copy of the Declaration of Independence under a wooden floor in the Gilman-Ladd House.

Lien entered the museum and asked the front desk lady if Thomas Ginnam was available to meet with him. She said he was over in Portsmouth talking with a coin shop owner and he'd be back early this afternoon. Lien Euksevel headed home to his property at Zebulon Thing Corner. He called the museum after lunch and was told that Thomas Ginnam was back in his office. He was invited to come down right away to meet up with Mr. Ginnam.

Tom Ginnam was excited to hear about the newfound elephant token. As he was looking with a magnifying glass at the token, Euksevel asked him a question. "Sir, can you please tell me more about the roots of your Society of the Cincinnati? I've been through your museum here with my family looking at your history of our nation's fight for independence from England. But I've never heard of your organization's history. How did a city in Ohio bring its name here to New Hampshire? Seems odd."

Ginnam said, "Oh, it has nothing to do with Cincinnati, Ohio. Here's the origin. The early leaders of the American Revolution were up here in New Hampshire gathering people together before starting the war with England. The name of the society came from a Roman senator from around five hundred BC, about twenty-five hundred years ago. Lucius Cincinnatus was a hero of the Roman Republic. He led his country's army to defend against foreign invaders. He was known to uphold the public's need for civic righteousness. When George Washington and others were highly frustrated because England's dictatorship was not representing the needs of the people in America, they colluded together to start a secret society to push the revolution and to start a government fully represented by citizens.

"Our Society of the Cincinnati was actually started years before the naming of the city in Ohio. The city in Ohio was first established in 1788, after our country won the Revolutionary War. But, its first name was Losantiville. Two years after the city's opening, the governor of Ohio changed the city's name to Cincinnati to honor our historical, humanistic Society of the Cincinnati. Our society began back in 1783. President Washington was the first premier of the Society of the Cincinnati."

Ginnam flipped the token over a couple more times, then asked how someone found the token. Lien shared the details of his son Nirad and their dog Mason digging into the ground and uncovering a granite slate that was covering a stone with a spot that had this token in it.

Ginnam explained the histories of several 1694 elephant tokens. He told Mr. Euksevel that there have been decades of confusion among the coin professionals on the New England Elephant Tokens because some counterfeit versions were created over a century after the originals. Ginnam told Lien that he might have a recommendation for this one, but that he has to talk with his manager before he can share his idea.

Mr. Ginnam was out with his manager for about an hour with Mr. Euksevel's elephant token. They both entered into the office to give Lien a recommendation based on their analysis and discussions.

The conversation immediately took on a huge aspect that Lien would never have expected. Ginnam introduced his manager, Roger Stevens, then said, "Well, sir, we have reviewed several aspects of this token and the place that you found it. Like I said before, we can't fully confirm that the PCGS process would correctly address this token as an original made in London at the Royal Mint in 1694. So you might not be able to sell it at auction for the price you'd hope. But Roger and I have another notion that we need to share with you." He handed the conversation off to Mr. Stevens.

Manager Stevens came forward immediately with an incredible recommendation. "Mr. Euksevel, thanks for showing us this piece. I have been researching these copper tokens for years now, and this one is very important to us, even if the PCGS process doesn't align it with the other three New England tokens that have been auctioned this century as original tokens. A couple of our other Cincinnati staff members and I have been working on a plan to tie these particular tokens into our museum to show people how it relates to our country's origins and philosophies of freedom for everyone. This might seem weird, but we want to offer you a reasonable price so that we can put this token with others to keep the history of America's elephant in this heavenly town forever. I'm able to offer you ninety-four-thousand dollars, if you hand this piece over to us today."

Euksevel was super amazed. "Wow, you guys! I'm shocked! I won't negotiate for anything higher than that. Let's go with it! My wife and kids will be really happy with the outcome of seeing this elephant in the forest at our home."

Manager Stevens and Mr. Ginnam did not share with Euksevel the full historical details of the New England Elephant tokens and their ties to Exeter, New Hampshire, the Republican Party, and slavery abolitionism. They set up a transfer of ninety-four thousand dollars to Euksevel's personal bank account.

After he had the Zebulon Thing elephant token under his ownership and Mr. Euksevel had left the museum, Manager Stevens went into his office, opened a cabinet door, and moved a time-worn wooden box out to his desk. He opened the case and lifted out a leather bag of tokens, and a historical novel entitled *The Elephant Freedom Journal*. He compared the newly found token to those in Mehna's bag of tokens and confirmed that they are definitely of the same copper die creation.

Two other museum staff members who had worked on the Folsom Tavern's marketing team for two years were both of African American decent and both natives of Concord, New Hampshire, the state's capital. Throughout their first year at Folsom Tavern, Manager Stevens always shared with these two staff members the journal's essence of the life of the awesome woman who created this country's successful fight against slavery exactly three hundred years ago.

Over months of the staffers Burt and Susan reading the journal, including that last three vital pages, these nice people came up with two incredible ideas to start the next phase of Mehna's mission. Having dated for years, they now planned to get married. Their first idea was related to development of their future family. Before their marriage, Sue and Burt both changed their legal last names to "Abhoola" to honor the African hero that they felt so close to. Because the second idea they created needed the Secret Ella Society to approve it, Manager Stevens worked with them to prepare their presentation for the Secret Ella Society conference in November of that year.

They learned over time that Mr. Stevens had been facilitating secret-society political conference meetings for decades, ever since he was hired onto the museum's business staff in 1977. The meetings had been hidden from media in order to allow for Republican Party's brainstorming and negotiations to occur without the left-wing news outlets making false reports about the Republican underground society. There were at least five right-wing DC legislators at the quarterly Exeter Inn meetings over the past one hundred years, since the Exeter Building Inspector, Douglas Westman shared Mehna's box with righteous staff members at Folsom Tavern in 1891.

CHAPTER 37

SECRET ELLA SOCIETY CONVENTION, NOVEMBER 9–11, 1994

EACH OF THE SECRET ELLA SOCIETY CONFERENCE MEM-
bers were assigned to the committee by the head of the Republican
National Committee. Roger and Tom were setting up and facilitating
these meetings at the Exeter Inn on Front Street for over twenty
years. The conference was usually three days long so that they
had time to review the past few months of false news reporting by
Democratic news outlets and time to brainstorm and create strategies to offset the left's falsehoods that end up in voters' heads.
For this year's final Secret Ella event, five DC members arrived, but
only three of them had ever been to Secret Ella Society meetings
before. On day-one, Roger initially asked the team to begin their
review of the deceitful political reports published since the last
Secret Ella Society conference back in early August.

When he unified them for lunch on this first day, he let the
team know that two more museum staffers would be joining them
tomorrow with a new proposal for preserving liberty. Then he
shared the Secret Ella Society conference rules. "So here's our
society's decree. Four of us American Independence Museum
employees are your teammates on this society, but I must always
remind all members that the operator of the museum, The Society
of the Cincinnati, has no part or position in our secret society. It's
just that strong right wing supporters have always been employed

there, and we've done our own support for freedom, without making it a part of the museum's business."

After lunch, Manager Stevens restarted the discussion of the conference's foundational realities. "To merge us all together on the objectives of this conference, let me share with our new legislative members the true history of our elephant icon. It's probably more historical and more freedom-defending than you might think. We need to introduce you to a woman who started our Republican Party in Africa over three hundred years ago. When we get you there by the end of this three-day meet-up, you will also understand the reasons why your party started this Secret Ella Society conference one hundred and thirty-three years ago."

Roger shared the foundations of the Republican Party which have ties all the way back to a young lady born in Africa in 1673. He gave the two new members copies of Mehna's journal, but did not include the final three pages yet. Two of the other Secret Ella Society members had been to the conference's quarterly meetings for the past year, but they too had never been shown the final three-pages of the journal. The fifth member was Congressman Jason Beach who had been carrying the Secret Ella Society conference information back and forth from Exeter, New Hampshire, to Washington, DC, for over nine years. He knew of and honored Mehna's entire journal plan, including the final pages, for a long time.

Manager Stevens said, "We won't discuss the deep details of the entire journal until after you've all done your own review of the journal including the final three pages that I'll give you tomorrow when my other staff members join us. You'll see that this week's revelations will launch Miss Mehna's next five hundred year plan for freedom protection."

After he gave them a few hours of understandings toward the Republican Party icon's true beginnings, the rest of the conference's first day was centered on discussions by team members about non-fact-based news stories from left-wing newspapers and television stations who call themselves "news" programs. Everyone in the room knew that "freedom of the press" was being overcome by press falsehood. Several discussions ensued to develop tactics for the party of the elephant in Washington, DC, to try to inform the voting public of the actual truths which are being hidden from them.

After ending the quarterly fake-news defense review, Mr. Stevens updated the DC team on the new ancient elephant token found right here in Exeter earlier this year. He handed them the token that Euksevel's son found in April, then said, "You will really have an incredible evening when you review your copy of the freedom journal and think of this Ella token that you're looking at now. Tomorrow we'll also be sharing with you some new information we've received which will launch the next phase of Mehna's plan."

Secret Ella Society Convention Day Two: The Dive

The second day of the undercover meeting took the team to a whole new world. Mr. Stevens began by commenting about their reading of Mehna's journal. "So now you all know how and why our party's icon was created by Mehna Abhoola, the world's most honorable and successful pioneer for liberating humanity!"

Even though they were all super eager to see the final pages of Mehna's writings, they still each shared highly emotional outcomes from their reviews of Mehna's manuscript. Each of the members started mentioning what they read last night with words like "Wow!" "Incredible!" and, "Amazing!"

Roger Stevens reacted to the emotions in the room by standing up and hugging the society's bag of tokens which only had a dozen of Mehna's pieces still in it. He handed out copies of the journal's last three pages to each of the five society members, even though Jason Beach had read this many times. They started reading the document that had been endorsed as the beginning of freedom's next phase.

The Last Three Pages of Mehna's Freedom Journal

Page 37

♥ Love you, Marty. So sorry for this hurt, but I will be going with you to America. Like the two angels in King Tutu's golden stool of Ashanti. I will be in the tokens with Ella for eternity to end the evil of racism forever.

♥ When Ella and I meet up with the Grand Abolitionist Party, which this journal and its holders will have enabled, then we will finally be at the real beginning of the war to end slavery.

♥ If you are reading this and you are the wonderful, brave people starting up the right battle to free all humans in America and beyond, then I ask you to please clutch a New England Elephant Token and give me a hug of your love!

♥ If my blood comes out of the tokens hundreds of years from now, please name me Ella.

Page 38

I am Martin Walpole, Miss Mehna's close friend. Before I left for New Hampshire several days ago, she dove into the liquid copper in my friend's reverberatory furnace to bond her blood and her brain into the New England Elephant Tokens before the tokens cruised with me to America. That night, when I found her departed in the hearth adding her life to the tokens, my friend Norbert and I pulled her body out. To make sure that she will be in the tokens for thousands of years, we extracted some of our queen's blood from her burned body and dumped some of it into the liquid copper. As I was crying so deeply, Norbert made another twenty-five tokens with this powerful liquid copper carrying her legacy. He implanted more of her blood into the belly of the elephant on the twenty-five new tokens before each one was pressed on the die tool. Before he pressed the new tokens, Norbert rebuilt the die tool to make the elephant step back from the token's edge to make it look better. The new die had the *D* on the word *God* leaning slightly right. Now we know which tokens are Mehna's life forward. It was so, so sad, but I'm so proud. She made her own decision to send herself to the future war against slavery in America. Please, team of abolishment! Honor her life and win her war against slavery. If the slavers keep pushing to divide races around the world, then please support Mehna's future plans so she can keep fighting their meanness.

Page 39

This is Zebulon G. Thing. I'm adding this note onto the last page of the Ella journal in the year of 1882. We want the tokens in which Mehna lives to be safe until science might someday be able to bring her back to humanity. Because I've been attacked at church by Democratic supporters and since we've seen the Democratic KKK gangs killing only Republicans, I'm afraid that Mehna's tokens will be attacked and stolen if the party of slavery knows where we have them hidden. So to defend Mehna Abhoola, I just placed one real Ella token on the hill at Zebulon Thing Corner in a granite box underground next to the granite bench.

Roger stepped in as he saw that each member had finished reading the final pages and how they sat with emotional facial expressions. "How incredible is this that we just got this new token of love from a local historical farmland? Some of us in this committee have actually known forever that this token was buried out there on Oaklands Road. But we've agreed for eighty-five years with Zebulon Thing's idea to hide one of Miss Mehna's tokens from anyone who is part of either the secret Democratic society or their tricked gang members. The timing of Mr. Euksevel finding this one now is really fascinating. Just like we know that God brought Harriet Tubman here to support creation of the Republican Party, God now had a local boy's dog dig out the Ella token this month. We might need every one of these twenty-five tokens to initiate Mehna Abhoola's future plan."

Mr. Stevens took a minute of silence to let the emotions of Miss Mehna's fight for freedom set in.

"Here's why we need as many of the twenty-five tokens filled with Mehna's life as possible. At this committee's request, for the past few years, Mr. Gimman and I have been communicating with some college science professors who are exploring the potential use of historical DNA in human birthing. They have already confirmed that they've found human DNA in each of the New England Elephant Tokens which we've shared with them for testing. These groups have been trying to invent ways to place DNA from anyone alive or dead into any human egg or sperm so that the processes of in-vitro fertilization can someday let people have babies from whatever DNA source they desire. It's helpful that we have this new token of love found right here in Exeter, because we might need more of Mehna's DNA to set off her next plan of attack.

"This topic brings us to the point where I want to introduce you to two of my staff members. I was going to introduce Burt and Susan to you today, but it's late enough now that they will join us tomorrow for conference day-three."

They ended the conference meeting, and then all headed down to the Exeter Inn's Epoch Restaurant & Bar and had hours of conversation about what they've seen in the journal and what it means to the future of their country.

Convention Day Three: The DNA Plan

When everyone had entered at the conference room for day-three, Manager Stevens let the members know that his museum staffers were ready to join the conference. He went down to the restaurant, and brought the Abhoola's up to the Secret Ella Society team.

He introduced the new team members, "Hey folks, please welcome Susan and Burt Abhoola. Yes, I said Abhoola! The same name you read in the book. This wonderful couple is highly aligned with the Mehna Abhoola family and her fight for equal righteousness. That's why they got married last year with their new legal last name, Abhoola."

A Washington, DC, legislative member named Barbara stood up and said, "Oh my gosh!" She rushed over and shook hands with both Burt and Susan. "You've changed your name to Abhoola! That's incredibly honorable from what we've read in this book over the past two days."

Susan Abhoola spoke up to start sharing the presentation they practiced with Mr. Stevens. "Because of our high gratitude for Miss Mehna's life to end slavery and to make us as free as we are today, Burt and I want to be part of the Abhoola world, so we changed our last names, and are so proud. We now have developed a proposal to support your Secret Ella Society's groundwork on Miss Mehna's final plan. We want to help you help her defend the freedom of all citizens in America for the next five hundred years." She pointed to her husband, Burt, to get him to continue the presentation.

Burt said, "There's a new underground science hiding in the basements of colleges and private businesses around the world.

Nine years ago in 1985, a British geneticist and college professor of genetics started deep science into DNA analysis and proof of identity. Since he started the science, other groups are in force to see if DNA from any person, dead or alive, can be placed into human egg or sperm. Your partner Jason was here two years ago when I joined your society. Hello, again, Jason. Your society approved a project to have us work with some science outfits to investigate and develop options for use of Mehna's DNA from Ella's belly in the tokens. Thanks Jason for keeping the DNA project under approval of this society for years now. When Susan and I met Jason back in 1992, we started to work on the DNA discovery project for the society. Now, Susan is going to share with you, our Abhoola plan for the future."

Susan said, "Thanks, Burt. You da man! Okay, team. The first test tube baby was born in England in 1976, almost twenty years ago. Since then there have been continued science philosophies around the world working on new human birth prototypes. We might still be years away, but we're working with several DNA and in vitro fertilization experts who believe that they are getting closer and closer to the point where historical DNA can be placed into male or female human birthing. The reason we all want to share this with you is to ensure you're continually updated on the progress of our efforts to have our first child, your Ella or Martin baby. As African American's, Burt and I feel that we must honor our ancestors, the ones like Mehna Abhoola who lost family members to black African kingdom terrorist leaders and their white British, French, Dutch, and Portuguese enslaver allies. We will give you updates on the status of our family project at each quarterly Secret Ella Society conference meeting here in Exeter."

Several discussions ensued due to the deep emotional enlightenments that came out over this three-day secret meeting, the last one of 1994. Manager Stevens closed the society gathering after he shared the organization's requirements for confidentiality. Jason

Beach took the new strategies back to Washington to attempt to offset the Democrat's and leftist news outlets' lack of truths. Each of the quarterly secret society future meetings included updates on the DNA science and Abhoola family status.

CHAPTER 38

MEHNA'S 1694 PLOT RESTARTED

NOVEMBER, 1999: THE SECRET ELLA SOCIETY CONFERence was updated on the world's scientific status on DNA birthing. Susan Abhoola told them that some innovators are close to the point where DNA can be removed from a mother's egg and new DNA can be placed into the cleared egg. She said that the egg can then be fertilized and placed back into the mother for pregnancy.

November, 2000: On November 1, 2000, Susan Abhoola learned she was pregnant. Weeks later, the day Susan's pregnancy was shared with the Secret Ella Society conference group, one of the Republican ladies came up with a recommendation to honor Mehna Abhoola's next generation.

"Congratulations, you two!" she said. "Since you told us last year that the scientists you work with were getting close to placing DNA into human eggs, I've been setting up a recommendation for you and Mehna. Now that you've shared your wonderful info today, I'd like to honor you and Ella and Mehna with something our citizens will respect for hundreds of years.

"As you've all seen for years, Queen Mehna's journal has several pages where she drew examples of three stars that she had patched on her forehead when working at several London coffee shops. I researched 1694 in London and found that most women in London had stars patched onto their foreheads. You've all seen where she drew her forehead with three stars onto the top of page twenty-five.

"Her three stars are aiming one point down, and two points up. I'm asking us to see if our RNC will honor Mehna's life, her commitment to end slavery, and her future life by turning our three icon stars to match hers from over three hundred years ago. Will you help us get icon Ella's stars to match Mehna's forehead? Here's what I'm saying."

The lady legislator handed out a card to each member showing her recommendation for rotating the stars thirty-six degrees to the right to honor Miss Mehna and her supporters.

One of the gentlemen senators on the committee stepped up after looking at the card. "Well, this is noble! Think of it this way. The first important phase of Mehna's war against slavery and racism began at the 1853 Exeter meeting with Abraham Lincoln and Amos Tuck who started our party of freedom. She authored the launch of that phase to be represented by the team flipping Ella to the right. Now we're entering into the next important phase that she created way back. I agree with your recommendation to honor the launching of this next Ella phase where she will forever be defending our country of freedom against the racial division strategies of the Democrats. Ella is facing right and the *D* in *God* on her tokens is leaning slight right. So now let's lean Ella's stars slight right.

"We're the party of righteousness for all humans. We will bring your recommendation down to the capital and share it with our RNC leaders. I'm sure they will agree to honor the Abhoola family of freedom and righteousness."

In 2001, the Republican Party icon's stars were rotated to the right, thirty-six degrees. The Democrats' left-funded news outlets started reporting to the public that the stars were turned upside down to show the icon as anti-American.

Susan and Burt Abhoola's daughter, their first child, was born on July 31, 2001, at Exeter Hospital. They introduced her to the world with the name Ella Harriet Abhoola.

At the last quarterly Secret Ella Society conference meeting this year on November 10, 2001, Susan and Burt showed up with their beautiful three-month-old baby daughter. The conference members all rose and cheered to show their honor and appreciation for all that the Abhoola family had been doing to bring Miss Mehna's long-range plan into fulfilment over the next century. The cute little baby will be a huge part of the Secret Ella Society's future, so the team knew they would see her again, many times.

Because of the importance of her life, her parents decided not to have another child. Her life in Exeter included childhood swim teams and gymnastics. By the time she got to junior high, she was the fastest swimmer on the team. Ella also was a good student at the top of her classes each year.

September 2016 to June 2017, Freshman School Year

When Ella Abhoola reached high school at fifteen, her parents sent her to a private school in Wolfeboro, New Hampshire, called Brewster Academy where there were more unpolitical civics classes than were found in most public high schools where teachers, staffers, and students were often faked out to the left.

Throughout her first few months in Wolfeboro, one of her parents down in Exeter called her each evening after school and asked about her classes, especially the civics class on government processes. During the civics class discussions, her mom or dad always gave her updates on the controversies within American politics.

Her parents told Ella that their Abhoola life is all about protecting human rights for all people, especially for Americans because of two very segregated political parties. After many of these calls from her parents, Ella established her own four-year plan to do ongoing research of the political directions and momentums in America. Her parents always told her what's going on, but they didn't yet share the names of the two divided parties, because they wanted her to do her own research to find out which arm is causing racial and minority division.

On the eve of the 2016 presidential election in November, Ella and several other Brewster students stayed up and watched the results of the election. President Trump won! She and one of her friends cheered and applauded the new president's win. Three other friends watching the election showed frustration toward President Trump's victory, so they left the room after telling Ella they still wanted to be her friends.

Secret Ella Society (SES) Meeting

Roger Stevens was still the manager of the Society of the Cincinnati, and he still facilitated the Secret Ella Society events every three months. With this being her first year in high school, the committee began providing invitations to Ella, through her parents, for each conference. The team members felt overwhelmingly that the Secret Ella Society belongs to Ella and her sister Mehna, more than to any of themselves. While Ella was in high school, her secret society team made sure the Exeter meetings were on weekends or vacation weeks, so that their iconic member could be at almost every meeting going forward. They scheduled the fourth quarterly meeting of this year to be after the November election, so that they could celebrate victory for the people or work on defending American freedom if the Democrats were to win.

Mr. Stevens started the conference by introducing Ella and her parents to the team members, some of whom were new to the Exeter meetings. "Hey, Abhoolas. Thanks for bringing your wonderful daughter down to this party event. Hello, dear Ella. Your parents may have told you that this team met you back about fifteen-years ago here in the same room. Thanks for coming back. This is a great time for our country, with President Trump's victory last week. His win means that our country will start being great again by re-establishing the strength of our country's security and stopping the racist divides that President Obama has been so good at implementing."

Ella stood. "Good to see you, Mr. Stevens. I agree a ton with your honoring of President Trump's victory last week! Here's why I agree so much. Throughout the first two months of high school, I have researched and found so much false-information being processed on TV and the internet regarding this presidential election. I have learned for sure that our current president, Obama, has for the past eight years been constantly using policies to separate people by skin color to meet their goal of earning more votes. I am displeased by the hate he and his administration have for years been showing against light-skinned men and women, America's law enforcement officers, and military volunteers and veterans."

September 2017 to June 2018, Sophomore School Year

At her first Secret Ella Society meeting after starting her second year in high school, she gave an update about school life. "Hi there, folks. I want to let you know that I've started an after-school committee up at my high school so that I can see if my student friends are being faked out by news outlets. My team up there did its own research on some of the religious news angles we've been seeing. Here's what my friends wrote about President Obama's histories that could have prevented his election wins if people had known the truths. Let me read."

Of course he claims to be Christian, but his support for Iran's nuclear weapon development included him giving Iran one hundred and fifty billion US taxpayer dollars. He fully supported Iran's backing of ISIS and several other Islamic terrorist outfits. He never said anything against their continued government's call for "Death to America" which they still say today. That he never responded to their calls for America's death gives us the full understanding that he was always angling our country toward democracy downfall and Islamic-style dictatorial takeover.

"Hey team. The way I see it is that his response to their continued call for death to America was his gift of one hundred and fifty billion dollars. So I have to believe that he agrees with their push against our country of freedom. Here's another item my friends wrote from their research."

Even though he went to a Christian school in Indonesia as a child, he was registered there as a Muslim. If real news about his Iranian dictatorship support had been shared for his first four years in office, he would never have won his second term. Our voters would not have voted for him if they had known that he would support Iran's nuclear program, their disgraceful impact against women's rights, their terrorist allies, and their desires for ending our country because of their hate for any non-Muslim religion, cap-italism, and individual freedom.

She ended the reading of that note from her friends' investiga-tions. "My four friends up there in Wolfeboro are really intrigued by the research we're doing each week. Even though their par-ents grew them up as Democrats, our opinions have been merged together by us doing and sharing our research. I'm just letting you know what I see going on in our world. I trust ninety-five percent of all voters to be good people. If they all get the real truths of what's going on and what goals the politicians have, then their votes will be valuable and right. But they just don't get the truth from the left media. Those are the nice people who vote wrong but wouldn't if they always knew the truth.

I am so offended that the Democratic voters are being ill-treated by total world socialists. My parents have shared with me that we need strong, strong emotions and resilient efforts to fight for our freedom and protect our country, and that you in the committee here are going to restart Mehna's battle to save our constitution, our borders, our religious rights, and our economic fortitude."

Summer of 2018: Ella meets Mehna: July 31, 2018

On her seventeenth birthday, before she started her junior year in high school, Ella's parents held a very special birthday event. They spent several days with her in a room with giant whiteboards, sharing the entirety of Mehna's journal and the history of Abhoola DNA that led to this family's incredible life of history and future. They gave her the original freedom journal and the sack of the remaining four New England Elephant Tokens. By the end of the first day, Ella emotionally recognized that these tokens were today still part of her wonderful ancestor's incredible life.

After that remarkable meeting with her parents and now living daily with Mehna and her journal, Ella instantly took on a deep constitutional yearning, because she felt that she must defend all people from the Democrats since she was so ingrained with her ancestor Mehna's life toward equal liberty for all of humanity. Because of everything she learned from her parents and the historical journal from 1694, Ella found herself walking around with one thought constantly in her head: "We need a special day for the New England Elephant Token to engage Mehna Abhoola's final plan for freedom." She repeatedly convinced herself, "There will someday be a giant NEET Day for all of our country's nice people."

As she dug more deeply into the current 2018 political standings, Ella began to research many stories from newspapers and news channels that report on politics. By watching multiple news channels aligned with various political parties and doing her own research to find the true facts, Ella soon understood that CNN and MSNBC were in high support of the racist party in America, the Democrats. She proved to herself that these are news channels which put out completely false information aimed at the forty-fifth president of the United States. President Trump and his family were under constant attack by clearly phony news, but most of the public were not watching both sides of political parties' news, nor researching the facts on issues like Ella did.

Ella went to her Secret Ella Society conference this summer. "Hello my friends! Great to see you. Maybe you've heard that my parents shared the full Mehna Abhoola freedom journal and token plan with me on my seventeenth birthday, last month. I have the journal now, and I've been hugging my sister Mehna in the tokens every day. And now I know that Harriet Tubman also embraced these same tokens. Wow!"

Everyone got up and came over for the Ella hug, known to be just like the Harriet hug that helped build this freedom team.

Ella moved on. "Thank you all so much! Like I've told you at our first few meetings and now that I'm on board with Miss Mehna's plan to defend freedom, I've become very engaged in political historical research. Here's a new one I found. In President Obama's first year as president of the United States, Iran had a 2009 communist election. The laws in Iran allow the government to decide whose votes they will count. During Obama's time in office, many Iranian women were arrested and put in prison for voting against the government's choice of a tyrant. Hundreds of women who voted for Mir-Hossein Mousavi were arrested and imprisoned, and their votes were removed from election results. From my findings, because Iran is President Obama's personal ally, he never said anything to our public about what his friends in Iran do to their women, and he made sure that Democrat-controlled news outlets never reported anything in America about the unfair practices they use there in Iran.

"Crazy! It bugs me so much that our voters here in America are not shown everything about someone who is our president if he is a Democrat. They only create false challenges toward our Republican Party to share with the public."

Ella raised both of her hands and said, "Yes! You heard me say *our* Republican Party. I'm only seventeen, so I can't vote yet, but I'm with you! This is our party of freedom for all! Thanks so much for all you do."

On day two of the conference, after the members went through their falsehood news reviews and response objectives, Ella mentioned how glad she was that the lying news outlets had been given an accurate name "fake news" by awesome President

Trump who had been attacked for two years by the Democrats' news outlets. She told the committee that they will hear her use that term quite a bit in her future life.

Roger Stevens said, "Ella, my queen! You're so right on. Please keep going forward with your deep, high-quality research."

September 2018 to June 2019: Junior School Year, Seventeen Years Old

During her junior year at Brewster Academy, Ella was much more engaged with the quarterly secret conference meetings in Exeter, since her parents shared the entire Abhoola history with her this past summer. This year, she had worked with school guidance counselors to find a good law school for her college degree. Doing her own research for the past few years about the commentary by political news outlets, Ella decided that she should apply to Harvard University law school, because she wanted to be able to spy internally on their historical hard-left socialism that they might be teaching to all of their students. She also felt that she might be able to spy on the Democrats' hard-left secret society, like Harriet Tubman did to the southern Democrats during the Civil War.

The past two years were a huge attack on the US constitution with the Mueller investigation. Ella had been watching and researching all of the ongoing reports against the president. But she didn't see anyone on either side of the political agendas telling what she saw as the most likely objective of the leftist's fake investigation. Everyone thought they are just attacking the president, but Ella believed that their primary objective was to win the 2018 midterm congressional election by pissing off the voting public after lying that the president had been colluding with Russia to win the 2016 election. Ella's research confirmed that most key aspects of the investigation could have been published before the 2018 midterm event. The Democrats won the House of Representatives because the President's innocence from the investigation was not shared with the public prior to the November election.

Only a week after the January 2019 inauguration of the Democrats in the House, Mueller said he was ready to publish the report. Ella wrote a paper for her secret society members showing how she believed that the Mueller investigation knew before the midterm last year that the president was not guilty of any Russian collusion. She recommended that the society ask the Department of Justice to determine if hiding information from the public until after the election was an intentional strategy of those Trump-haters to win that midterm election. She sent her paper to Roger Stevens.

In May of 2019, Ella drove from Wolfeboro down to Exeter to attend this year's second Secret Ella Society quarterly conference meet up. As she did at the beginning of each conference event, she gave her education update, then Ella told the committee that she is choosing Harvard University for her law degree, because she wants to see what the deep state Democrats are doing to fake the students there to the left.

One of her society members reached in to give Ella a head start toward the Harvard University life.

"That might be the best call for you, Miss Abhoola, but you'll have to be very careful down there. Just recently, the university's administration removed one of their African American educators from his job as law school faculty dean, because the left-wing-trained students all started complaining about his position on defense attorneys standing by the American principle that those charged with crimes are innocent until proven guilty. He had been telling students that when they became defense attorneys, their duty would be to represent anyone accused of crime, even if it's an unpopular person. Because fake news always accuses people of guilt long before any court results, these students are being trained to believe that the goal of the new socialist America is to hold people guilty until proven innocent. Of course, we all know that this is the big strategy of the left against our great president today. We've all seen the fake Mueller investigation shared for two years calling the president guilty, regardless of the facts. So Ella, just be careful when you get into that college. Stay hidden on your positions for American individual freedom, or they will attack you, maybe even physically."

June 20, 2019: Democrats' Reparation Event

The Secret Ella Society quarterly-meeting agenda this summer was focused on addressing the left's continuing creation of victims and victimization. The Democrats did this to make people think lighter-skinned people should reimburse billions in cash to anyone whose ancestors were enslaved in America. It was another of their many skin-separation strategies so that they can keep pushing all of America into racial divide.

Ella began the conference. "Here are some of the results of my research since our last meeting. You all saw this week that the Dems held a political event in Washington on the topic of repa-ration, asking white Americans to be held accountable by paying huge assets to black Americans like me for the years of slavery before the Civil War. Why don't they ask for reparation from the Americans whose African ancestors kidnapped and sold millions of Africans to the Europeans?

"Here's an example of that. News outlet producers always consider President Obama a black president, but when they are arguing for reparation from white Americans, they won't ever tell the voting public that his mom was a white American. Her par-ents grew up in Kansas, one of the South's slavery states, so she and her son might be from slave-owning ancestors. His dad was from Africa, not America. Kingdom leaders in Africa and slave-owners in America could both be his ancestors. If so, shouldn't he be under the toughest demand for supremacist reparation? But I know that these deep state Democrats can't agree with that, because they only want to accuse and abuse the Republicans and lighter-skinned Americans. Anyone who looks at the whole history of proslavery in America will see that only Democrats would ever have to be responsible for African American reparation."

"Here's another thought from my research on true versus fake. They are openly working to end all border security, and to get more people from the world to come here now. This worries me so much. During this week's Democratic nominee debate for the 2020 election, the entire faction said they want to make it legal for anyone in the world to enter our country without documentation and without any process for true citizenship. And at the same time, they said they want to provide free medical healthcare and free college to anyone in the whole world who decides to walk, crawl, drive, swim, boat, or fly across our borders without legal entry. Their public voices for free everything and open access means that millions of people around the world are right now packing their backpacks and hooking up with Soros family's funding arrangements to get to our country. For the hard lefties, our country is not the United States of America any more. Within years, if they continue to fake out voters, our country of true citizen freedom could be done and gone."

June 29, 2019: Ella investigated the reporting of TV news outlets during the week, even though she was also hiking through the White Mountains with some friends for days on end. She saw all of the left news outlets complaining that President Trump was meeting again with the North Korean dictator, Kim Jong Un, to try to stop their nuclear weapon construction efforts. They made the public think the president was trying to build relationships only to get closer to communist dictatorships. Ella learned that Obama never met with the North Korean leader in his eight years in office, while they were manufacturing and testing nuclear weapons, which was the reason that America's current president had to drive to end their nuclear weapon development.

While President Trump was working on international relationships to ensure that nuclear weapons are not set up anymore as they were during Obama's eight years in power, CNN and MSNBC trotted out another falsehood to support their hard left's violence against any conservative. Their associates, called Antifa, physically attacked eight conservatives at a political event in Portland, Oregon. These news channels intentionally hid the news, never showing the public the leftist attacks on conservatives. Several people were put into the hospital, but these results were hidden from the public to keep the violence against conservatives going forward. Five days later, CNN reported on-line that they had not been able to confirm that the attackers were from their Antifa associates. Videos on true news outlets clearly showed that Antifa did these attacks, but CNN and MSNBC did not show the truth to their viewers.

Because Ella Abhoola watched all sides of political news channels so she could find out the real truth, she was disgusted, as always, by the Democratic Party's fake-news strategies of lying and hiding. She wrote some notes to herself that she wanted to share with her Secret Ella Society at the next quarterly conference.

We need to show all public voters that the Democrats started the violent Ku Klux Klan so they could attack and kill Republicans.

We need to show our people how ongoing violence by leftists toward conservatives is always hidden from us by the devious news outlets.

Once the good people of the world, including the tricked Democratic voters, know of the real truth of leftist violence, then Democratic voters will walk away from those idiots who support their deep state strategies and violence against American citizens.

I will get these facts out to the public somehow, someday, on a very NEET day.

July 3, 2019: Ella received an evening phone call from her high school friend, Bonnie Seven. Bonnie was feeling let down. "This is disappointing! President Trump set up a really fantastic celebration of our country's independence and military defense for world freedom. I love what he did. But my parents' news channels, CNN and MSNBC, only talked today about how he shouldn't spend tax dollars on celebration of our country's past military successes for protecting freedom and democracy here and around the world. How the hell can they tell the people that he should not honor our country, the world's protector of liberty?"

Ella looked at Bonnie. "Come on, left voters! Tell these crazy liars to stop the hogwash."

Secret Ella Society conference on July 19, 2019

Ella gave her first in-depth speech to the Secret Ella Society. "President Trump has focused the Republican Party this year on improving criminal justice reform to stop the long range of the Democrats' racist measures where minorities are given higher imprisonment assignments than anyone else. The deep Democrats and their controlled fraudulent news broadcasts can't give President Trump any credit for his support for one of the most important equal human rights aspects that any president has ever done. The Democratic secret society leaders do not want things like unequal criminal justice to be removed from our country, because they want racist factors like this to remain in place so they can keep blaming the other political party. This is the same as all of their lying and cheating that creates racial division among our people. They only care about voting results, not about the lives and rights and loving relationships of our people. The deep Democrats focus on keeping or initiating negative impacts on people's lives, so they can keep falsely blaming their opponents for them. I promise you that I will someday figure out ways to let the voting public know every day what the fake news outlets are lying about or hiding from our people. You will be surprised, and super satisfied, when a future event, which I'm calling NEET Day, changes our country's whole perspective on cultural dis-union and socialism illegality.

"I need to let you know how I really feel about all this stuff you've been sharing with me for the past couple of years. When you hear me speak with you about politically terrible Democrats, please know that I'm talking about the secret Deep State of the Democratic politicians. Not the good people who have for hundreds of years been tricked to call themselves Democrats and to un-intentionally vote for the secret-ass society's desires for slavery, dictatorship, and the end to our constitution.

"You've all taught me by now that we here at the Secret Ella Society are the deep state of our Republican Party. We're so much more freedom-based because you here in this committee have been the deep state, but you've shared our party's deep ideologies with all voters, except of course the CNN and MSNBC news watchers who are not given anything factual. A party's deep, long-range ideologies are what the Democrats' deep politicians and their news outlets will never share publically. Thanks for setting me up with this information so that I can be aware of fake-ism during my upcoming college years."

September 2019 to June 2020: High School Senior, Eighteen Years Old

By the end of her junior year at Brewster Academy, Ella had created a close team of political associates after years of her counterparts learning that so many issues put out by any political party needed to be intensely investigated before anyone could understand with confidence what was really going on. She didn't push either political side in any direction for their first three years in high school, but she did convince her friends over these years that they need to do their own investigations of information from political news outlets, on TV, internet, and newspapers.

She became so pleased with her relationships with these four friends of hers in school. Before her parents drove her this year to Brewster Academy, Ella created a written proposal for an agenda model of their group meetings, showing names of team members, topics, and strategies for research when political issues crop up. Her research strategies were defined in the agenda as being only done by two persons merged together from opposite parties. To honor her friends and pull them close together, her agenda paper provided a name for the team. She decided she wouldn't share her full agenda with her friends until October, because she wanted to let everyone get going in school their senior year before she kicked off her full plan for collaboration.

August 19, 2019 was the first day of their senior year in Wolfeboro. Her parents, Susan and Burt, drove her up to Brewster Academy early on Friday, August 16. After they had lunch and she checked into her dorm room, Ella started looking around to find her close team of friends whom she hasn't seen throughout the summer months. She saw none of her friends yet, so she gave a list of their names to the school admin staff and asked them to invite her team of friends down to the Wolfeboro Dockside restaurant for dinner after they show up and check into the academy and their dorms.

She headed down to Dockside after setting her bundle of stuff in her dorm room, then she watched some news while waiting for her friends. She saw a disgusting report on politics while waiting for them. A Democratic senator from Illinois held a fundraising event that day. After his event, the senator's fundraising team posted a picture on the internet of an American Hispanic aiming a gun at President Trump's head, showing the Democrats' historical desires for violence and murder. She only saw this report on one channel. The other news channel on TVs across the chamber did not show this report. She was so emotionally engaged when she saw this photo promoting assassination. This crazy photo put out by Democrats joined with Ella's awareness of the many attacks by Democratic gangs on Republicans over the past one hundred and fifty-five years since the Civil War. Before she could calm down her deep feelings about this senator's supporters, her first student friend entered into the restaurant.

Bonnie Seven saw Ella sitting over by the large glass windows with the beautiful view of Lake Winnipesaukee. She rushed over and they shared hugs, showing their happiness of seeing each other to start the school year.

Bonnie started, "Ella, my dear! So good to see you, Queen Moses. I'm calling you that because you remind me of Harriet Tubman, who was the Moses of her people. You are the Moses of people today, and you have Harriet as your middle name! Thanks for setting this up and for all you've done for us over the past three years. I just saw Frank Damadon back at the admin office getting himself set up for his dorm room. He'll be right over here soon. Are you okay? You look worried."

Ella said, "Hi Bonnie, dear. I'm okay. I just saw something terrible on TV, so I'm feeling emotional about attacks on our citizens. Those murders last week in Texas and Ohio of thirty-five people are so sorrowful. But now, we have political supporters building expectations for more killings. It makes me worried about all of our people. We'll talk about that when our friends get here." Bonnie was a deep Democratic supporter, as were her parents, so she chose not to respond yet to Ella's comments on today's TV news reports. The other four team members showed up for dinner. After they had all hooked up, shook hands, and ordered their meals, Ella began their senior-year team conversations.

"Hey, my friends. So great to see you. Here goes our final year here! But hey, maybe you've been stressed all three years here where I've put a bunch of pressure on us to navigate our political understandings to a place where we can unionize our feelings and beliefs. I was thinking that I might be less engaged with politics on this team of ours over this final year in high school. But today, something new came up. And for the past several months, our political shams have been ridiculous. Because of the political attacks on our president and physical attacks on conservatives around our country, I'll be hoping that we can keep teaming up with more political analysis and brainstorming. Has anyone seen what happened out in Illinois today against our President? Some Democrats posted a picture on-line of one of them aiming a gun at President Trump's head on a puppet."

Frank Damadon, a light-skinned guy from Claremont, New Hampshire was first to reply. "I'm sure that what you saw was Fox fake news. I know that citizens' real-news channels would definitely have shared that with us if it really happened, but they haven't. So it means that some Republicans created that photo you saw and posted it online so that they could blame the Democrats as being more violent than Republicans. That's how the right-wing party works, and that's why my parents have never watched Fox News through their entire life."

Even though he said those things, Ella was relaxed because she knows he's a nice guy. "Thank you, Frankie. You know that I'll try to keep us close together, no matter what each of our opinions are, and you probably know that I'll ask for more and more research from this whole team to confirm each of our positions and opinions as the year moves on. Let's just keep our discussions going on and we can use our togetherness to help set up each of our college and career pathways, especially those of us that might drive toward government jobs. Our collaboration will be especially fun, interesting, and vital for those of us who turn eighteen before the presidential election next year, in November."

CHAPTER 39

FUSION SQUAD KICKED OFF

ELLA SCHEDULED TWICE-WEEKLY AMERICA-FIRST MEET-
ings throughout their senior year which she would facilitate to
merge their political sentiments together based on accurate
research. For the first two months, their passionate and intriguing
afterschool gatherings were focused on all aspects of information
shared from leftwing and rightwing news outlets who were trying
to polarize the 2020 presidential election.

It was Ella Abhoola's deep kindness of character that kept all
five of them very close, regardless of their original political tra-
jectory, usually driven by students' parents and their teachers. In
October, after her tightfitting team had met dozens of times this
school-year, she shared her perspective of her friends' alignment.

"Good evening, my friends. I hope you had a good day in class.
I'm going to suggest something outrageous for this close knit
team. Let's think back to how much success we've had together
collaborating our political agendas. That room you guys had the
school superintendent set up for us with those giant white boards
has really taken our research and brainstorming to new highs. So
here goes my idea. I believe that we are so mutually motivated
now by what we've been doing. You may have heard me use the
term "fusion" before when honoring our close ties and our deep
research efforts. I'm suggesting that this senior year, we are the
two-party fusion squad."

Ella handed them each a three-by-five card as she continued.

- Two-Party Fusion Squad
- Ella Abhoola, Fusion Squad Facilitator
- Bonnie Seven, Democrat
- Frank Damadon, Democrat
- Greg Fields, Democrat
- Billy Mizner, Republican

"As our engaging year here moves forward, to set us up for our first year at college, I think we should start a new research method. I'm asking that we document the side that you want to protect against falsehood. So on these cards, I've put down what our Fusion meetings will look like with research material, one way or the other, left or right. So with these assignments, as one issue is being researched, we'll have to make sure that both sides are fused together with the facts. See what I mean?"

Bonnie reacted. "Ella. Billy would be so overwhelmed if he has to provide all of the balance that's on your card. But here's something I'm glad to share with all of you. Because of the great togetherness and hard-fact scrutinizing that Ella has set up for us, I'm on board with her new Fusion Squad concept. That's us! But hey. Because of all the things I've learned over the past year with all of you, and this summer at home, I have flipped to the right, just like the story Ella shared with us about the elephant icon flipping right in 1853. So look. Here's an option. Now that I'm going to take on the Republican falsehood protection research, I think you and me, Frank, should be one of the research duos. That puts you two, Greg and Billy, on the second research team. So both teams will be bringing all the facts to our Fusion Squad facilitator. This great lady."

Frank Damadon was glad to say, "Awesome ideas, both of you. And thanks Bonnie for setting up with me, because we've done some great research closures in the past. So now, let's do it again." Ella and her four friends designed their Fusion Squad process over the next several meetings.

Life is changed in America and the world by anti-humane attacks.

By mid-January of 2020, the Fusion Squad was very established as a way of detecting all news-outlet falsehoods, and uniting the team together on what's best for American citizens. But this century's third-decade began with two life-challenging activities which changed America, the world, and the Fusion Squad's high school year.

From January through March, the first life-challenging disaster was due to fully political attacks by the Democrats on America's president so they could try to impeach conservative American citizens' 2016 voting results. Ella's Fusion Squad investigated all news reports and the facts, so each member was absolutely sure that these impeachment cases were the continued falsehoods that had been ongoing since President Trump won his 2016 election. From his Democratic Party and fusion squad insights, Frank Damadon said that he believed most left voters now knew that the news reporting against the president was fake and disgusting. He said that many more voters would support President Trump in this next election than any president before.

In March, the world's most significant life-challenging attack by the COVID-19 coronavirus pandemic closed every school in America and made people stop hanging together. The squad's high school told them that they might not graduate until later this year or in 2021. While concealed at home during the months of coronavirus, Ella still communicated daily with her Fusion Squad friends about watching and researching the news reports.

Mr. Stevens told Ella that while she's at home he'd appreciate it if she could share with him the results of her fusion team's concealed investigations, because she could help him complete the Secret Ella Society's quarterly fake news reviews. During the first few months of the COVID-19 pandemic attack, she shared with Manager Stevens the squad's findings of the false news reports by CNN and MSNBC, where they were using the American deaths to blame the president.

Ella's Fusion Squad Report: Because this year was a presidential election year, the Fake News outlets CNN, MSNBC, and their newspaper allies immediately started to use false racism tactics on coronavirus news reports to continue their 2020 election victory endeavors. These news channels began lying and holding back true information to attack President Trump's efforts to save American lives. CNN reported that the President was being racially bad by stopping China from sending sick people to America as of early February. This meant that the owners of these news companies wanted to have many more Americans die this year so that they could ramp up their blame on this great president before the election.

The routine racial segregation commitments by the Democrats during the coronavirus human deaths made Ella realize that she was aware of some deep aspects that President Trump should share with America. She wrote a potential speech element that she hoped Manager Stevens could share with the RNC and the President.

If President Obama had protected Americans during the 2009 swine flu disease by using the one hundred and fifty billion taxpayer dollars that he eventually gave to Iran, maybe he could have prevented some of the twelve-thousand American swine flu deaths. He definitely could have set up the medical safety programs and recovery products that we needed here this year. The next president that I will hand this White House over to five years from now will have a massive international virus-safety program, with venues, laws, and spare parts to protect all of our people against these rotten virus attacks. No future president will ever be in the weak defense of citizenry like we were handed by previous leaders. Fake News...please tell your folks the truth, that over the next five years as your president, I will create full protection programs and products for the viral safety of future generations of Americans.

While they were all concealed at home hoping to get back to school, all five members of Ella's Fusion Squad, Ella, Bonnie, Greg, Frank, and Billy, were accepted into Harvard University's school of law.

Having gotten out of school in March, and having seen for months her fusion squad's investigation results, Ella felt that she had dug her way into the political hurricane America was going through. Because of the constant racial divisiveness, Ella knew that what these Democrats were doing to humans was exactly the same disappointment that the African kingdom kings and England's Royal African Company did to millions of people. What the Democrats were advancing to get more votes was what Ella planned to take on in college and after, so that she will help humanity like her sister Mehna did. She was now sincerely convinced that Mehna is asking her to bring about a new war against the Democrats' racial-division strategies which they use only to increase their votes so they can make more personal wealth for themselves.

After President Trump, Vice President Pence, all governors, and millions of Americans worked incredibly hard to offset the coronavirus, some schools were reopened by June or July. Ella and her fusion friends did three more months of high school, then graduated in October.

Roger Stevens began the Ella society fourth quarter event by honoring Ella's graduation. "Great job, Miss Ella! Congratulations on your graduation." The entire team stood, cheered, and applauded. "And now you're heading to law school. We're looking forward to meeting with you after you settle into Harvard and begin to see if they still use political strategies hidden within the college processes. Did you see anything in the debate between President Trump and the Dumbocrat that inspires your ongoing battle to defend our country?"

Ella stood up again. "Thanks so much, my friends for cheering at my graduation. I'm ready to move on now that I'm able to vote and to react to the stuff that I see coming out against our party of equality. Thanks for asking about the debate, Mr. Stevens and for sharing that new name 'Dumbocrat,' which is so accurate and meaningful. The most inspiring part of that whole argument was the awesome professionalism and human civility presented by our great president. The inspirations I feel from the responses done by the left are pretty much just that I don't understand how any decent US citizen voter would ever agree with anything the dummy is planning to do to our country. Of course, I understand that his desires for bringing in millions more non-citizens every year, giving them free medical services, welfare, and beyond will ensure that he gets all of those anti-American illegal votes. Why would true citizens in our country vote to turn us into lower wage, lower military, lower security, and lower defense by giving our total country away to millions of people from all over the world who want free everything? Ridiculous. His passions are not American. We need to figure out how to let voters know that the left's nominee is completely in line with the Secret Ass Society whose ultimate goal is to remove all weapons from people so that they can remove our constitution, and put in the full socialist dictatorship that they've been aiming toward for over a hundred years!"

This Secret Ella Society conference was working to figure out strategies to help all American citizens get the best plan for making and keeping America great forever forward. The team talked in detail about how the Democratic nominee and all of the other deep state Democrats were only openly working on getting more votes with all of their lying, cheating, and hiding of facts. Some society members knew for sure that he was also sometimes telling the truth, like when he admitted that he wants to tell countries outside of the US that if he is ever president, they can come here without a legal entry process and they will get free healthcare, free welfare, free college, and voting rights without being legal citizens.

The Ella society shared with her something they've always known, that the Democrats' true long-range goal is to tear down the US Constitution and to replace it with dictatorship-controlled socialism so that they would themselves be the millionaire elite, which they always call the one-percent when they attack the Republicans. At the end of this three-day Ella society event, the whole team worked on setting Ella up to prepare for her time at college, so that she would be safe while hanging out with the Democrats who would attack her physically if they find out who she really is.

Ella said goodbye. "Thanks to all of you for your help. I know you're right about the potential violence that I will see if I don't hide well at school. I have learned, as you know, that the deep state of Democrats, and many of their faked voters, have been attacking, killing, and beating up Republicans ever since 1836, even before they lost the Civil War. So, you're right. I should not wear my MAGA or KAG hat or shirt at or near the crazy school, so that I can stay very underground as I observe their deep state planning. Goodbye, my friends. Love you all. Thanks so much for helping all American citizens keep Mehna's plan flourishing so future generations will still have our great country of freedom and friendship."

CHAPTER 40

ELLA ABHOOLA AND FUSION SQUAD AT HARVARD UNIVERSITY 2020

NINETEEN-YEAR-OLD ELLA ABHOOLA ENTERED HARVARD University in October, months later than schools normally start, as did her tight-knit friends from Brewster Academy. After only two weeks of school in Cambridge, Massachusetts, the Fusion Squad's facilitator set up white-board rooms and meeting times to restart this political school year.

The team members had known each other for four years. They were each satisfied to again meet together several times a week at college on occasions such as lunch, dinner, and Ella's repetitive fusion events. Some of them were also together at times in law-school classes. They started meeting every Thursday evening at six to participate in their fusion process to investigate each week's political factors.

After about a month of Fusion Squad members living the college life, Frank Damadon told Ella that he met a fellow student whom she should consider to be a new member of the squad. Frank said the guy's name is Barry Zonkers, and he told her that Mr. Zonkers was in the Navy for four years before he started college here at Harvard.

She asked, "Frank, how does this Zonkers guy give you the impression that he'd be good with our team?"

Frank really wanted her to hear this. "Barry and I have been hanging out and just getting to know each other. As we've spoken around everything, some political issues came up. Barry is challenging his own past of being a strong Democrat. He's been telling me for weeks about how he feels that he might walk away from the left because of everything going on. And now he feels like there are some issues going on here at school in classrooms and events that are also challenging his connections to his and my party. So with his current perspective, I feel that he'll be really motivated by your Fusion Squad methodology."

Ella asked Frank to invite Barry Zonkers over so they could be introduced before he joined their formal weekly events. However, before Frank had her meet that guy, someone approached her the next day out in a hallway between classes.

"Hello. Excuse me. Are you Ella Abhoola?"

She nodded.

"I'm Barry Zonkers, the guy your buddy Frank may have mentioned. He's been sharing some neat things that you're facilitating to straighten up political curvatures. I've been amazed by what Frank's told me about your political fusion work. Wow."

Ella was really satisfied that this man who approached her turned out to be the guy that her squad member Frank had already confirmed as being a nice person who won't attack her for political mutiny. Ella held out her hand. "Hello Barry. Yeah, that's me, Ella Abhoola. Good to meet you. Hey, we'll keep talking, but when you just now said that Frank's been sharing neat aspects with you, I have to say that when you meet my Fusion Squad, you'll be given details about something else far more NEET than ever before. Let's have you hook up with Frank on Thursday evening after class so that he can show you our underground brainstorming chamber. We meet each week there from six to about nine."

They shook hands one more time. "Okay, thanks, Ella. I'll see you Thursday night. Have a great day."

As they headed away from each other, Ella's head was filled with a new deep feeling that she had never taken this far. She liked his nice approach of hooking up with her and her team of fusion friends.

After they all met at several Fusion Squad meetings, Ella and Barry were hanging out at lunch breaks and speaking about her fusion strategies and his current standings between parties. She handed Barry her fusion squad card revised with Bonnie now being Republican and asked him which party would be listed next to his name.

He looked at the squad card and responded to Ella's question. "As you know, I've always been a strong Democrat since my family has always been to the left. But now, I'm just not able to stay there, because of all the weird things going on, against President Trump and with the hard-left ideologies, which I can't stand behind. I'm so disappointed with my prior party that I must say my family and I have always been crazy to support the Democ-*rats*! Because of their concealed political dogmas, we didn't know that there were so many rats on our side."

Barry wrote his new party affiliation next to his name, then handed the card back to Ella.

Two-Party Fusion Squad
- Ella Abhoola, Fusion Squad Facilitator
- Bonnie Seven, Republican
- Frank Damadon, Democrat
- Greg Fields, Democrat
- Billy Mizner, Republican
- Barry Zonkers, Republican

"Because of where I've seen my party going over the past several years, I will be fully engaged with your fusion efforts. So incredible what I see you doing with your friends to bring everyone together. I'm psyched about joining your team. And, look. I can maybe add a feature to your teamwork. For the first two months here, I've been joining up with a couple of left-wing student groups who meet together regularly in some of this leftist school's underground accommodations. If you'd like, I will continue to attend some or most of their meetings, and then I'll share their perspectives with your team. That okay?"

Ella really started to feel that this guy was going to be an important close friend. "Barry, that's better than just okay. Your offer will be a key aspect of bringing secret society information out to where we on the Fusion Squad can investigate and analyze what's going on."

As time moved forward for two months, Barry contacted Ella more frequently, about every day. She was really feeling close to this man because, like her, he used political facts to steer his beliefs. They started dating just about every day for lunch, dinner, or events like the Boston Red Sox games at Fenway Park. On the third weekend in October, Ella invited Barry up to Exeter, New Hampshire to meet with her Secret Ella Society team. While they drove back and forth, Cambridge to New Hampshire, Ella started sharing the full story of Mehna Abhoola and the New England Elephant Token. The first time north, she drove him out to Oaklands Road in Exeter to show Barry where the Zebulon Thing Corner elephant token was discovered in the woods twenty-eight years ago. The last aspect of the story of Mehna Abhoola which she shared with her new boyfriend took Barry to a new height of emotions.

Barry said, "Oh, my goodness, dear friend! Your life of this DNA from a magnificent African lady who started your party of the elephant is amazing to me. Now I see why you're wearing these elephant earrings. It's colossal that your earrings are over three hundred years old, and such a deep aspect of your life.

"Wow! These are your sister's incredible motivations which led to the humanitarian Republican Party and the end of slavery. I'm overwhelmed by your life of righteousness, sweetie."

As their freshman college year moved on, Barry remained engaged within his leftist networks because he admired his girlfriend's fusion-squad approach so much that he wanted to help bring the school's political strategies out to her team for their reviews and potential merging with facts.

CHAPTER 41

2020 PRESIDENTIAL ELECTION RESULTS

AMERICA'S GREAT LEADER, PRESIDENT TRUMP, WON HIS second presidential election, even under the heavy cloud of untruth presented for the previous five years by the fake news establishment. After the presidential impeachment hoax by Nancy Pelosi and Adam Schiff and the news falsehoods during the coronavirus attack, many more voters in 2020 realized that the deep Democrats and their news outlets were the real racists in the country's political pavilion. The mainstream media still constantly used the words racist and racism to describe anything this great president did to defend the freedom and life of all American citizens. Their continuous un-true use of skin color to advance their political strategies was starting to show many more voters who is the true party of scam and hate. Ella Abhoola was so driven by these news outlets' increasingly awful styles that she set a problem statement, causal analysis, and several corrective actions into her head. In her life of patronage for Mehna's plan of freedom, she was committed to steering herself through school, a law career, and maybe a political overlay to a point where someday these scam issues would disappear. Ella constantly promised herself that she would forever honor her sister's lifelong war for humanity by fixing the world of racial politics on a NEET day.

President Trump's second victory was via a huge avalanche of votes from both parties. He got over one hundred million votes and the socialist left nominee got less than twenty million. President

Trump won by the Electoral College, four hundred thirty-seven to ninety-four. To fully support this great president, the increasingly less-faked voters also elected the highest numbers of Republicans in history to both the Senate and the House of Representatives. The president now had both congressional teams supporting his continued drive to fully recover the weaknesses of our country that were set up by the previous president, the hard-left legislative millionaires, and the corona virus.

With full congressional backing to support the American citizens' calls for making and keeping America great, the President set up full funding and planning to finally seal our borders which the Democrats had been making less secure for hundreds of years. America's southern border with Mexico would be fully sealed within two years with a high-quality wall which included underground defense to stop the tunnel human-trafficking that hard-left Democrats had never tried to prevent.

President Trump also launched an international professional team that would be working more closely with the South American and Central American democracies to coach their leadership on helping their own economies and peoples to support decent living in their own lands. Of course, the newspapers and TV shows that wanted to drive socialism and racism did not show the American public that the President wanted all humans to be living decent lives in their own home countries. Left news media continued to lie because they wanted to keep calling him racist even though their own voters were starting to understand how great he is and how racially divisive their leftist party is, the party that they walked away from in this year's election.

Ella and her friends were fortunate to be able to start college late in 2020 after the virus attack had been shut down. By schooling through some added summer months, they were able to still meet their 2024 graduation year. Throughout their college life together, the entire fusion squad observed the college's practices of only allowing left-wing discussions anywhere in the school. Ella was not able to speak openly with the deep-left secret teams of college students, nor during the college's civil politics classes. However, just from her conversations with individuals outside of classes and meetings, she was besieged as an enemy of the college's political foundations.

2021: After the Republican takeover by voters, witch-hunt investigations researched the 2019/2020 congressional attacks which were only to impeach President Trump and to fight his attempts to stop the Democratic National Committee and their politicians like Biden from international anti-American collusions. When the legal investigations were completed in April of 2022, Adam Schiff, Nancy Pelosi, and other politicians were impeached and removed from their offices for lying, cheating, and attacking the American citizens who voted for President Trump.

July 2022: Politicians Arrested and Prosecuted

A Department of Justice two-year investigation determined that President Obama's administration officials had colluded with foreign countries to falsely attack President Trump before and after the 2016 election and prior to the 2020 election. Days after they were all found guilty of starting the Mueller investigation by creating false documents and fake witnesses with help from Russian and other foreign officials, several of them were also found guilty of having created the fake Trump/Ukraine impeachment attack. President Trump developed a proposal to commute the ten-year prison sentences of Obama, his vice president, his secretary-of-state, and several other criminal administration officials.

Mr. President tried to negotiate a deal to commute the prison times from their ten-year sentences down to six months, so that they would be removed from prison before the next mid-term election. President Trump said he will propose this commutation only if Obama and each of his guilty staff members agree to share with the public the full facts of their work with and financing of leftwing political news companies, their ties with Soros business teams, and their deep lying and cheating secret society strategies. The negotiations resulted in Obama being the only one whose ten-year sentence was reduced to six months. He said he would not agree to let his other previous staff members be part of the negotiations and the releasing of facts because he could not trust that they would camouflage his involvement in the collusions and his administration's long-range illegal FBI policies. President Obama didn't want his secretary of state, his vice-president, and the six guilty FBI members to get the six-month commutation, so President Trump gave each of them a seven-month commutation. He said that their additional month was because of their illegal deplorability against our constitution.

June 2024: Fusion Squad Graduation Party

The evening before their graduation from university, Ella's team of friends and her boyfriend, Barry, set up an event at a restaurant within walking distance from school. Barry invited Ella's parents, Susan and Burt Abhoola from Exeter, New Hampshire. She was so surprised and happy to see them there with her Fusion Squad. Her friends and Barry started to present speeches giving honor to Ella's really great alliance efforts. After each short speech of honor, the team clapped and cheered to share their honor of Ella and Mehna. Unfortunately, there were over two dozen hard left students and several radical teachers at this restaurant who became aware over the years of Ella's push against the Democratic deep state trickery.

After the second cheering and saluting affair, before Barry started the third one, Ella's father got up and walked over to him. "Hey, Barry," he whispered. "I have to share this. I'm seeing a couple of these men and women around here in the room walking around, talking to others while pointing at us and showing faces of anger. Do you think this could be dangerous?"

Barry looked around the restaurant and saw several people staring over at the squad with looks of frustration. "Thanks, Burt. Good point, since we've seen years of attacks from people who have bad tastes but don't know it because of fraudulence. I'll ask someone else to speak next so that I can sit back and monitor the potential intrusion from these kids who have been taken hard left by their college staffers."

Barry asked Bonnie to do the next speech of honor for Ella. Bonnie was so tied to her friend that her decree of Ella's righteousness brought even higher more energetic cheering and celebration from the squad. Just as the team stood and cheered facing toward Ella, over a dozen students and two teachers from the University jumped up quickly and raced really hard yelling and screaming right at the whole Fusion Squad, and Ella's parents. The pro-Antifa Democrats tried to tackle down squad members, but Barry and her dad were posted right in front of Ella, punching and kicking every rat that raced toward their girl, the fusion queen.

Even Bonnie kicked, hit, and tackled several men and women from the attack. After most of the battling had stopped, one of the teachers laying down after Burt slugged him several times in the face started screaming at Burt and Susan. "Why are you damn blacks even here? You should not be part of our college, you racists!"

None of the Fusion Squad members were injured, and neither were Ella's parents. The restaurant owners did not contact the police about this political attack, because they were part of the deep-left state of Massachusetts.

After this standard leftist attack, Barry told Ella, "My dear, I'm with you as a true Republican for the rest of my life." At twenty-three years old, Ella Harriet Abhoola graduated from Harvard University law school. Each of her fusion friends and her boyfriend Barry also graduated with great results.

2024 Election Season

She started her attorney journey with a job at a law firm in Portsmouth, New Hampshire. Even though President Trump had proven to more than half of the country's voting citizens that mainstream media are political falsifiers, not real news outlets, Ella continued to remain active in doing her own true-news investigations.

The 2024 Republican nominee, Harold Robert, won the next presidency because of his well-known great ability to protect freedom for all and because of the morality of President Trump's sharing with the public all the years of leftist scams. Ella was very excited about supporting the new President during her work life to protect American citizens from the Democratic socialist dictatorial takeover.

January 20, 2025. Inauguration Day

The day after President Robert's 2025 inauguration when President Trump left office, the Secret Ella Society members, Ella, her boyfriend Barry, and her Fusion Squad all traveled to Boca Raton, Florida, to meet President Trump and his family. This was Ella's first time meeting this wonderful president who took America in the right direction of righteousness for all.

Down in Florida, President Trump gave a great tribute to Ella Abhoola, because he had been told the whole story of Mehna and African Americans seeing the elephant of freedom.

While there, Ella shared several more items with retired President Trump, his family, and her people. "Mr. President, thank you for meeting with us. Up in Cambridge at Harvard, some of us were able to talk with a few students and teachers who were part of the secret society meetings they hold hidden in the basement of some buildings there. Because of what I've learned in my own research toward the world of political news programs and their directions, I want to tell you all that I think their secret team should be called the Secret Soros Society, similar to what we have here, our Secret Ella Society. Here's another suggestion. We've heard that back in the 1860s a Republican hero called Elephant

Joe jokingly suggested that Amos Tuck should consider changing his name to Amos Tusk because of all Amos did for our elephant party of freedom. So, now I'm suggesting that you should consider changing your family name to Trunk to honor your support for Mehna's plan for freedom of humanity. Ha, Ha! Just kidding. Love you and your family, President Trump, and all you've done for humanity and our country, sir."

CHAPTER 42

ELLA MARRIES BARRY

AFTER BARRY HELPED SAVE HER LIFE BACK IN SCHOOL, he and Ella became so close with everything including their political understandings that they decided to become matrimonial for life. They were married on November 10, 2025. Because of the power and importance of the Abhoola family-wave, the new couple both chose to be legally named the Abhoola's—Ella and Barry.

Two weeks after their marriage, Ella and Barry Abhoola were both at the next quarterly Secret Ella Society conference meeting. Before the team got into their quarterly fake news investigations, a teambuilding conversation started up.

A senator from Virginia said, "Congrats, you two, on your marriage. So, Mr. Barry. I know that talking like I'm going to do now is what the Democrats do to keep talking about skin color. But we'd like to hear your take on their continuing racist separation strategies. Because you married this wonderful African American lady, and you're from French and German light skin ancestors, what has your life been like toward other cultures?"

Barry had a key example to share. "Well, folks, I'll share some of my life, which got me to my wonderful wife. When I was a kid growing up in New Hampshire where I never met a darker skinned person, my foremost heroes were the Red Sox players, like David Ortiz and Mookie Betts. I had never met an African American, but I loved those guys on TV as a kid. Then, when I joined the navy and went to boot camp, things happened. There were about eighty-five recruits there with me. Early on at camp, my best new friend turned out to be a nice black guy from Ohio. For nine weeks, we hung out together for all the boot camp activities that we could. In the evenings, we'd go out behind the shower rooms and wrestle really hard. So fun. I loved John, the first African American I had ever met. Unfortunately for him, there were a dozen other black recruits who were not happy with John being friends with a white guy like me. They all hung out together and aimed middle-fingers at white guys often for reasons I couldn't understand. They spilled shaving cream on almost every white guys' pillows. And they never hung out with anyone but their color of men. I didn't know then that these behaviors were political, but my position now is just that we have to stop letting the Democrats teach people that they are victims and that they must stay segregated from other skin colors. My friend John and I had no skin color. We just loved spending time together. I wish the Democrats' deep state and their racist news outlets would stop creating the skin color separation issues, and just treat everyone the same, fair and decent. We would just all be super friends, like John and I were, if the deep left would quit their division strategies."

Stevens responded to Barry's case. "Thanks, sir. No surprise there. That's what we see happening everywhere. People are growing up with their parents, the tricked ones, unintentionally raising racial turmoil. I have another similar example which happened just recently. My brother lives down in Bradenton, Florida, in one of those gated communities down there. Last week, his ten-year-old grandson, Cameron visited their home. My brother was walking to the mailbox while his grandson went across the street to try to play with two boys about his age whom he saw outside. Those boys' parents were born in Turkey, then they were brought to America legally as teenagers by both their parents. Now their family members are totally American citizens. As my brother was walking past the three boys just as his grandson got over to the other two, he overheard an awful comment from one of the boys before they had received any talk from Cameron. The kid said to his brother, 'We won't play with this kid. He's an American, so he hates us. No way will we ever play with any of them.' These kids were born in America, just like my brother's grandson. So, the only way they could be trashing other kids like they did is from their parents teaching and sharing anti-American sentiments to their children. Obviously, these kids' parents must be fully tied to the minority-separation news outlets, just like the men you met in boot camp, Barry. So I agree with your position that we have to stop the Democrats from teaching people that they are victims and that they must stay segregated and attack white Americans."

In 2028, when Ella was twenty-seven years old, Republican President Harold Robert won his second term in office. Ella and Barry's first child was born on March 22 that year. They named their baby boy Harold Robert Abhoola, to honor the current president who was doing a great job for America.

Four years after her job as a lawyer, several Secret Ella Society members contacted the New Hampshire Governor and shared with her the extensive skills of Mrs. Abhoola. The governor appointed Ella Harriet Abhoola as New Hampshire attorney general.

During her two terms, eight years in state office, Ella picked up her fight against politicians and news outlets who did not believe that telling the truth to the public was important. She gave weekly updates on the internet and Twitter showing which news reports were not true and which facts were kept away from the voting public by those leftist media companies. But she knew that so many Americans would not ever see the truth because they only watched leftwing media outlets. Ella continued to create her life-long plan for making sure all voters were provided true facts about the political ideologies of both parties, and to ensure that voters know for sure that news outlets have been lying to them for over one hundred and fifty years.

As attorney general in New Hampshire, Ella still kept her Fusion Squad engaged. She hired Bonnie Seven and Greg Fields for her staff when jobs opened up for which they were qualified. Frank Damadon and Billy Mizner both worked in Boston, so they were able to meet with the rest of the Fusion Squad whenever Ella set them up. They were hanging out together and very pleased when the Republicans won the 2032 presidential and legislative elections. This victory put good strong leadership in place for twenty years, all the way back to President Trump's first win in 2016.

2036 Election Year Collusion and Ella's Response

The Democratic deep state hadn't had the presidency or any part of congress since President Trump won in 2020 his second term. Therefore, to get their uninformed voters and illegal voters to ramp up their support, the Democrats started in 2033 to rebuild the same anti-American positions that they used against President Trump and President Robert during their sixteen years in office. For the three years heading into the 2036 election, they restarted these strategies by using their excellence of presenting falsehoods to the public.

- Teach uninformed college students and voters that America sucks.
- Convince unaware voters and college students that the American flag is a racist icon.
- Express to unaware college students and voters that the American military is inhumane.
- Persuade neglectful college students and voters that all men and women of our law-enforcement teams are racists and people haters.
- Convince the ill-informed CNN and MSNBC viewers that all of the American voters who chose to vote against the Democrats for the past fourteen years are deplorable monsters that deserve physical attack.

- Tell the uninformed that taking away your health-care insurance will be a great new world.
- Teach the ill-informed that the Trump KAG Wall should be torn down so that all American citizens will pay taxes for the medical needs, college, and free welfare of all people from any country that sneaks their people here through America's borders.

This election year, 2036, to attempt an election recovery, several deep state leftists colluded with socialist politicians to create a new independent party. They funded CNN and MSNBC to have them make trajectories to fake out the people such as young conservative voters who were tricked to pull votes away from this year's Republican nominee.

Since they were successful with secretly getting more than half of the US states to have issues with unsecure, in-accurate, and illegal voting, the Democrats won the 2036 presidential election and the House of Representatives by a slim margin. Because of the left's fake independent party nominee, just as occurred in President Clinton's win in 1990, a higher percentage of Electoral College voters voted against the Democrat, but Beto O'Rourke still won the presidency.

When Ella was thirty-eight years old, she launched Mehna Abhoola's next phase of freedom defense because of all the rotten terrible things the deep left was doing to hurt her country.

By now, the new empress was highly respected. As New Hampshire attorney general, she had intensified her drive to educate the world about her ancestor, Mehna Abhoola and Mehna's plan to free the world from evil-doers such as the black kingdom leaders who stole her dad and brother and sold so many of her friends and African people to other cultures.

For the past two years under O'Rourke, the United States of America had been melted down by the Democrats into one of the worst economies ever and the weakest military and border defensiveness since Obama tore down the country back when he was supporting Iran's military growth. Because of Ella's love for her country and the good people, even those who are tricked into supporting anti-American politics, her emotional concern toward the current Democratic leadership kicked off to a new high level of passionate embattlement. Ella, the sister of Mehna Abhoola, decided that the elephant in the room will finally again be attacking the left's push for socialism, dictatorship, and racial division.

CHAPTER 43

ELLA ABHOOLA'S 2039 PRE-ELECTION SPEECH

BARRY ABHOOLA HELPED HIS WIFE AND THE SECRET Ella Society by setting up a political launch event in the lobby at Major Blake's Hotel in Exeter which was called the Squamscott Hotel back when America started seeing the elephant in the 1800s. The day before the event started in June of 2039, Republican supporters including Ella's Fusion Squad members were rambling around Exeter's beautiful downtown area. Several of Ella's local supporters were wearing the MAGA hat supporting the country's need to beat O'Rourke. Others were wearing KAG hats and shirts that represent the wonderful terms of retired President Trump.

As had been their deep state's expectancy for the past one hundred and fifty years, a gang of leftwing supporters attacked the individuals wearing the MAGA and KAG hats and shirts. Their attack put three New Hampshire citizens into the hospital with broken arms and smashed heads. Since the Fusion Squad had seen attacks in the past, they secured themselves enough in the streets, and ended up not injured or killed by the Democrats. The left's news outlets did not share this round of violence with their public onlookers. This attack was remarkably similar to the Democrats' outburst against slavery abolitionists in 1836, right here in Exeter at the Methodist Church only a quarter mile away, the attack which helped motivate Amos Tuck into creating the Republican Party to defend his democracy.

Because of this continuing violence by the Democrats against free-speaking Americans, with several of Ella's supporters now under healing, her scheduled event was postponed for several weeks so that she and Barry could work with local town government and law enforcement officials to create a safer event. Just like happened to Amos Tuck when he was attacked due to politics, Ella's deep emotions exploded much grander to help all Americans walk away from the Democrats. Because of the now-elevated significance of her speech event, Ella and Barry decided to ask town leaders to let her speak to people outdoors at the historic bandstand in the town's center. Because of the chronological decency of this great town, the rescheduled Ella event was set up at the renowned town-center bandstand.

The state's attorney general and her husband, Barry Abhoola, came down from Concord, the New Hampshire capital, days before their rescheduled Ella event so that they could meet with the three citizens who ended up hurt by the Antifa-styled attack weeks ago. Everyone who was injured was doing better now, and they were so triggered from what happened that they each chose again to go to Ella's speech event tomorrow. Ella's parents and her Fusion Squad were all here for the event. Many, many more kind conservatives showed up at this event to help defend against the violent Democrats' next attack.

Roger Stevens, long-term director of the American Independence Museum, was first to walk up to the bandstand microphone. "Hello, you wonderful people. Your great New Hampshire Attorney General has some important information to share with you today. Please welcome Ella Harriet Abhoola back to her home town, your historical heaven on earth."

Ella stepped onto the front of the bandstand, and shook hands with Roger while the crowd was cheering and clapping for their really strong constitutional representative. She moved up to the microphone as her five Fusion Squad friends sat down right next to her.

"Thank you for being here, everyone." With her arms straight up overhead, she elevated her voice. "I am announcing today that every citizen in America will be way more safer and happier in January of 2041 when I will be your next president of the United States!" The crowd again cheered, loud and clear.

"Thank you, thank you! We all need me to do this because of the past three-years of the current administration and congress making America worse again. It's fantastic and crucial to be with you here in Exeter, New Hampshire, this wonderful historical community where local heroes worked with President Lincoln, right back here in this hotel, to battle evil people who wanted to carry on slavery and racial turmoil forever in America. The same battle is still on today because of the Democrats' racial discord." Ella turned and pointed back at the famous historical hotel.

"How amazing it is that our wonderful Republican Party was started right here on October twelfth, in 1853. You Exeter people must really know that it is so significant that we're meeting up exactly where Presidents Washington and Lincoln launched their freedom battles for all of this country's people. Just yesterday, my great husband Barry and I went jogging right down there on Front Street, onto both Washington Street and Lincoln Street. It is so gratifying to have run along with those supermen and now to be with you today to start a spirited battle to fix our country, like these great presidents did and like President Trump also had to do and did because of evil politics.

"Today, I'm going to show all of America why and how we need to vote to stop O'Rourke and his cronies from continuing to make America worse again! Our country is in serious trouble. With under three-years in office, O'Rourke has increased our poverty, raised our violence at home, weakened all of our country's international defensiveness, and again attempted to build more skin-color division like his racist buddy Obama did for eight years.

"Since this jerk has been president, we have less defense, we have less competence, and most citizens don't know what's happening. I'm sharing with you now the deplorable things that O'Rourke has done against our country.

"He has weakened our international trade deals to the point that we're again losing more jobs to China, Mexico, and beyond. He has refused to keep America first by not ever negotiating toward world economies, NATO defenses, and environmental safety from huge carbon-emission countries like China and India.

"As soon as they saw this ridiculous president take over our country, Iran and other terrorist groups such as the Taliban and Isis immediately started attacking their people and neighboring nations. They know that O'Rourke is the same anti-American as their friend Obama, so they know that he will not take any actions to end their religious drive to murder the entire non-Islamic world.

"Our great presidents, Trump and Robert, built our military and border security as strong as ever. But in the past two years, O'Rourke and his evil vice president have laid off forty-percent of our military members, most of whom wanted to keep their jobs to protect our country. And these ridiculous leaders have worked hard to increase illegal immigration. But these teardowns are not the only aspects of our nation's defense that O'Rourke has tried to eliminate for his entire political career. Here's his primary goal against free life.

"The right to bear arms, our Second Amendment, has been horribly attacked over the past century by using fake information. Crazy President O'Rourke has been one of their strongest cohorts to take your guns away. Here are the real facts that you can't get from leftwing media.

"Only a few of the Democrats, the hard-left socialists, understand the true reason for the fight to take guns away from our people. O'Rourke and his gun-stealing allies use false facts under the cloud of mass murders to hide their true intentions. For this rotten, unreliable president, *progressive* means moving closer and closer toward socialism, toward communism, into hard-core dictatorship, and away from freedom, democracy, and capitalism. He wants to take guns away from us citizens to get to his deep-state goals.

"They hide the real reason for the Second Amendment from the voting public and from the ill-informed politicians in both parties. The real reason for ensuring we-the-people have weapons has always been to protect democracy from a socialist dictatorial takeover. Our founding fathers understood that an authoritative, unrestrained federal government could someday take the power of the people away by using the military to dismantle all legislation, to end our rights to vote, and to put their desire for fulltime dictatorship into place.

"The Second Amendment established the principle that the government does not have the authority to disarm citizens. This was and is necessary to ensure that freedom and democracy, for the people and by the people, would never be overtaken by any dictatorship, left or right.

"President O'Rourke and Vice President Harris are nibbling away at our rights to own guns so they can move us closer to having their dictatorial armies stop democracy. The deep state left politicians know that eventually, when we the people can't rise up in arms against the government takeover, their communistic, socialistic dreams will have a path to what they call "progress."

They have done well to trick voters into thinking the Second Amendment gun rights are only for individual defense, not to protect against government takeover of democracy. It is my belief that the deep-state Democratic leaders and their news outlets are very pleased each time mass-murders occur in our country, because each of those terrible events keeps them on track to continue attacking our gun rights, which they do without letting people know that our personal weapons are necessary to protect our constitution and individual freedom.

Because of the world's history on gun rights, I will never let our Second Amendment be stolen away! If the African tribes of my ancestors in the sixteenth and seventeenth centuries had been given access to the same guns that were traded to the African kings by selling slaves, then the kingdoms' armies would not have been able to walk around the continent and enslave millions of its own people. America! Do not ever again vote for the Democrats who want to demolish democracy by taking away the people's rights to protect our country from government takeover. Their policies are the same ones that enslaved and killed millions of people for hundreds of years. Never again. Never!"

Ella finished her discussion on gun rights, then began sharing other progressive misdemeanors.

"In his attempts to reestablish Obama's dreams for our country, this president has directed fake news outlets to drive people into threatening and attacking our law enforcement officials who risk their lives for us every day. America! Vote for me next year to protect and honor our law enforcement men and women who love our country."

The grand crowd took off with giant cheering again to honor America's law enforcement personnel.

"Great folks! Our country has so many awesome people like you! Now, guess what. With only a few years in office, President O'Rourke has lowered your household incomes by over four-thousand dollars a year. And taxes are going way up again."

The crowd booed.

"Your vote for me will restore your income that O'Jerk has stolen from you. Even though he funded and started this secretly, you've probably heard that he spent five-billion tax-payer dollars in his first year to remove hundreds of miles of the Trump KAG

Wall. Now that the wall is coming down, Vice President Harris has met dozens of times with Mexican government officials behind Schiff-styled closed doors to convince them to stop securing their southern border and to start recruiting migrants and drug cartels from around the world to enter the US illegally. In just two years, O'Rourke and Harris have brought our country's annual opioid deaths back to thirty-thousand lives lost per year, which President Trump ended significantly during his years in office.

"America! After next year's vote, I will rebuild the torn-down parts of the Trump KAG Wall and put an end to all of California's underground human and opioid marketing." The crowd rejoiced again for several minutes to show their support for America's border protections.

"Thanks for your support of our borders. Hey, great folks! If you agree that we the people must protect democracy and capitalism from leftwing government takedown, let me hear your even more cheers!"

Ella raised her hands way up as did the thousands of cheering conservative supporters who were filling all the streets within sight of Exeter Town Hall. After minutes of the highly emotional public cheering, she restarted her speech.

"Next, I will cover with you my family's three-hundred-and-forty-five-year Republican battle against slavery, racism, and the hidden inhumane strategies of the Democratic Party. It has really been that long, because we're talking about good fighting evil, even before we had political party names. Here goes.

"Late in the seventeenth century, families in today's Ghana region of Africa were victims of the Bank of England, the Royal African Company, and the local African tribal kings. Those entities worked to advance their own economies and cultures by human trafficking and slavery sales.

In 1691, a brave African woman in her teens told groups of young kidnapped African's, as they were being boarded onto ships headed for Maryland in America, that their freedom and happiness would start when an elephant shows up in America and they start seeing it.

In 1692, after growing up in an African kingdom that sold rival tribal members to the English, and after her dad and brother were kidnapped by the local black kingdom leader, this great lady, my ancestor Mehna Abhoola, decided that she must make her way to London to create a plan to end slavery. She learned to speak English and began to build her five-hundred-year plan to end world racism and slavery. She is the key founder of our Republican Party that still today fosters the basic freedom and equality fundamentals for all humans. Her plan has been carried forth by her underground society for three hundred and fifty years holding true to the New England Elephant Token, these amazing copper tokens that she made in London and sent here to Exeter in 1694."

She held up a token. "Look at this Elephant Token. You will be amazed at its history, struck in 1694 at the start of this godly African woman's forever-plan for freedom and happiness for all humanity. Miss Abhoola went to London in a secretive way and made friends with people who agreed with her that slavery, human trafficking, and racial division are wrong."

Ella shared the history of Mehna Abhoola's freedom journal, a 1694 token found three miles away in 1994 in Exeter's Oaklands Forest, and the 2001 token-DNA research results.

"I am the offspring of Princess Mehna Abhoola. I'm here to continue Princess Mehna's plan of uniting all humans by way of trust, truth, love, equality, freedom, and democracy.

"Until this new information that we're revealing today came to light, the history of how the elephant became the GOP icon has always been documented and published as being from Thomas Nast, a conservative illustrator for the New Yorker newspaper. He created a cartoon in 1874 showing an elephant in the newspaper to represent Republicans. Nast called both the party and the animal smart, persistent, and meticulous. But guess what! This new discovery we're about to show you reveals an amazing series of events. Events about the GOP icon's astonishing history, and about the Democratic history of falsehood and fake culturism.

"The iconic American phrase 'seeing the elephant' has been under analysis for many years to find its origin. Look this one up, folks. Fourteen years before Mr. Nast drew the Republican elephant cartoon, the phrase 'seeing the elephant' was used at the beginning and throughout the Civil War by the Union soldiers to show overwhelming sentiment for their fight to end slavery forever in America. So here and now, let me share with you the amazing origin of the American party of the elephant. Today, it is remarkable that we're here in Exeter, the exact location where America started seeing the elephant of freedom, right here where we had great humanitarians like Abraham Lincoln, Amos Tuck, and Harriet Tubman creating merger plans for virtuous political abolitionist groups.

"When I'm your president, to honor Mehna Abhoola, Harriet Tubman, and their three-centuries of anti-racism supporters, I will launch a fabulous New England Elephant Token affair, a very NEET day, which will make all of us want to vote for each other, not against each other, for the next three centuries.

"Before I tell you what I'm going to do for you after I become president, I want to show you even more problem areas we have today because of O'Jerk and his falsehood party.

"By the time all of our citizens hear these aspects of truth, we will all then be heading for the very important NEET event after I am your president so that we can bring everyone together to offset our current problems of racial divide, which are terrible for all of the people of love that we have.

"Here we go with sharing political plans of attack against our democracy. We, as voters, need to know what the long-range dogmas are for each party. The evidence is so clear. If you do your own investigation into any stories posted by CNN and MSNBC and the facts that they hide from you, you will clearly see that their goals for the future are to end America's freedom. Of course, most left voters, and most of their politicians are not allowed to know of the deep-state goals for ending democracy. Use true facts to add a higher value to your voting rights.

"I recently read a leftist book written over forty-years ago with which most political Democrats still try to align. This book has many influential political-victory concepts. Here are four of his concepts that we know they believe in and use very well today, both publically and in colleges to pull students away from the Republican Party. They are better at using these philosophies of battle than we the righteous are, because we don't think these lying and cheating processes are fair for our people.

"The communist author wrote that underprivileged people must build political influence by attacking the living. That idea of his shows us how the deep-state Democrats try to create lower-class minorities and motivate them to use physical attacks on their conservative and law-enforcement opponents. This statement is exactly what the Antifa attackers and others have been living up to for the past twenty-five years. It's also the same as President Obama did by driving the public left to hate our law enforcement heroes.

"This guy also wrote that their party should look for ways to upsurge self-doubt, nervousness, and vagueness within the public's heads. This portion of his book really explains how fake news became a valuable fundamental strategy for their party to get into power and try to remain in control."

Ella held up a picture of Thomas Nast's 1874 cartoon of the fake Democratic icon. "In 1874, in his political newspaper in New York, Thomas Nast revealed the Democratic mascot as a jackass hiding under a lion-skin costume, showing the public that the party then used news cover-ups to hide their party's true character and intentions. America! You can now see that these strategies of taking people down a false-path has been in our politics since at least the 1870s when Mr. Nast reported on them. The Democratic Party has continued for over a century to push their racial-division agendas. They have been getting much better at their cover-up strategies since televisions and internet have joined into human life. These divisive fake news practices still in use today are meeting up with that author's plans to increase self-doubt, nervousness, and vagueness in our voters' heads.

"All these years of the lying and holding back facts to cause voters' self-doubt and false victimization means that there are continuing secret strategic dialogues by some leftist entity. The consistency of the faking and lying for so many years means that it is a real underground strategic group that clearly uses falsehood as their main goal for winning votes. They must be paying the news media outlets to support the lying. The deep state lefties must lie to their own politicians who may never know of the long-range goal to close democracy with a dictatorial takeover. How fake is that. You secret politicians call yourselves Democrats, but your long-term strategies clearly show that you want to end our democracy.

"The next item I want to share that this leftist architect wrote in his book says that mockery is civilization's most powerful firearm to force the other party into vote reduction. He wrote this for the Dems to believe that falsehood is the most potent weapon to pressure their political enemy. I also think it's rotten that colleges use this man's strategies to steer young Americans into a terrible, unexpected direction.

"Today, that will change as we share with all Americans the total age-old trickery of the deeply secret Democratic politicians. Millions of our country's voters have been deceived for hundreds of years into voting away from the very human, caring, fiscally sound party of fairness, equality, and national defense.

If the information I'm opening up with you today will somehow be shared with all of our citizens, all of the previously faked-out voters and politicians on the left will walk away from their secret society's goals of racism, dictatorship, socialism, and beyond.

"Okay, friends, the last item I'll share which that awful man wrote is where he said that the most important drive for successful election strategies is to sustain a constant pressure on the opposition. This one we know very much to be why and how the Democrats treated President Trump and President Robert with fully false attacks throughout each of their two-terms in office.

CHAPTER 44

Abhoola Speech Covers Historical Calamity

"There you go. Now you know. From the first aspects of this speech, you can see the long-range desires of each party and their methods of steering people toward their wishes. Now I'm going to share a valuable list of historical events from both parties. The reason that I must share these many decades of facts is because of the past thirty-five years where our entire public has been tricked into thinking that the Republican politicians and voters are the ones of racial division. So, right now, I'm erasing those years of fake-out by issuing these genuine events to you.

"Only a few deep-core racial-division strategies over the past century and a half are needed to convince any kind, open-minded voters who the real white-supremacy party has been and still is today. Here are facts that will revise people's wrong-opinion of the rightwing being the evil one. I will start each event by saying which year it occurred. Every one of these are true facts. Look them up, good people, and share them with your Democratic friends.

- In 1828, southern slave owners created a governing body to keep slavery flourishing for years to come. The new Democrat Party also worked to prevent full-citizenry from Native Americans.

- In 1836, when a church pastor right here in Exeter was holding a godly slavery-abolitionist event at his church, Massachusetts Democrats attacked the church with rocks and clubs to end the antislavery event.
- In 1850, the Fugitive Slave Act was designed and passed by the Democratic Party to criminalize anyone who helped escaped slaves get into a free and safe life.
- In 1853, the good people in close ties with Harriet Tubman and other fugitive slaves knew that ending slavery would only happen by tying all decent politicians together into one team to battle the deplorable deep-state Democrats. Harriet Tubman, Abraham Lincoln, Amos Tuck, and Mehna Abhoola started the Republican Party on October 12, 1853 right here in Exeter, right in this hotel behind us.
- Starting in 1861, hundreds of thousands of lives were lost in the Civil War, while the Democratic Party pushed to support the cravings of the Confederate states for continued enslavement of darker-skinned people.
- In 1862, the Democrats in Congress opposed freeing slaves in Washington, D.C. by using false information. Your great New Hampshire Republican Senator John Hale called out the lies and hate of the Democratic speakers, then he ended up getting enough votes to free the DC slaves from the Democrats.
- In 1868, Democratic businesspeople from our southern states started the Ku Klux Klan. KKK Democrats murdered Republican politicians in South Carolina and Arkansas that year. They also murdered seven African Americans who tried to engage in conservative political careers.
- In 1878, women's voting rights were voted down by Democrats. They battled against women's rights to vote for forty-years until the Republican Party won a landslide in the Senate and House to give women the right to vote.

- In 1892, higher percentages of Democrats than Republicans pushed and passed laws to prohibit the legal entry of Chinese persons into the United States.
- In 1894, Democrats in New York arranged for leftist voters to illegally vote several times in each election. When a federal polling officer attempted to stop their cheating, the New York Democratic senator hired local leftist gang members and had them kill the polling officer.
- In the early 1900s, the Harvard University president created college rules which prevented both African and Native Americans from living at the deep-left college.
- In 1902, the new progressive arm of the Democratic Party was launched to revive white supremacy against minorities which they achieved for the next twenty-two years.
- On June 2, 1924, Republican President Calvin Coolidge signed an act granting full citizenship to all Americans born in the United States regardless of skin shade. He had to do this to offset the continuing racial-division strategies of the Progressive Democrats.
- In 1945, Democrats continued to openly try to stop the federal government from creating laws which would prevent states from obstructing minority voting.
- In 1964, by facilitating a two-month filibuster, Senator Al Gore Sr. and some other Democrats tried unsuccessfully to obstruct the Civil Rights Act of 1964. After Gore's two-month battle, a higher percentage of Republicans than Democrats passed the act.
- From 1964 to present, disgraceful media has constantly lied to the public, reporting that the Civil Rights Act was passed only by the Democrats. They've deliberately ignored the truth that a higher percentage of Republicans have always supported the freedom rights of our people.

- In 1965, same as the prior year, a higher percentage of Republicans voted for the Voting Rights Act to end the left's decades of trying to expand minority-voting barriers.
- In 1969, the Democratic president approved only a five-year extension of the Voting Rights Act. In 1975, the Republican president increased the time-extension of the voting-rights bill to seven more years.
- In 1982, our great Republican President Ronald Reagan felt that the Voting Rights Act needed more lengthy involvement, so he extended the bill by twenty-five years. In 2006, Republican President George Bush extended the bill by another twenty-five years.
- In 2011, to keep racial-division strong, President Obama added more skin-color aspects to our affirmative-action laws so he could convince colleges to use race in deciding who can go to their schools. He did this to reverse President Bush's 2008 position which ended the rights of colleges to use racism for admissions. This doesn't mean that Obama was against people of various skin colors. It really means that he just wanted to keep making more cases of segregation so that his political scam-party could blame his human turmoil on the Republicans.
- In August of 2018, under President Trump, the US Supreme Court investigated Harvard University's continued use of racism to determine who can enter the school. The college was using Obama's directives to deny Asian Americans entry to the school, so President Trump ordered his administration to stop the unfair practice that the college has been using for hundreds of years. President Trump's Attorney General commented on the court's decision. He said, "No American should be denied admission to school because of their race."

- In October 2018, just days prior to midterm elections, recently retired Obama went on his allied TV news channel and reported to the public that the Democratic Party was responsible for creating and passing the Civil Rights Act in 1964. He and his news allies were clearly lying. This was just one of their thousands of lies each month.

- In 2019, a TV news response by a hard-left woman who lost the 2018 gubernatorial election in Georgia contained multiple falsehoods, none of which were corrected by the destabilizing left media. She told the American public on a leftwing news channel that the President Trump administration was racist because of wanting to secure the southern border. Then, just like Obama did, she told the public on national TV that only the Democrats were responsible for passing the 1964 Civil Rights Act. Liar lady, or she just doesn't know the truth.

- From 2016 to 2020, the Democratic Party and their secret Soros society members in the FBI and CIA continued to attack American constitutional rights by colluding with Russia and Ukraine to create false information about the American president. Of course, we all know now that several of their people in power were found guilty of these conspiracies due to Obama's, Clinton's, Schiff's, and Pelosi's illegal drives against President Trump.

- In 2033, President Harold Robert was accused by several news outlets and Democratic congressional men and women of supporting Afghanistan's underground sales of opioids to America. Without having any true evidence, they created stories where they said that he gave billions of our tax-payer dollars to support illegal drug sales. They created several false documents and social media lies by colluding with Afghanistan leaders to drive the FBI against

President Robert, just like they did with Russia and the Ukraine against President Trump sixteen years ago.

- In 2036, as most Americans know, the Democrats and their Soros-funded news outlets organized, financed, and promoted a fabricated independent party with a nominee using fake conservative insights to trick some Republican voters away from their core base so that the Democrats could renew their chance to win the presidency.

"There you go, America. I just gave you over two hundred years of political facts showing the party of racism and democracy downfall. There are many more historical facts that show how awful our political processes have been, because of the divergent use of freedom of the press to trick voters away from goodness.

"Please, please, please, voting citizens, do more and more of your own bipartisan research between now and next year's election so that you can vote the right way. This is how we will someday stop colleges and high-schools from forcing young voters in one direction by any political deep-state. They will grow up learning to not be tricked, like their parents will no longer be misled after I become your president and I launch your NEET Day American recovery plan."

As Ella raised her arms way up, a local band in Exeter's historical bandstand started playing America's national anthem, "The Star-Spangled Banner." The entire town center cheered and clapped intensely to show their support for Mrs. Abhoola, the United States of America, and democracies around the world.

"There are very clear examples of facts that anyone can look up. Of course, if anyone is working for the Dems or their politically controlled news outlets, they won't let you look up the facts and report the truth against their party. If you report the truth about your party's awful history, or goodness of the Republicans, you'll lose your job.

"Fortunately, the voting public started to become somewhat aware of these party situations when President Trump clearly showed us how the media was reporting false information. After his eight-years in office, there were far fewer written and voiced discussions about skin shades. But by 2036, they got back into their rotten skin-color attacks by increased funding of their fake news allies. In America today and over the past forty years, freedom of speech and freedom of the press are used to promote freedom of lying by CNN, MSNBC, the *Washington Post*, and other Soros-backed media outlets.

"When I become president and forever thereafter, everyone will be loved by everyone. We are from now on, all the same human race. That's it! We will from now on call-out the left whenever they start to re-push racial activism. After I launch your NEET Day in 2041 or forty-two, no one will agree to be voters who support the lying mainstream media.

"And, hey, you young voters who have grown up to support the left. You need to ensure that you're aware of how and why your parents and grandparents were always lied-to by their news media outlets. You should walk away from the left, and vote for me to protect your families and future generations from evil dogmas.

"Before the end of this grand affair, I want to remind America that Harriet Tubman was one of the strongest Republican-sided abolitionists ever. As a previously enslaved African American, not only did she free hundreds of slaves with her Underground Railroad process, but she became the first women to lead an American army troop into battle. She acted as a spy to find out what the slave owners were doing to win secession from the US of A.

"Our angel, Harriet Tubman would *never* agree with any of the Democratic Party's ideologies or cheating strategies, especially those by which we've been torched over the past four decades. America! If you ever see Mrs. Tubman on one of our country's cash bills, make sure that you honor the fact that she was a strong

Republican and was viscously attacked by the Democrats with the Fugitive Slave Act in 1850.

"Please! Vote next year to honor Harriet Tubman, by voting for me, Ella Harriet Abhoola, as your next president. Your votes will result in NEET Day unionization acts for your American friends, families, neighbors, and future generations of unionized people who will vote to ensure true love for all. You'll never again allow the hidden hate like we see today from O'Rourke and his deep state allies.

"Now that you've heard about the real Democratic Party, I'm sure you agree that we need to end their push for making America worse again. When I'm your president, we will all be making America great again, just like President Trump had to do for eight years after the Obama era. Never again will our citizens vote for making America worse again.

"Now, let's get back into my ancestor Mehna Abhoola's fusion plan so we can save America's constitution from Democratic tear-down. Our citizens today are finally becoming aware of the major differences in how both parties treat each other and our citizens. We, the party of the righteous elephant, do not accuse Democratic voters of being awful people, only of being vastly unaware of the true facts of their party's deep political schemes.

"The top leaders of the left deep-state have been accusing our nice people who have rights to vote of being deplorable. Listen, America! Their politicians calling all conservative voters *deplorable* means that they are accusing you of being disgraceful, dreadful, unacceptable, and terrible. Do they really think all voters who don't agree with them are so rotten, or do they just accuse voters this way to keep driving people apart? As your next president, I will end the unfriendly calamity the Clintons, Obama, Pelosi, Schiff, O'Rourke, and their deep-state communists have caused.

"No person with righteous, honest, and caring human character would ever vote for the real ideologies of these deep Democratic

Party politicians. Starting today, more and more of the leftwing of voters will walk away from the deep cheating strategies of their party as these historical realities that I'm showing you are shared throughout our nation.

"I must say this again. It is not the Democratic voters who are responsible for the deep, dark, immoral concerns of their party. Even leftwing voters would never agree that each of these racial-division behaviors is a good thing for our friendly civilization. I definitely do not and will never accuse Democratic voters of being true racists and un-constitutionalists, like the left voters have been hoodwinked to believe that we on the right are.

"Starting with my presidency, there will be no skin colors in America. We are, from now on, all just human beings and friends. Seeing and treating everyone as completely equal has been the real strategy of the Republican Party since its first days under President Lincoln. As President Trump taught us this century during his wonderful eight years and beyond, we must strive to be all one nation with a fair, comprehensive, and steadfastly competitive culture which encourages every person to do and be their best."

As she put on her red NEET hat, Ella said, "To get there and stop the political scams, we will be using the next NEET phase of our champion Mehna Abhoola's foundations.

"When my presidency starts up and your grand NEET Day launches, all of our citizens will finally be voting and living together and demolishing the Democrats' racial-division strategies. Our country will finally realize that we're close-knit humans, all of us, regardless of how close to the sunny equator our ancestors lived.

"The other one-percent, the elite left moon bats, will stay concealed in their secret society with the Soros family, will keep hiding in college basements, and will continue cheating, falsifying, and funding illicit news, so that they can push for their dictatorial takeover of the world's greatest democracy.

"Thank you, everyone, for today's celebration of our country's grand future. From today's revelations forward, ninety-five percent of all Democratic voters, and their politicians, will change parties, to the party of the New England Elephant Token.

"You people are so awesome. I will be the next president of your great country. Thank you! Goodnight!"

The Abhoola pro-American crowd went into a colossal cheering celebration.

By a giant landslide, Ella Harriet Abhoola won the Republican Party's primary nomination for president in the 2040 election.

CHAPTER 45

2040 PRESIDENTIAL DEBATE

IN JUNE OF 2040, THE AMERICAN PUBLIC'S MIND WAS
opened way up by the first presidential debate between
Democratic President Beto O'Rourke and New Hampshire's State
Attorney General, Ella Abhoola. President O'Rourke was sixty-five
years old at that time, but he never reminded anyone that thirty
years back, he always argued that seniors should not be running
for president because of their age.

Before the debate started, Mrs. Abhoola tweeted, "America,
please vote for or against the deep state philosophies of your party,
not for the hidden dogmas that they won't share with you. Don't
let lying steal the value of your vote."

As the presidential debate set off, each nominee began with
a five-minute opening statement. Abhoola was first because CNN
wanted their ally O'Rourke to be able to finalize each discussion
with the news outlet's expected response. Ella started off using
the same opinion she sent on Twitter before the debate began.

AG Abhoola began. "America, please vote for or against the
deep state philosophies of your party, not for the hidden dogmas
that they won't share with you. Here are the deep Democratic
dogmas. If you won't walk away from the Democrats and you continue to vote for them after you know these facts, then you're
admitting that you agree with these goals of your party:

"You want voting to tear down the Trump KAG Wall and get us back to where over one-million world migrants are crossing our boarders every year so that your party can get more votes.

"You hope to tear down voter-ID laws because they cost too much for the Soros family and Democratic lobbyists to pay billions for the millions of illegal entries per year to create and assign fake driver licenses and fake voting IDs. Make sure you support all demands and desires of the socialist Soros world. That's why you vote Democrat.

"You want to remove all firearms from all Americans so that millions of us cannot defend our constitution. When your party in the future attacks our federal government to start your new authoritarian regime so you can remove all voting rights and throw away our constitution, you don't want us to fight back with guns. You won't share with our citizenry that our Second Amendment calls them 'A well-regulated militia.' And the law says, '*A well-regulated militia...shall not be infringed.*' You must know for sure that if our people knew this meaning of the Second Amendment, they would never have voted for you.

"You want to pay far more taxes than you pay today and you want to improve the influences that the lying and cheating fake news outlets have on tricking our citizens.

"You want to reduce the size and strength of our military teams to prepare for the dictatorial takeover by several communist, socialist countries.

"Hey, lefty voters! I do not believe that you would ever vote for those strategies and outcomes. But I do know that you do not believe what I just said about your party's goals. I am not and never will be like this President's ally, Hillary Clinton, who has always raided hundreds of millions of American citizens by characterizing you as 'deplorable people.' Because I disagree with her evil ways, I am not saying that you Democratic voters have ever been intentionally trying to tear our country down and hold racism active for the entire history of our republic government. Not intentionally responsible, just hoodwinked into voting for rotten results."

President O'Rourke's debate preamble started with calling all conservative voters deplorable. He said that everything Ella had just said was false information. He called her a racist and a liar.

CNN asked the debaters the following question to begin the first dispute toward next year's election. "The majority of Americans have for years been wanting Congress to perform high levels of reparation against white people in America to set up reimbursement for the people who were slaves over a hundred and fifty years ago. Please share your plan for having white Americans payback the enslaved American civilizations."

She provided fact-based responses to defend against the lies President O'Rourke would use, which was what the Democrats had been known to do for the past thirty-five years. "First off, you, CNN, are lying again to the public by saying that a majority of Americans agree with reparation against the white American culture. That is not at all true. You know that Vice President Harris is the big pusher for reparation, and this idiotic President agrees with her. Now, with all of the internet research we can do, we find so many historical facts that have been ignored or hidden by this man's allies. Like President Trump taught our people about your sharing of forged information way back when he beat your party's run for president in 2016 and 2020, I need to remind the public right now of some facts that remain hidden. Vice President Harris's ancestors were not American slaves, and one of her ancestors in Jamaica was very likely a rich plantation slave owner. I'm convinced that you and Harris push separation of peoples only to try to get more votes, so that you can remain rich.

"I told you during our last debate about the African kingdom leaders who sold African tribal members to Europeans to enrich themselves. Now, I've learned from my research that there were free black Africans in the American colonies as far back as 1654.

And guess what? The children of free African Americans grew up not knowing about the de-humanizing culture of slavery driven by the Democratic Party for hundreds of years. For over a hundred years, many free African Americans became slave owners. In business competition with white slave owners, there were hundreds of black slave owners throughout the colonies. Look it up people, so that you don't let any political team or this president tell you their lies or hide the truth.

"So, Mr. President, respond to this. You Democrats have been talking about reparation for many years. Now that I've shared with you these facts that you either never knew or refuse to admit knowing about African leaders selling their people and African Americans owning black slaves, do you want to push for reparation from those folks? Yours and our vice president's ancestry are possibly families of slave owners, so your and her reparation will be required to send millions of your personal dollars to black folks in Texas and Jamaica whose ancestors may have been enslaved by your families. Or will you still just push reparation only toward the lighter-skinned conservatives?"

President O'Rourke said, "America, my friends. We've been trying for twenty years to get the racist Republican Party to support a complete reparation process where funds will be provided to all African Americans today whose great-great grandparents were enslaved here by the awful white, conservative Americans back in the 1700s and 1800s. Of course with President Trump's racist positions, he made sure that this fair reimbursement process would not get passed to support the families of the previously enslaved."

President O'Rourke ended his response to Ella's comments and questions, then he looked at the CNN debate staff and swung his head to the left. CNN reporters moved on to another topic—political racism—so they could ensure the president would have an opportunity to attack the Republicans with minority division strategies.

Attorney General Abhoola began using video screens behind her to show the public more facts which they had maybe never seen.

The video screen showed eight worldly cultures who have been proslavery over antiquity and which cultures have been enslaved. The proslavery cultures were shown to be Romans, Muslims, African kingdom leaders, Hispanics, English, Europeans, black slave owners in America, and American migrants. The video showed the world's enslaved peoples as having been Africans, Muslims, including Muslim women today, Christian Hispanics in Spain enslaved by Muslims, and Native Americans who were enslaved by Hispanics in Central and South America.

Ella pointed at the video screen which showed the list of cultures and skin colors. "Mr. President, either you have been tricked into believing that slavery and racial division are light-skinned ideologies, or you know it's not true, but you lie with CNN. Here's what you should be sharing with the public, but we know you can't as a Democrat. The racial issues that you blame only on light-skinned Republicans were caused by evil cultures, regardless of skin shades, dark or light. It's all about evil powers overtaking goodness in our world. Now that I'm showing the public the real history of slavery and racial divide, voters will be walking away from your incorrect use of skin color. Here in America, it's only been you Democrats who have been proslavery since our country's life began. You're done with politics now, unless you walk away from the Democratic Party."

O'Rourke said, "Turn that screen off. You're lying. Only non-Hispanic white people enslaved black people. And during and after President Obama's time in office, your party of that gross fat dumb animal lied to the public by calling our president a racial divider, a user of skin color. I will challenge your lying this year and you will have no chance of winning votes from good people."

Ella's response was clear. "I don't enjoy my own showing of historical racial division, but that last video screen image showed the colors of cultures that did the slavery thing hundreds of years ago. Worst of all is that the skin-color division in our country over the past thirty years has been only driven by you Democratic politicians and your news outlets. I'm going to be eliminating skin color as a problem in our country, but that only means that I'm going to continue showing the people that all citizens must be treated the same, which you disagree with, Mr. President."

Ella walked over to her smaller screen and showed how she would be binding all our people together after she wins the election.

"We're taking your decades of division away. We all need to consider red, white, and blue as our colors of equity and friendship between all cultures in America."

O'Rourke pointed at Ella. "I expect that this terrible right nominee will not support her own ancestors with reparation or anything else, because she is also a racist like Trump and Robert. My plan for billions of dollars of reparation will be implemented the first week after I win my second term when you vote for real decency from your Democratic Party, which it always has been to tear down the evil right and their deplorable voters. You Republicans should not even have voting rights."

Ella said, "After I become president and our citizens shut down your rhetoric, people will know that we're all the same race, Earth's humans. If any of you do your own research on what I've been revealing to the public, you will immediately understand which one of us is the liar. I want all citizens to do their own research on every political topic, real research—not fake news. The more that people can vote based on true facts, the more fused together we will all be for America's future generations."

Ella Abhoola changed the larger video screen viewing, so she could respond to President O'Rourke's position on racism.

"Now, sir, look at this fact, which you will choose not to share with your voters. I'm going to show you something of your past president whom you say is not a racist. I'm turning this screen on to show our people your position. Here goes."

The video she pointed at showed two paintings of black women, each holding a white woman's head and the knife used to behead.

"Mr. President, why does your political party have no problem with Obama befriending and hiring this artist who paints these portraits of black ladies beheading white ladies with knives? When I was in high school in 2017, he employed this black super racist to paint his museum portrait, a fact that will never be shared by fake news media. The President's artist friend told reporters in 2012 that these paintings of beheading are sort of a play on kill-the-whitey thing. I dare you, sir—try to lie and tell the pubic right now how this was a non-racist decision by your skin-separation president.

O'Rourke responded. "You showing racial stuff to the public is rotten. You do the racial thing by sharing fake information to our people, most of which you lie on purpose, and some which you do because you've been tricked for your whole life by right-wing political scam."

Ella put onscreen a map showing all of the United States and Puerto Rico. She pointed at the screen and stared right at the President's eyes. "These are the wonderful people that I'm representing as president starting in January." The screen quickly switched to a map of South and Central America. "These are the wonderful people and criminals and terrorists that you're always representing first. Our people north of here are never represented first by you or your party. You're all about support for human trafficking and illegal drug businesses."

"We all understand that your support of people from other countries over American citizens is clearly only so you can increase your vote totals by telling the whole world that they can come here for a free, non-working life and get cash support from working citizens. I wouldn't be surprised if you secretly own a backpack manufacturing company in China, because since you have been president, millions of backpacks are being given to the world and they are packing up and heading to our country for free-cash support."

O'Rourke just waved his hand at the CNN facilitators, asking them to move on, because he knew that he could not tell the public that he's keeping our borders secured. CNN's next question was about capitalism pros and cons, and socialism pros.

Ella responded first. "I'm putting another couple of factual pictures onscreen and I'll show you the reason that voters should only be going one way." She turned on the large video display behind her and she pointed at this picture on screen.

The picture on the screen showed two columns of a one-acre of land within a town of socialism and a town of capitalism. The socialism showed no changes to the acre of land, until the bottom where homeless bodies were shown laying in the acre. The capitalism column showed the acre being built up supporting banking jobs, constructions jobs, maintenance jobs, and utility jobs. The final capitalism acre showed workers expressing joy with arms up.

Ella said, "Here's the real truth that the left is wrong about. Human prosperity is improved by creating assets from nothing. Prosperity is not stolen from low class workers by top level asset creators, not taken away from low and middle class, like the liars say, and the unaware Democrats think. Every citizen in America has the ability to create or attain assets. All people are more wealthy, not just the business creators, by building and creating more assets in our country. The Democrats and fake news always say that the top one-percent gets too much. But look here. Without a capitalist market, we have nothing. No jobs. Nothing but poor lives for everyone. We need to teach people the truth of the differences in socialism and capitalism. Creating more and more valued properties adds more assets to all of our great people. The socialist decree of doing nothing does not add the availability of more assets to anyone. For example, we would not have cars or TVs or cell phones or internet if we did not have human competition and motivation established by capitalism. Competition is good and healthy due to allowing all citizens to push for a better life. Hard socialists don't understand that working-people's competition drives higher wealth and happiness for everyone, not just business leaders and risk takers."

"But don't forget. There are examples in the world that fit the core progressive's economic model. Competition is removed from society to ensure no one can motivate to exceed anyone else. The idea of working hard for education and higher wages is removed from society to ensure that no one grows beyond poor and that no one challenges their political elite. Freedom of work, education, travel, and everything else will be stolen from you if the progressives' secret model is ever implemented. We must expose and eradicate their three-hundred-year-old clandestine plan, and that's what my one-hundred-and-fifty-year plan for the future will do starting on January 20th of 2041 when I become your next president." Ella's response time ended.

President O'Rourke headed into full socialist response by accusing Republicans of trying to take top jobs away from darker skinned people. His entire comeback used the topic of skin color as the cause of his opinions of why socialism is necessary for the whole world, especially this country. While the President was fighting back, Ella added to her video screen a new graphic model of human reality.

CNN facilitators asked President O'Rourke to wait for a second, then they ordered Abhoola to close down that video presentation.

The President said to his CNN allies, "Thanks for taking that picture of total falsehood away from our public." He blew out another full set of confusion regarding the differences both parties take on economics.

When CNN took a commercial break and both nominees were off stage in a hallway, Ella raised her voice and shared with the president her deep thoughts about how American citizens have been treated by the left.

"Mr. President. Your first few years have been so disappointing, because of the dreadful messages you have always sent to American citizens who love our country, our flag, and our constitution. Stop your racial separation support!"

When they returned to the stage after Ella's comment, O'Rourke drove back by saying Abhoola's message during the break was the type of violent attack that he gets from all Republicans. The president said that only Republicans attack other people, not Democrats. He ended the debate by telling the public that Ella had lied about the KKK murdering Republicans, the Democrats' killing of a poll officer in New York, the years of Antifa attacks on conservatives, and the ongoing attacks on KAG and MAGA hat and shirt wearers.

Ella's response tried to smooth out the anxiety created during this discussion. "Sir, I must apologize for sending that message toward you with my high voice. I know for sure, based on what you just said, that you do not know the real truth of political history in America. I really believe that you might be a nice person who cares about all humans. But from the super research results confirmed by my Two Party Fusion Squad, I know that you have been misled for decades away from the real deep secret aspects of your party. To me, you're not bad or mean, just fully tricked into your beliefs. Same as the voters who support you. They are good people who don't know the real truth of what political deep states are doing. To try to get our people, including politicians like yourself, to recognize and overlook all political trickery, I hope you and I can collude together for the rest of our lives, regardless of which of us wins the presidential election."

The president took some time to think about what Ella had said. "Okay, Lady Ella. I'm going to tell the pubic here now that I am impressed by your use of fake presentations. You've put a lot of pressure on me with these video screens. I wish I had done that to show your inaccuracies. And I'm overwhelmed with your proposal to work with me to eliminate or override fake news. I will work with you on that in the future. But I have to tell our people now that everything you've lied about or hidden from the public in this debate is not because you're a bad person. It's just because you've been tricked your whole life by some deep state society behind the Republicans. When we hook up and embattle fake news, you're wrong and will be very disappointed about where that will end up. Fox News and the *Washington Times* will be the outcome of our investigations on who is lying to and hiding from the public. I can't tell the public that you're a good person because of all your false information sharing. But I like your idea because you will change your right-wing position as soon as you and I collude into showing you the truth of political history in America."

Ella's last comment came out. "Good response, Mr. President. Thank you. Let's find out which one of us can be turned left or right, and then we'll pull the public together beyond the party of scam. I agree. Once I'm president, when you and I start spending some unionized time together, I'll let you know that we'll have a huge elephant in the room on a day you'll be calling NEET Day. We will sanctify the unification of honest political teams." CNN closed the debate.

CHAPTER 46

2040 ELECTION RESULTS AND A NEET NEW WORLD

ELLA HARRIET ABHOOLA WON THE US PRESIDENTIAL election by a giant landslide, becoming POTUS 49. With this election, President Abhoola was so proud and grateful that her sister Mehna Abhoola had won another key battle for humanity, three hundred and forty-six years after she started her plan-of-attack by good against evil.

As Ella won the presidency, Republicans won all Senate and House open seats, and thus both legislative bodies were more than seventy-five percent right and righteous.

After winning the presidency, she wanted her Secret Ella Society to be not secreted. She ordered Roger Stevens to rename his conference in Exeter, New Hampshire, the Grand Old Ella Society. She opened her deep society to the public, to news outlets, and the other political party because she wanted to start showing her commitment to political openness to the public.

President Abhoola's Fusion Squad joined with her at the first Grand Old Ella Society conference meeting after the election. There was a giant celebration of the elephant in the room! Mr. Stevens had all of Room-219 bestowing elephant photos, and freedom-honoring pictures of Harriet Tubman, President Lincoln, Amos Tuck, Elephant Joe Josephs, and President Trump.

After an hour of celebration at the conference, President Abhoola started her sharing. "I'm very glad to see all of you fused here together again, after all that you did together to bring us to this wonderful outcome. I've asked all of us to come to the conference this time, because we've got the path to freedom now opened in front of us, after it's been blocked for the past four years. I want us to head down the path. Our Fusion Squad friends will be staying here in Exeter for as long as necessary to work with you Society folks to design several fusion chapters to fix our country. We will launch the improvements that you help develop on a day to honor your town here." She pointed to one of her earrings. "The New England Elephant Token and my sister Mehna will expect us to launch a world-changing NEET Day, no more than three years from now, to repair and defend our country and its peoples' freedom forever."

President Abhoola Puts America First

When President Abhoola was elected, forty-six of the USA's fifty state governors were all Republicans. Every state legislature had at least eighty-five-percent Republicans in office. Even with these giant election-wins and the President's push for more honesty, the political-left news media outlets continued to use their sneaking strategies. Her Fusion Squad's close monitoring of the medias' reporting helped them to continue designing and building massive government repairs to meet the President's goals.

NEET Day Explodes in 2042

After two-years of wide-ranging efforts by her magnanimous fusion squad, President Abhoola and her Grand Old Ella Society proposed a major change to the US federal government to restore the country's First Amendment rights, which were torn down by Fake News outlets. To honor the 1853 elephant in the room at the Squamscott Hotel, Congress passed the president's proposal on October 12, which became known as the Freedom of the Press Recovery Act. The main target of the act was to put a cash value on citizens' votes. After the Act was in full public knowledge, when people did their own research to find out the true needs of America and the truly accurate and fair way to get there, then they earned considerable federal tax relief when they voted using facts, not lies. The approach put a higher value on citizen's votes.

From the Act, a new federal office, the Freedom of the Press Investigation Department (the FPI) had to present a TV program every day with a facilitator and two or more investigators, at least one from each political party, left and right. The public could watch the FPI investigation channel at no cost. As political news outlets shared stories on TV, internet, and newspapers, each report was placed into open investigation the next day on the FPI channel. The fusion of these political rivals assigned to the FPI determined which of yesterday's reports were true, and which were not. The more hours that legal voters digitally confirmed their viewing of the FPI program, the greater annual federal tax relief bonus they achieved.

From another feature of the Freedom of the Press Recovery Act, if any citizen proved that they watched and listened equally to at least the two main political waves of news-outlet information, they earned more tax relief. People could save hundreds to thousands of dollars annually from federal taxes if they verified that they were voting based on true facts, not misrepresentations. The Freedom of the Press Recovery Act placed an asset value on American Citizens' votes, because of President Abhoola's position that fact-based voting would always result in the best outcomes for all American Citizens, now and for generations.

If the Freedom of the Press Investigation processes determined that any political news outlet lied to the public during more than twenty-five-percent of their monthly reporting, then they lost one-month of media independence as they were forced by the new law to shut down their TV, newspaper, and internet presentations.

Seven months after President Abhoola's NEET Day launched the Recovery Act for governmental improvement, she continued to discuss with her administration's Fusion Squad and her Grand Ella Society how she was supremely concerned about news outlets who were still using skin color to separate people to try to get more votes. She asked her deep state society to work with her Fusion Squad, which they've done several times in the past few years, to design a law which would prevent any public reporters from using skin-separation talk to separate citizenry. The Federal Human Unification Act was passed by Congress in August of 2042. After the Unification Act was passed, news outlets were monitored for their use of divisive words such as racism, racist, racial, bigotry, supremacy, Black, White, Hispanic, Muslim, and Asian. The FED FPI channel persistently showed the public daily, weekly, and monthly how often each political news outlet talked about skin color and cultural segregation.

President Abhoola was very proud to have created processes and expectations for happily-merged humanism which would override divisive racism practices. Because she was very knowledgeable and engaged with the constitution, and with the importance of protecting American citizens with ideologies such as military, boarder security, international economic defense, law enforcement, firearms rights, and education, President Abhoola added another public exposure event to her Federal Human Unification Act.

The revised Unification Act put another event on the FPI channel. This event required Democrats and Republicans in both arrays of Congress to hold bi-partisan brainstorming events created on giant white-boards in front of nine Congressional members from each party and while exposed to all American citizenry on the FPI TV and internet channel. This process, called Ideology: Confusion into Fusion, began an entirely new close relationship between all people who became aware of deep state issues previously hidden from voters. Voters began soon after the NEET Day kick-off to realize that having citizenry vote for their country's necessary and appropriate philosophies is far more important than just voting based on news outlets' untrue reporting.

To transform citizens' political mindsets from confusion into fusion, America's ideologies from both parties were now fully exposed, challenged, and analyzed openly in front of the public. The process brought legislators together in determining and negotiating the best goals for American policies, today and into the next several generations.

Another important aspect of the FHU act required fusion-classes to be presented in all public and private high-schools and colleges. By this law, students were always reminded of America's history of forced separation, and shown how that would not ever happen again as they are taught how to move political confusion into fusion.

Grand Old Ella Society Conferences Swell after NEET Day

After a year with the NEET Day acts and programs in place, several results began to persistently improve all of the United States of America's peoples' lives. Two years after she launched this holiday of political fusion, President Abhoola came to her home in Exeter, New Hampshire, which she did several times a year. Her visit here, as usual, included meeting with her Grand Old Ella Society and Roger Stevens. As they joined up with five congressional men and ladies, Roger roared when he and the President entered the room. "President Abhoola! Congratulations and thank for what you've done for our country as America's first female president! All citizens are finally seeing the elephant to keep everyone free!" Mr. Stevens turned around and pointed at a video screen showing the team their successful objectives for unifying the people.

The video showed a list of all four new NEET acts, the Freedom of the Press Recovery Act, the Freedom of the Press Investigation

Department, the Federal Human Unification Act, and the Confusion-into-Fusion Ideology Program.

The screen provided celebration for the new world. For over an hour, there were wide-open conversations about how well these great acts were treating all of America's people and political processes. The President was really excited about sharing a few new NEET results that some of her staff members may not have heard yet.

"Hey, team. Great job you and our Fusion Squad have done to get us to these friendly places that my sister Mehna in my earrings is now very delighted to see. Here's a couple of onset results that are starting to show how awesome our FPRA is and how it's brought on the alteration of the public's political beliefs from confusion into fusion.

"Election results are starting to show that over ninety-percent of our citizens now understand that we the people must have weapons to prevent takeover of our constitution, even by elected politicians. Because of the Confusion to Fusion program, people now understand that if any federal government entity ever tries to attack our democracy to start dictatorship, we with firearms will fight back to protect our constitution and individual rights. There will no longer be any voting push, except by deep secret progressives, to remove our Second Amendment rights.

"Here's the other NEET result that I was called about earlier today. Because of our FPRA and FPI outcomes, the New York Times, CNN, MSNBC, and dozens of other news outlets are all shutting down this month from bankruptcy, since no one is watching or reading them anymore. After we started our Unification Act, their excessive use of cultural separation talk and false reporting ended up taking them out of business. Yay, team! Now we know for certain that Mehna's 1694 New England Elephant Token plan for love, and our NEET acts, have accomplished the world's next great achievement for humankind."

President Abhoola's new acts of citizen unification also resulted in the Democratic Party falling apart. The secret society of asses revised their party name so that they could try to start tricking the public again into thinking they are good. The new party name was the Valid Party. This name was just like decades of CNN calling themselves "The Most Trusted Name in News," which the American public started to realize was false after President Trump's eight years of great work to show the truth about them.

After the real fake news outlets ended their daily falsehoods, others such as CBS and ABC started sharing only fact-based information and stopped hiding real political details from the public. They made these changes because they agreed with the President's desire to renovate America's freedom of the press. They began being factual even though most true reports showed patronage to the Republican Party, which was the opposite of what they had been doing for the previous half-century.

2044: At forty-three years old, President Abhoola won her second term as the President of the United States of America with over 90 percent of votes. Roger Stevens was seventy-nine years old, but still attended the next several SES conference meetings so that he could honor President Abhoola whom he met as a baby forty-three years ago at one of his Secret Ella Society events.

Throughout her second term in office from 2044 to 2048, President Abhoola's Freedom of the Press Recovery Acts consolidated most voters and developed close ties between people who used to be hauled into opposite beliefs.

2094: On her birthday, July 31, 2094, President Abhoola was ninety-three years old. She reflected herself as being four hundred years old, as she sat with her 1694 New England Elephant token earrings and a bracelet on her right arm. America now celebrates each October 12 with a holiday called NEET Credence Day to honor Mehna's, Harriet's, and Ella's grand plan for merging all humans into Mehna's plan forever. This huge trunk and tusk celebration credits Mehna Abhoola's plan for humanity, the Exeter, New Hampshire 1853 abolitionist forum, President Lincoln's 1864 end to slavery, President Trump's colossal work to heal our country, and President Abhoola's launching of NEET Day government revisions fifty-two years ago in 2042 which ended the Democratic Party's fake news and racial divide in America.

Since her election and her NEET Day launching of political party mergers and cultural unions over fifty years ago, constitutional foundations became more closely tied to all aspects of American life. President Abhoola's love and devotion for America re-established President Donald Trump's great accomplishments after the Democrats won their final election in 2035 and attacked American citizens' priorities for four years. President Abhoola's great affection for humanity brought on the past five decades of a solid economy with great job availability and strong boarder security to protect US citizens from socialist countries' invasions. Ella bestowed America's re-honoring of the constitution in core education programs, and she established very tight US relationships with democracies throughout the world. Human beings everywhere now saw that America had become the most anti-racial-division country in the world by having the voting-public terminate political racism tactics. Even outside of the United States, political-scam media outlets were almost completely detached from human life.

For the past fifty-four years, almost all of America's voters had deeply respected what President Abhoola did for America by continuing to embrace Mehna's 1694-plan for freedom and love for all forever. For the past twenty-five years, over ninety-percent of America's voters had agreed with and voted for the conservative Republican Party, the party grown huge by Ella's cultural-friendship and fusion objectives.

The President's family shared her 2094 holiday response. "Thank you for Keeping America Great forever, people! It is so respectful that we're all so close together today, with essentially the same goals for safe and happy futures of our country's next twenty generations and beyond. It's so great that you all are still seeing the elephant! That keeps freedom alive! Love you and your acceptance of our country's forever NEET life!

President Abhoola passed away two weeks after America's NEET Credence Day. The Republican Party national pact honored her life and passing by modifying the party's elephant icon to represent the real 1694 Ella, the elephant that God merged with Mehna Abhoola, Harriet Tubman, and President Ella Harriet Abhoola to respect all of humanity forever.

THE END
LET's KEEP AMERICA GREAT!

'AMERICA'S TOKEN OF FREEDOM'
HISTORICAL AFTERWORD

SOME OF THE CHARACTERS AND SITUATIONS IN THIS novel are fictional; however, the historical contexts of these events are accurate.

1. Zebulon Thing Corner: A historical book named History of Newfields New Hampshire published in 1912 by Reverend James Hill Fitts covers the amazing history of Zebulon Thing Corner, a farmland in Exeter and Newfields, New Hampshire which was owned and operated by the Giddings and Thing families in the 1700s and 1800s.

2. Ashanti Empire: Research indicates that seventeenth century African kingdom leaders in the Ashanti Empire had control over fields of gold so that they could buy modern weaponry from Europe. Their power plan became a successful trade network increasing the slavery market. The slave trade was a source of wealth greater than gold for the Ashanti Empire leaders.

3. 1694 Royal African Company: A historical book called *The Constitutional and Finance of the Royal African Company of England from its Foundation till 1720* was published in 1903 by W. R. Scott. Mr. Scott. He reported this about England's Royal African Company:

   From 1691 to 1697 a series of disasters were encountered partly through the war and partly by disorganization of trade by persons who infringed the exclusive privileges

*of the company. The position of the company both finan-
cially and legally was comparatively weak and the assistants with some strategic ability petitioned Parliament in
1694 to bring in a bill to establish the company rather than
wait for the expected request for the formation of a regu-
lated company.*

4. 1694, Freedom of the Press: In England, the Licensing
    Order of 1643 was ensuring that the press was not lying to
    control or destroy the government. In 1694, King William
    ended the 1643 Licensing Order and opened freedom of
    the press to ensure that his government could use press
    reporting to align the public with his desires for power and
    directions.

5. 1694 Politics: Revolvy.com website has a document titled
    First Whig Junto showing how major political schemes
    in England changed in 1694. The website says: "*The First
    Whig Junto controlled the government of England from
    1694 to 1699 and was the first part of the Whig Junto, a
    cabal of people who controlled the most important political
    decisions.*"

6. Abolitionist Attack: History of the town of Exeter, New
    Hampshire was written and published by, Charles Henry
    Bell, in 1888. Mr. Bell reported the following about the
    1836 attack on Reverend Storrs in Exeter:

    *The Rev. George Storrs, a noted advocate of the abolition
    of slavery, attempted to deliver a lecture there on that sub-
    ject. A crowd of proslavery men, idlers and boys gathered,
    and determined that he should not. As he persisted in his
    attempt, he was interrupted by hooting, by the flinging of
    stones at the windows and blinds, and by streams of water
    from the fire engines.*

7. Underground Railroad in New Hampshire: National Park Service at nps.com shares that the Underground Railroad was engaged with the Cartland Farm in Lee, NH:
    Moses Cartland was one of New Hampshire's premier rhetorical antislavery activists, but he took action as well. Cartland records provide documentation of the life of Oliver Gilbert and the Cartland's aid to other freedom seekers. Gilbert stayed at the site during the risky years following the Fugitive Slave Law. He escaped in 1848 from Maryland, traveled through Pennsylvania to Boston. Gilbert visited the Cartland site in 1852. He cooked for the household that included boarding students for Moses Cartland's school.

8. Cartland Farm Great History: In 2014, the University of New Hampshire Scholars' Repository published a book called *Oliver Cromwell Gilbert: A Life*. The document written by Jody Fernald and Stephanie Gilbert of the University of New Hampshire shares the historical details of the Underground Railroad in New Hampshire and its actions in Lee, New Hampshire by Moses Cartland, John Greenleaf Whittier, Oliver Gilbert, and Fredrick Douglass.

9. Robinson tokens: In 2003, The American Numismatic Society published a document called "The Hunt for Carolina Elephants, Questions Regarding Genuine Specimens and Reproductions of the 1694 Token." Neil Fulghum wrote the following about the New England Elephant Tokens created by Alfred Robinson in Hartford, Connecticut in 1861, at the start of the Civil War:
    The makers of some Elephant Token copies remain undetermined. Others are well documented. Among known early makers of Elephant tokens in the United States is Alfred S. Robinson of Hartford, Connecticut. Around 1861, Robinson produced copies of Elephant tokens in an assortment of

metals, using dies cut by Joseph H. Merriam of Boston. All, however, were the New England type.

10. Elephant Joe: History of Buffalo, New York can be seen on a website, buffaloah.com. The site's page written by Chuck LaChiusa in 2009 highlights that Elephant Joe Josephs was a sign painter, sometime artist, a public singer, was staunchly Republican and that he was captain of the local rail splitting team for two Republican presidential candidates, Lincoln in 1860 and Garfield in 1880. Mr. LaChiusa reported this: "Josephs understood the publicity stunt. His shop at the foot of Exchange St. in Buffalo was decorated top to bottom with visual word puzzles and pictures of elephants. A publicity wizard, Elephant Joe could make people 'see an elephant' where there was none."

'America's Token of Freedom' Conclusions

In England in 1694, all of the events related to freedom of the press, the new Bank of England, the Whig Junto government takeover, the passing of Queen Mary, and the financial calamity of the Royal African Company possibly had some initiating aspects that led to creation of copper elephant tokens during that colossal year of government and business recovery attempts.

Harriet Tubman's escaped slaves took a train or ship from Boston to Exeter, then they had to travel on land along Zebulon Thing Corner to get to the Cartland Farm in Lee on their way to Canada.

In a New Hampshire location where human champions were working to free the slaves, an abolitionist party was created and an ancient token was in a farm called Zebulon Thing Corner along the Underground Railroad. While the elephant token was there and the freedom trail folks travelled through for years, the elephant became the icon of the new party of freedom for all.

CPSIA information can be obtained
at www.ICGtesting.com
Printed in the USA
LVHW011933280620
659168LV00001B/30